THE HAPPY TREE

by

Rosalind Murray

NATAL PUBLISHING LLC
ARS LONGA, VITA BREVIS

οἵη περ φύλλων γενεὴ, τοίη δὲ καὶ ἀνδρῶν.
φύλλα τὰ μέν τ᾽ ἄνεμος χαμάδις χέει, ἄλλα δέ θ᾽ ὕλη
τηλεθόωσα φύει, ἔαρος δ᾽ ἐπιγίγνεται ὥρη.
ὣς ἀνδρῶν γενεὴ ἣ μὲν φύει ἣ δ᾽ ἀπολήγει.[*]

PART ONE
'Green Felicity'

I

LEAVES are falling down from the laburnum tree at the gate; yellow leaves, white gate, and red brick of the houses opposite; it is very ugly. In the spring the flowers are yellow instead of the leaves, and the hawthorn bush, to the side, is bright pink, and across the road is lilac. The red-brick houses have facings of yellow stone, squares of yellowish stone round the doors and the windows. All the colours are wrong, all the shapes are ugly, even the trees are not real trees.

Once I would have minded it so much, to live here, looking out at that laburnum tree, and that house opposite, that bow window, and the yellowish stone facings of the windows, and the lilac bush that has grown all crooked, and the pink hawthorn, and the laurels with patterned leaves; but now I do not mind. Now I do not see these things or think about them at all; only to-night I am seeing them, because somehow I have come awake to-night, for a bit.

To-night I realize that for nine years I have lived here, looking at that house, every time I go out, and have never really noticed it before. But even now that I see it, I do not mind. I do not mind about anything very much now, except, I suppose, John.

To-morrow I shall be forty; my youth is gone; irretrievably, irrevocably, gone; and even that I do not mind. It used to seem to me so difficult not to feel too much, and now I cannot feel at all. Is this simply growing old? Is this what always happens when one grows old? But if Hugo were alive still, would it be like this? I do not think that it would.

To-night things come back to me very clearly, in an odd, detached way, things that have happened to me, as though they had happened to somebody else, while I looked on. Yearsly comes back to me much more than usual, and Guy and Hugo, and our childhood there. Some things I have been almost afraid of thinking about too much. Now I can think of everything and am not afraid.

It is like what I have heard happens when people are going to die, or be executed. Is being forty like that? Does it mean that I do mind being forty, though I think I don't?

Hugo said that we must hold out till the end; I have had to hold out longer than he did, and it has seemed, often, that if I let myself think, or feel much, I couldn't do it. That was before this deadening came, that makes it easier; but now I am not afraid. Something is past, some danger is past, and now I know that I shall be able to hold out till the end. I do not believe in immortality, and yet I feel, somehow, that Hugo will know if I keep my promise.

Walter is in bed, asleep; and I am by the window, alone. There is a bright moon coming up now behind the houses opposite, and in the moonlight the colours are changing; the yellow and red grow paler, and less violent. Even on this road there comes a quiet and beauty of the night.

And my life up to now comes before me very clearly; the people and the places, and the choices and mistakes, and I seem to see it all in better proportion than before; less clouded and blurred across by the violent emotion of youth.

Guy, and Hugo, and Cousin Delia, and Sophia Lane-Watson, and Diana, and Walter, and George Addington, and Mollie; and Yearsly, and Hampstead, and here; but Hugo goes through it all; when I try to think of my life without Hugo, it is impossible; it is as though there were nothing there at all.

And really, so little has happened to me; my life has been a very ordinary one; no adventures, nothing dramatic, just the same sort of life as most of the women I meet in the street, and think so dull. The lady who lives opposite, in the house with the bow window, has three grown-up sons, and two daughters. She is much older than I am, her life must have had more in it than mine. Does it seem to her, I wonder, as intricate, and poignant as mine does to me?

I suppose that it does, when she thinks about it; and I suppose that is only seldom, just as it is with me.

Perhaps before her fiftieth and sixtieth birthdays she thought about it, and perhaps she thought it very interesting.

I wonder if I should think so too, if she told it to me.

II

The beginning is Yearsly. People say that places ought not to matter—still less houses, but I think they do. Yearsly has mattered to me, and it did to Guy and Hugo. It stood for something very stable, very enduring, and very sympathetic. Yearsly without Cousin Delia might have been something quite different; it is quite different now; but I think of them together, complementary to each other. Cousin Delia's personality pervaded everything at Yearsly, and everything there seemed somehow an enhancement and expression of her; and yet each was distinct. Yearsly had something that it had had long before she came there, and Cousin Delia had something, and a great deal, that she must have had before she came, and would have had wherever she was: she has it now.

The house at Yearsly was of grey stone; it was a long plain house built at the beginning of the eighteenth century, with a door in the middle and a row of high sash windows on either side of the door. Above this was a second row of windows, and a kind of Classical stone cornice overhung the upper windows. The roof was steeper than is usual in such houses, and was also grey; grey slates or chips of stone, with patches of green moss on them.

Once it had been a much bigger house, with a long bedroom wing stretching back, northwards, at the east end of the house, but that had been burnt down in 1830, and never rebuilt, and when I first remember it, this centre block was the entire house.

In the middle of the house was a hall, stretching from back to front, and the two main doors, the 'Front' door to the north, and the 'Garden' door to the south, faced each other across it. Standing on the south side of the house, you could look right through to the clouds at the north. The garden door stood open almost always, except in winter.

The hall reached up to the top of the house, and the big staircase wound up and round it, ending in a square wooden gallery from which the bedrooms opened.

In front of the house, the Garden Front, stretched a long lawn, with a wide gravel path down the middle; at the end of the path six stone steps led down to a lower lawn where we played tennis, and, at the top of the steps, one on each side, stood two lead statues; one of Diana with a bow, and the other, a hero leaning forward with a shield. The lead of the statues was perishing away, and there was a great crack across Diana's head, but they stood out clear, and almost black, from all the south windows of the house.

Below the tennis court was a piece of meadow sloping down to the Mellock river, with its two lines of willows, flowing at this point due east, and almost parallel with the front of the house. A little further on, it turned sharply southward, wandering away through the low-lying meadows beyond the hill.

At the east end of the house were beach trees: the nearest grew within a few feet of the wall, and their branches threw green lights and shadows into the end windows, and filled the rooms on windy nights with a swishing sound like the sea.

Further from the house the trees thickened up into the 'High wood' which stretched along the side of the hill, southward, above the course of the river, for a little way.

This wood was a particular home for us: we played in the trees like birds or squirrels, and built great nests of sticks in which we sat.

We had special trees too—good trees and bad trees, which seemed to us like people. There was one in particular, a very big one, which we called the Happy Tree, and that we loved the best.

Hugo had given it the name: lying on his back one summer's day, his bare feet kicking on the moss:

'On a drear nighted December,
Too happy, happy tree,
Thy branches ne'er remember
Their green felicity . . .

Green felicity, Green felicity, Green felicity . . .'

he kept chanting the words, beating softly on the moss with his feet.

The pale green sunlight flickered through the world of beech leaves on to his face; his hands were clasped behind his head, and his dark blue jersey was open at the neck:

'It is green felicity . . .'

Guy, half way up among the branches, said:

'What are you saying?'

And Hugo answered:

'Green felicity . . .' and then:

'On a drear nighted December,

Too happy, happy tree . . .

'Oh,' Guy said, 'well, I suppose so . . . but I don't see why too happy?'

And I said:

'But it just is . . .'

And Hugo said:

'It just is . . .'

'All right,' Guy answered, 'too happy, if you like. . .'

And afterwards we always called it the 'Happy Tree.'

Below the trees the hillside was smooth and green. A grass path had been cut in it, many years ago when the house was newly built. In those days all the hillside had been kept closely mown, but in our time the grass grew long and was made into hay. Only the path was kept still a little shorter than the rest; we used to race along it . . . there was room for two abreast, but it was not wide enough for three.

The path ended in a little stone pavilion which we called the 'Temple'—why we called it so, no one could remember . . . it had four glass doors and steps all round; inside there was a mosaic table and four statues in the niches between the doors. The doors were always locked, for the roof was unsafe, and nobody ever went inside; only Guy could remember going inside once, with Cousin John, when an architect or expert of some sort came to look at it.

At the other end of the house, to the west, was the walled garden, and in the sunny corner between the end wall of the house and the garden wall was the rose garden that Cousin Delia had made.

In that there was a sundial and some little stone 'putti,' and there most often we would find her. When I think of Yearsly in those long ago days, I think very often of her in the rose garden, with her long gardening gloves, and shady hat, and the half smile with which she would look up when one of us called to her, and her quiet grey eyes in the shadow of her hat.

She was never in a hurry, and never too busy to answer questions; if we wanted her she was always there. I used to wonder, even then, how it was that she had so much time, for my own mother was always busy . . . I wonder even more now.

Cousin Delia was very quiet, but she never repressed us nor made it seem wrong to make a noise, as so many quiet people do. I think it was partly that she was not quiet on purpose, or with an effort, but simply from a kind of serenity. She was happy, I am sure, and people round her were happy.

My mother once said that it surprised her that a woman of Delia's intelligence should be contented with such an 'idle stagnant life.' I felt very angry, even then, and tried to defend her, though I don't think I managed to explain what I meant.

The truth was, I think, that she was never idle, only the things she did were not the kind of things that my mother would count.

She was interested in so many things; in flowers and animals, and little precious things in the house; little pieces of china, or even old chairs; they seemed to have a value for her which they had not for other people, not as objects, but almost as friends; they lived and felt and were real for her; you could see it from the way she touched them; and then, of course, she had Guy and Hugo . . . and they meant so much more to her than I ever meant to my mother.

Beyond the rose garden was the old wall; high and baked and a little bulging in places. Big espalier apple trees were trained across it, and pear trees too. There were two wrought-iron doors that led into the walled garden; one led out of the rose garden, and the other, in the centre of the wall, was called the 'Jasmine Gate,' because of a great bush of white jasmine which hung round it and over the wall.

Inside the wall there were more fruit trees; apples and

pears again and plums and cherries; there were also currant bushes covered up in nets, and vegetables of all sorts.

And then there were flowers; a wide herbaceous border ran the length of the north wall, and it seems to me, even now, that the flowers in that border were brighter and bigger than any other flowers.

One year, too, there was a big clump of sunflowers, giant sunflowers, in a corner, away from the main border, and we made a house under the broad leaves, at least Hugo and I did, but Guy laughed at us . . . for he was older, and thought it silly; it was not a real house, like our house in the wood, he said; but Guy never laughed in a way that we could mind.

In the middle of the walled garden was a small round pond with a fountain in the middle. The fountain hardly ever played, but there were frogs in the pond, surprising quantities of frogs, and we used to call it the 'Frog Pond.' Twice we saw a mouse there too, on the little island of stones and weeds in the middle, where the spout of the fountain was. The mouse was running about among the stones, picking up something from under the weeds, and then it met a frog sitting stolidly on a stone, and it jumped back suddenly. We lay on our stomachs at the edge of the pond for a long time, watching for the mouse to come back, and then it was dinner time, and we had to go in. We only saw it once again, though we watched for it often, but the question of how it got there, and how it got away, occupied us a great deal, and its existence imparted a new interest to the pond.

Inside the house there was a special smell that I have never met anywhere else. It was a sweet, clean smell, and faint; what it came from exactly, it would be hard to say; lavender and pot-pourri, and old polished floors, and old brocade; sweet and faint and slightly pungent.

Sometimes I have caught whiffs of smells in other places that were just a little like it, and they have brought Yearsly back to me more vividly and suddenly than anything else, as though I had just come in by the garden door, and were standing in the hall.

The drawing-room was on the left of the door, as you went in from the garden. It was a very long room, with four tall windows along the side and one at the end, and there were two fireplaces with high chimney-pieces, white marble, with carved figures in faint relief, and over the chimney-pieces were high mirrors that reflected back the green of the garden from the windows facing them. There were yellow brocade curtains, very old and faded, and white shield back chairs upholstered in the same yellow brocade.

The room had been redecorated for our great-great-grandmother, Mary Geraldine, when she came as a bride to Yearsly, in 1802, and it had hardly been altered since her death, eight years later.

A portrait of her by Jackson hung between the two fireplaces, and there was a miniature of her on a little gilt nail by the further fireplace as well; a dark-eyed, laughing face, very charming, very romantic. There was an atmosphere of romance all about her, since her death in Spain when she was twenty-six. She had followed her husband to the Peninsular War and died of fever there. Her body had been embalmed and sent home to be buried at Yearsly, and the story was told of how, when the coffin was opened, it was seen that her hair had gone on growing after her death, long black hair flowing down below her knees, wrapping her round like a great black shawl.

Our great-grandfather had been a little boy, barely seven years old, but this sight he remembered, naturally enough, and he had told it to his children, Guy and Hugo's grandfather and my grandmother. My grandmother had told it to us. This impressed us very much and increased the indefinable glamour surrounding our young great-great-grandmother. Her husband had preserved everything after her death exactly as she had left it, and so it had remained down to our time. There were her handkerchiefs and pieces of lace, her little volumes of Italian poetry, even chairs and tables remained where she had put them; yet it was a happy sentimentality; there was no sense of a dead hand in the cult of Mary Geraldine. If Cousin Delia's own personality was gradually, quite imperceptibly, superseding the fainter older one, it was not deliberately nor of set purpose at all. The two personalities, quite distinct and different in themselves, seemed to blend and merge harmoniously, and Yearsly was the richer for both.

III

Cousin Delia never scolded, and never disapproved. It seems to me, when I think of that time now, that there were no rules at Yearsly, no forbidden places, nothing we might not do. It seems now, as though we had done just what we liked all the day long, only somehow we did not want to do naughty things. To begin with we did not quarrel. I cannot remember any quarrel between Guy and Hugo except once, over a dead robin—when Guy called the cat who killed it cruel, and Hugo insisted that it was not cruel, because it did not understand.

Even then they had not fought, but their voices had been angry, and that was very rare.

We did not want to annoy each other or other people, as my children so often do; we did not want to disobey, but then there were no rules to disobey. Sometimes I have thought that it was easy for Cousin Delia, because Guy and Hugo were so little trouble and so easy to manage, and that I could manage my own children that way, if they had been like them; but this explanation is not enough. Guy and Hugo would not have been so good with another mother. They were not very good at school, and I know that I was often naughty when I was not at Yearsly. I know that it was something in Cousin Delia herself that made the atmosphere; a kind of active peace and contentment that affected us, as it affected the animals and the flowers she had.

She did not play with us often, she seldom took us for walks; she left us much more alone, to ourselves, than I was ever left at my grandmother's in London, but she was always there when we wanted her, always in the background, doing her own ploys, and because she took pleasure in so many different things in the day, we took pleasure in them also; pigeons and tame birds, that came to her when she went out, and her big dogs and her flowers, and her beautiful embroidery of bright butterflies and flowers. Everything she touched or came in contact with became alive, even the chairs and the curtains, and the little china bowls. There was one chair in the drawing-room that was called the 'Little Chair.'

It was a little old chair of white-painted wood with a high back and very low seat, and she had covered it herself with an old piece of Mary Geraldine's gold brocade. This chair was not one of Mary Geraldine's; it had lain forgotten in a box room till Cousin Delia found it, but now it was a friend. So many things at Yearsly were like that.

Another thing about Cousin Delia was the way she took us as we were, and did not seem to want us different and better all the time, as I do with my children, except perhaps John. We were never afraid to say anything to her, for she was never shocked or disappointed with us. I wonder sometimes if she did disapprove of anything, or merely never thought of what she disliked.

I did not realize this so much until I married Walter, and found that he and his mother disapproved of so many things; and of course my mother did also, though differently.

She would read to us in the evenings, when it was too dark to be outside; sitting by the fire in the long drawing-room, with the lamp beside her. I can see her now, distinctly, if I shut my eyes. In the high-backed arm-chair, her chin resting on her hand, and her elbow on the arm of the chair. The lamplight would fall across her hair and shine redly through her fingers on to the book; and the ends of the room would be dark. Guy and Hugo would be lying on the floor, Hugo almost always on the hearthrug, with his chin in his hands, Guy more sideways, nearer the lamp, and I would be on a footstool beside the fender.

The crackling of a wood fire, wet sap spurting in the logs, the slight warm smell of an oil lamp brings those evening 'reads' back to me so vividly, even now, that I could cry to know how long ago they are, and how hopelessly past.

The books she read to us were very varied—*Burnt Njal*, the *Morte d'Arthur*, *Treasure Island*, *Ivanhoe*, are some I remember particularly, and sometimes poetry; but Guy did not care for poetry so much.

My mother used to say that Cousin Delia was a stupid woman. 'I have no patience with these beautiful cows,' she said once. But I do not believe that at all. She could not have read to us as she did, and made us understand and enjoy the books so much, if she had been stupid. I am not clever, I know, and it might not have mattered to me, but it would to Hugo, and I know he never felt her so. He loved her as much as I did, and admired her as much; and Hugo understood people almost always, I think.

After the reading we would go up to bed—running and chasing each other across the high, shadowy hall and up the wide stairs. We had candles with glass shades, so the grease did not drip when we ran. Sometimes I was frightened, when I was the first to run, and Guy and Hugo came after me round the great bends of the staircase; and Hugo was sometimes frightened, but never Guy.

We would separate at the top of the stairs and call 'Good night' to each other across the echoing space of the hall. Guy and Hugo slept together at the south side of the house. My room was at the opposite corner, looking out eastward to the beech trees, and at night I could hear the owls in the High Wood calling to the owls in the ivy—till the world seemed full of owls.

On the north side of the house was a small stretch of park, with a drive meandering through it. Once there had been deer in the park, and it was still surrounded by a high iron deer fence, but there were only cows grazing in it now, among the trees. They were Jersey cows, for Cousin John had a prize herd and took great interest in them. They would stand about the house, close up under the dining-room windows, and the soft munching sound they made could be heard distinctly during the pauses in the talk at meals. The dining-room was a panelled room, painted a pale green, with two windows to the north. Our schoolroom led out of it, with one window on to the rose garden and one to the north.

The nursery had been upstairs, where Guy and Hugo now slept, when they were very little, but I can hardly remember the earliest time, when I first came to stay at Yearsly, and afterwards, in the time I think of mostly, we were downstairs in that schoolroom, when we were not out of doors. We made things there; cardboard theatres, and plays and clay statues, and illustrated stories; and we would look out of the window into the garden and show Cousin Delia what we had done.

We used to have tea there too with our governess, Miss

Bateson. She was kind to us and we were fond of her, but she was not very important—not nearly so important as Nunky, who had been Guy and Hugo's nurse, and mine too when I first went to Yearsly, and who looked after us always, in a way, and said good night to us and unpacked for us and saw that our feet were dry. She stayed there always, long after Miss Bateson went away.

There was a round white teapot with bright flowers, raised up a little, on it, and a bright blue bird on each side. It never got broken till Hugo was at Oxford and his scout dropped it—but Hugo had it riveted, and I have got it now. We thought it lovely, and I still do, but Eleanor thinks it absurd, and 'funny,' so we don't use it now. I keep it in a cupboard, and I think I shall give it to John when he marries, if his wife likes it; but perhaps she won't.

We had very nice brown bread for tea, rather a light brown, and spongy—Mrs. Jeyes made it, the Yearsly cook, who had been there always and stayed always—the servants never changed at Yearsly—and milk and butter from Cousin John's Jersey cows, specially nice butter. Sometimes one of the cows would look in at the window, the north window, on to the park. Once Guy got out of the window on to a cow's back, and rode off on it—but the cow kicked him off very soon, and we watched him chasing it and laughing, but he could not get on again.

We had ponies, too, that grazed in the park with the cows. We used to catch them ourselves and ride about bareback on them. When we were older we rode out properly with the coachman, Mathew, and Guy became a great rider. I loved it too, but Hugo did not ride so much when he grew older. I was sorry he didn't, for I always did the same as he did, when I could.

The dogs were deerhounds. There were always two of them and sometimes three, and Cousin John had black spaniels as well. The dogs lived outside in kennels, or at the stables, but they played with us and were very much part of our life.

It is hard for me now when I think of those years at Yearsly to see them clearly and critically at all. It seems to me now that the life we led was a perfect life, as happy and complete as any children could possibly have. I know that it is unlikely to have been quite perfect, for nothing is; perhaps we were too idle; perhaps we should have been made to work harder and take lessons more seriously. I know Walter thinks we were all spoiled, that the realities of life were not brought before us, and that Guy and Hugo suffered afterwards for this. There may be something in what he says. I don't know. I only know that it was the happiest part of my life and I believe of theirs too, and that it has helped me afterwards, when things were bad and difficult, to look back to those times and live them over again; and as for Guy and Hugo, they were and are to me all I could wish for anyone to be, and I cannot wish anything at all different about them.

IV

The first big change came when Hugo went to school.

Guy had gone two years before, when he was ten years old. That made a break in our lives, of course; we missed Guy badly, but it seemed somehow in the order of things and natural. It had always been settled for Guy to go away to school when he was ten. He had accepted the idea, and Hugo and I accepted it for him. He was ready to go, and there was nothing tragic in the separation.

He went and came back, and went again and came back again. The term time while he was away passed not interminably, and he slipped back into our life each holiday time without a serious break.

With Hugo it was quite different. We had known that it was intended for him to go some time, but vaguely. Cousin Delia had said so at the time Guy went, and Guy spoke of it from time to time. But it had not seemed real or imminent, and had not worried us. Just as we grown-up people live always with the knowledge of death in front of us, yet do not think of it much, until it comes certainly near.

So two years went by after Guy's going, and we had grown accustomed to life with him only sometimes there, and were as happy as before, and as free from care. Then, a month after Hugo's tenth birthday, Cousin Delia told him that he was going to school with Guy the next autumn.

It was June. I found him lying in the hayfield, quite still, on his face with the long flowering grasses and the buttercups above his head.

I had known something was the matter, but I did not know what it was. I was up in our house in the Happy Tree, and I knew suddenly that something had happened bad, that Hugo was in trouble. I came down from the tree and looked for him, and for a long time I could not find him. I looked for him in the Walled Garden, by the Frog Pond, in the Ruin; I knew he was not in the wood; then I went down to the stream and walked along it; and then I began to wonder if Hugo was dead. Then as I came back from the stream I found him, lying like that, in the long grass.

I sat down beside him in the long grass and asked him what had happened, and at first he did not answer.

Two white butterflies were chasing each other backwards and forwards over his head. The buttercups nodded and swayed in the faint wind, and the soft, feathery heads of the grass.

They touched against my cheek, too, as I sat there, squatting on my knees. They were almost as tall as I was.

I bent down and touched him and spoke to him again.

"I am going to school in the autumn," Hugo said at last, and his voice sounded muffled as though it came from a long way off, and was not his.

It was like being shot—like the world stopping. I sat straight up again; even so the grass came level with my head.

I could not realize it at first; it seemed too dreadful to believe; and then a blind resistance came over me, an unreasoning impulse to protect him from this unbearable thing. I felt much older and stronger than Hugo and very fierce.

I snuggled down beside him and put my arm round his neck. He seemed suddenly very little and helpless, with no one in the world to protect him except me.

'You shan't go, Hugo,' I was saying. 'I won't let them. . . . They mustn't do it.'

Hugo shook his head.

'It is no good, Helen,' he said. 'I shall have to go. I don't want to. I am afraid of it—and nothing will ever be the same any more.'

I thought he was crying, but he wasn't, for he sat up then and looked at me.

His face was quite white and his eyes that were always big and dark looked bigger and darker. His whole face looked pinched and tragic as though he saw and understood so much beyond this one thing.

And I realized suddenly, for the first time, the relentlessness of time and the inevitability of change. I understood that I could not resist, and what that meant.

Something was passing, a door was closing, and nothing in the world could hold it open. Hugo was helpless, and I was helpless; and every one. We could not stand still and we could not go back; and what we had had, we could never have again.

I shut my eyes very tight and tried to understand, and a queer feeling came over me that in one moment more I would understand everything—the secret of life and the universe— something unutterably splendid and complete, but the moment passed, the secret receded. It had gone, and I could not grasp it; only the sense of helplessness remained, and of inevitability.

'Is this growing up?' I asked Hugo.

And he nodded.

'I think it is the beginning of growing up,' he said.

We sat very still for a long time, holding hands and not speaking. The butterflies had fluttered away, but the sun shone just as brightly; birds were singing in the willows by the stream, and somewhere up by the house the dogs were barking.

'Can you bear it, Hugo?' I asked at last.

And he answered:

'I don't know. They will try and take away my inside world, and perhaps they will take it away, and then what can I do?'

I said:

'Our inside worlds are too private for that. They wouldn't know about them at a place like school.'

He said:

'I have thought of that. One might keep it quite hidden away and pretend.'

I said:

'People don't know anything about what one thinks except here, you know, Hugo, and if they don't know they can't do any harm.'

'That's what Mother says,' he answered. 'She says no one can take one's inside world away ever; and nothing can matter too badly while one has that—but she says one must learn to live outside as well, and school does that—and Guy does that, of course.'

'Oh, Hugo, what shall I do when you are gone?'

'I suppose dying is like this,' Hugo said seriously. 'One going away—the other being left behind. It happens to every one and yet it is just as bad.'

When we went indoors I found Cousin Delia in the drawing-room. She was standing by the end window, looking out into the rose garden, and her back was to me.

I called her and she looked round. She held out her hand to me and I ran up to her.

'Must Hugo go to school?' I asked her, and she nodded her head. I looked up and saw she had been crying.

'Dear heart, he must—isn't it cruel?' she said, and I felt as though I had said already all that I was going to say, and she had answered all. I threw my arms round her and burst into tears.

'Oh, Cousin Delia, I can't bear it!' I cried.

She called me her pet and kissed me, and said again to me what she said to Hugo; it was kinder to him really to send him now, she said.

'Life will be hard for Hugo,' she said. 'I know that. I have always known it; but it will be worse if we put it off. We can't run away,' she said. 'We can't shut ourselves up for always. He has to go out into the world and fight some time, you know, Helen. Oh, my little Hugo—I would save him if I could!' She turned suddenly away and sobbed.

I had never seen her cry; she was so quiet and calm as a rule; my mother called her cold—and it frightened me, I felt more than ever that something momentous had happened.

That afternoon we sat in our Happy Tree and told stories

and talked very solemnly, about school and life and growing up. After tea Cousin John took us riding on our ponies. He was kind and cheerful as he always was, and did not seem to feel that anything tragic was happening at all. He never understood things as Cousin Delia did, but we enjoyed our ride and were happier after it; and the next morning when we woke up, the grief was less.

This sounds, I expect, a great fuss about nothing. What is it, you will say one little say—boy going to school? But even now, when I think of that day, it seems just as heartbreaking, just as momentous, as it did then. It is not, after all, the event itself that makes the tragedy, or significance, but the effect of that event on the people concerned. Guy's going to school was not tragic; Hugo's was. It was like going to the war; like being killed—at least in one way—something terrible to be faced and gone through with; and he did face it and go through with it; and it was not less painful because we were children.

V

We were happy again that summer, as the days and weeks passed by, but the shadow of the coming autumn was over us. We would remember suddenly in the middle of playing, and stop. One said without thinking, 'We will do that in the winter—or when the nuts are ripe'—or something of that sort, and then remembered that Hugo would not be there.

Guy was very kind to Hugo.

He said to me:

'I am sorry for Hugo. You see, I like school. It is different for me—but Hugo minds things more.'

Once, many years later, he said almost the same again. When he was in hospital and very ill, he said:

'I am worried about Hugo—it is different for a tough fellow like me——but Hugo minds things more.' And I remembered. It was like Guy, dear old Guy; he minded things quite enough in his different way.

The day came at last; the 22nd of September. The last week was a misery, but it passed too; and Guy and Hugo went off together.

Soon after that I left Yearsly and went to London to my grandmother, in Campden Hill Square. My mother was there too, mostly, but she travelled about so much that she did not really live in any place at all. She organized Women's Trade Unions and societies for Citizenship and things of that kind.

My mother had been at Newnham and got a First Class in Economics. She was very clever and competent. She lectured in Economics too.

I was a disappointment to her, I know, for I was not clever, and not interested in those things at all. I don't think she would ever have bothered about me much. I don't think she would ever have cared about children or wanted to be with them. She had not time. And I am glad of that, for if she had cared more, she would not have let me go to Cousin Delia as she did, when my father died, for she did not like Yearsly nor the Lauriers. If she had kept me with her I don't know what would have happened. I don't know how I could have grown up at all.

But now when I went back for a bit, it did not matter. It was really my grandmother who counted, and I loved her. She used to be at Yearsly sometimes before, when I was there, and I had gone back to her always from time to time. She was my father's mother, Mary Geraldine's granddaughter. She was not different and hostile, as my mother was.

I think that my grandmother must have been a rather wonderful person. My father had loved her very much. I have seen letters he wrote to her from Afghanistan just before he died, and letters when he was a boy, before he was married. She had grown up at Yearsly in the strange time after Mary Geraldine's death, when our great-great-grandfather was still alive and kept everything like a museum of his wife. His son and daughter-in-law lived with him and their two children. Yet they had not been oppressed by him. They had grown up unwarped and contented, loving their home and their strange old grandfather, and when my grandmother married the chain had not been broken. My father and Cousin John had been more like brothers than cousins, although they must have been very unlike in themselves.

I think now that my father's marriage must have been a

sorrow to her. I don't think she can have liked my mother really, but in the time I remember she never showed it. She made it easy for my mother to come and go as she wished, with no constraint upon her. She never appeared to disapprove of her—not even of her neglect of me. Of course I did not understand these things at the time. It is only now, looking back, that I see what a difficult situation it must have been, and how well she dealt with it.

I don't think it would be true to say that I disliked my mother. I admired her in a way, and I think her poor opinion of me had a very strong effect upon me. It was her own doing that I felt her so definitely in opposition to Cousin Delia, and that inevitably raised hostility in me. I think now that it was curious in so clever a woman that she did not conceal her feelings more.

It was only years afterwards that Grandmother told me of my father's wish for me to go to Delia when he died. He had sent for Cousin Delia and asked her to take care of me, to have me with her at Yearsly as much as she could. My mother did not want me herself, but she could not forget this.

VI

For about two years I was mainly with my grandmother. I had a governess and went to classes with six other little girls.

After that I went away to school. I was not unhappy, but that time did not seem to count. In the holidays, when Guy and Hugo came home, I went to Yearsly, and that was like coming alive again. The holidays were much shorter than the term time, but they stand out in my remembrance as the only real parts of those years.

I believe many children have this power of detachment, almost like a sort of suspended animation—a living quite apart in an untouchable world of one's own, when the outside world is too uncongenial. Certainly Hugo and I did it. Guy did not need to. It was not that he cared less for home, but he had room for more different enjoyments, more different people and forms of life.

These holidays at Yearsly stretch out, in one way, as an unbroken continuity, so that the time before school and this are not separated really by the big break which we felt at the time.

I have felt like that often with big and important events in life, or what seem to one so at the time. In one sense they are irreparable and complete, and nothing is ever the same again, and in another they seem after a certain time to have made no difference at all.

What is different 'and what the same'? I suppose there is no test—no way of knowing—just as with a person—they change and yet are the same. When I think of myself as a child, through all these years I am writing about, in one way I see myself as quite a different person——a child whom I watch and wonder at, sometimes, and from whom I am quite detached; and yet in another way I feel all the time, that that child and I myself, now, are one. And both are true.

Only Hugo does not change. He grows, of course, and changes to that extent, from a child into a man, but from the earliest time that I remember him, and I cannot remember any time before that, it is the same indescribable personality. He is different and more lovable than other people. Not cleverer, nor better, exactly. Guy could do most things better than he could, and many other people are as good; but no one I have ever met was like Hugo in the special quality he had. Guy felt it too, and Cousin Delia, and the Addingtons did, and, I think, Sophia Lane Watson. Some people did not understand Hugo at all.

Walter didn't, and some of the people at Oxford. I have heard people say he posed, and gave himself airs, and it used to bewilder me at first that anyone could be so wildly mistaken.

Hugo never posed. I don't think he could have, if he had tried. He cared so little what other people thought of him. He lived so entirely in a world of his own.

He was kind, and very careful about hurting people's feelings, when he thought of it, but often he used to forget altogether that anyone was there. He said odd things sometimes, unexpected sort of things, because what he saw struck him in some unexpected light. It would never have occurred to him to say what he said for any other reason.

It used to worry me at one time that Walter did not appreciate Hugo, but that was a long time ago. I see now, and have seen for many years, that they never could have understood each other. They spoke different languages—or rather they used the same words for quite different meanings.

Walter once said:

'Hugo has charm, certainly, but he is an unsatisfactory fellow. What is there behind all that?'

And another time he said:

'If Hugo had ever done a good day's work one would know where one was with him.'

And I could not explain. Hugo did work in his own way constantly, practically all day long, but it was not the kind of work that Walter could recognize or admit. Hugo was living and taking in and trying to understand all the time. If Hugo went for a ride on a bus—afterwards, when we were older— he found drama and beauty and queer exciting romance. He would tell one when he came back sometimes about it. The other people in the bus, people he had looked down on walking in the street, lights and shadows in a fog, sunsets in smoke, everything and anything was exciting and inspiring to Hugo; and some one else might have been the same bus ride and seen nothing at all.

It was not that he was exactly observant, for he wasn't. Often he noticed nothing when other people did. But he had a world of his own in which he lived a great deal, and sometimes—you never knew when—outside sights and sounds responded to something in it, and there was an illumination, a sudden quickening into life, of all around.

We who knew Hugo and loved him understood this. I don't think Walter could have been expected to understand; he was too different.

VII

Scenes stand out to me from those school-time years.

Chiefly in summer. The summer holidays were longer— and the summer days at Yearsly were lovelier than anywhere else.

The sound of the mowing machine in the clear mornings; haymaking along the grass hill below the wood;—tossing the hay and playing in it; romping in the little 'pikes' of hay with the dogs. One hot afternoon in particular—it must have been late in August, for they were cutting the corn in the field beyond the willows—paddling in the stream while Guy fished.

Then there were agricultural shows; one in particular I remember, when Guy rode his pony in a jumping competition and won the second prize.

That must have been September, for the corn was cut in nearly all the fields. We drove, Hugo and I, with Cousin Delia in the dog-cart. Guy had ridden over earlier with Cousin John. It was at Shelbury, nearly nine miles away, and we had tea in a tent at the show, and wandered round the field and looked at the horses and the cows—Cousin John was showing his Jersey cows—and flowers in a big marquee and cheeses and butter and eggs. There was the noise of the farmers talking, and the soft stamping noise of the horses, and lowing of cows, and the hot strong sunlight over everything; and then the excitement when Guy's competition came on. He had a grey pony called Griselda, and he rode very well. Hugo and I were breathless with anxiety when it touched the bar once and knocked it down. But there were two chances, and the second time he cleared it. When he rode up to us afterwards with his blue badge we were desperately proud of him, and some of the farmers came and congratulated him, for the boy who won the first prize was much older than Guy, and they were very close.

Afterwards we drove back in the cool of the evening, and all along the road there were people coming away from the show, and cattle and horses, and carts, and some called out good night to us as we passed, and we felt how nice they all were; and when we had turned off the main road on our way to Yearsly, the horses' hooves sounded on the road in the stillness, and we heard the rooks cawing over the trees in the High Wood, and saw them wheeling in great circles, getting ready for bed; and we saw the smoke going up very straight into the sky before we could see the house; and we were very happy.

Walter laughed at me when I first told him that I liked agricultural shows. He thought I was joking. It seemed to him, he said, an impossible thing to like. But I do and always have. We went to them often at Yearsly.

Guy was in the first eleven at Winchester. He sang and he danced, and he rode, and he shot, and he fished, and he played tennis—all well. Hugo and I did most of these things too, but not as Guy did. It seemed at that time that there was nothing Guy could not do. He was handsome too, not taller than Hugo, but much stronger and browner, and he held himself better, and walked as though the earth belonged to him. His eyes were grey—very merry eyes—and his hair bright brown. Every one loved Guy. Hugo worshipped him.

He said:

"There is no one in the world like Guy. He can do everything."

One had the feeling about Guy that the world must be his to do what he liked with; that he could do or have whatever he set his heart on. He threw his head right back when he laughed, and opened his mouth very wide. Anyone who heard Guy laugh was bound to laugh too. You could not help it; it made the world full of laughter.

He used to sing with Cousin Delia a great deal. His voice was a pleasure to her, and his love for the songs she loved.

I remember them singing the 'Agnus Dei' from Mozart's Third Mass one winter evening in the long drawing-room. Guy looked so tall and big in the lamplight, and Cousin Delia so happy; and he let himself go and sang with all his might. It was exciting and wonderful.

Sometimes people came to stay—various cousins and second cousins—and sometimes Guy and Hugo brought friends back from Winchester; but most of them did not count very much.

Guy used to hunt too, and made friends with people he met out hunting. They would come to meals and sometimes spend the night. We liked them when they came, but did not miss them when they went away. We were I think too contented by ourselves. Later when they were at Oxford they made friends who counted in a different way, and became a part of all our lives.

Hugo was very happy at this time. When I think of him in those years, it is generally happy. He did not laugh as Guy did, loud, with his head thrown back; his was a lower, more gurgling kind of laughter; but his eyes danced and his whole face twinkled.

I remember his laughing at me one day in the hay. They were making hay on the grass hill below the wood, and we had been helping, and he threw himself down on one of the new-made 'pikes,' and Guy and I had buried him; and he burrowed out, and his head came through all tangled and stuck over with hay, and his dark laughing eyes shone out of the nest of hay like some wild, but not frightened animal.

One summer we had a passion for Conrad, and read aloud to each other up in our Happy Tree. Another time it was Shakespeare that we discovered for ourselves. Hugo knew a great deal of poetry by heart, more than anyone I have met, but he was not a mooning, moping sort of boy as poetical people are supposed to be. He loved games and swimming and fishing and dancing too—when we were older and used to dance.

I think one of the special qualities about both Guy and Hugo was the way they enjoyed so many different things.

We used to fish in the stream very often—long afternoons with the sun flickering through the willows on to the clear bright water. There was a big pool to the east of the house, below the temple, with a willow slanting out across it, almost horizontally, from the bank, and the bank was rather high. There were perch there, and ling. Sometimes Cousin John would come with us and teach us the art of 'casting,' or tell us about places he had fished in in Norway, and in Persia. He had been in the diplomatic service when he was a young man, before he married. He knew endless curious unrelated things, about places and people and armour and folklore, and the history of weapons of all sorts

Guy would fish for hours at a time, sitting almost motionless on the slanting willow, but Hugo and I would bring books with us as a rule. We would fish for a bit and then read for a bit and then fish again. Guy thought that rather childish, but he never interfered with us or tried to stop us.

That was, I think, part of the special charm of Yearsly. No one ever interfered with anyone else. There was no pressure on anyone or anything to be different from what it was.

One thing we missed during these years was the autumn at Yearsly, when the trees in the High Wood turned red and gold, and the leaves floated down about you as you walked, through the still air, and rustled round your feet. There was a blue haze among the tree trunks and a nip in the air, and often the smell of bonfires, burning up leaves and sticks, and the dew on the grass would lie thick till midday, though the sun was shining. And in the walled garden, the dahlias would be out, and dark red chrysanthemums and michaelmas daisies, and old Joseph, the gardener, would be pottering slowly about the summer borders, clearing up, and rooting out and burning up piles of finished flowers, on the rubbish heap behind the potting shed.

We had to go back to school now, at the very beginning of autumn, leaving with the trees still green and coming back again when they were quite bare.

In the Christmas holidays there were carol singings. Cousin Delia trained the people in the village to sing carols, and they would come in and sing in the hall by candle-light, sometimes with lanterns in their hands, on Christmas Eve; and Guy would sing with them, and Cousin Delia would teach them special things, besides carols. Once it was Bach's Christmas Oratorio. And Guy sang the solo parts. I think that is the most beautiful music I know. They stood there in the shadow of the hall, about twenty people altogether, with their lanterns on the ground. The light flickered upward on the dark wood of the staircase and on faces here and there, but it was mostly shadow, and the sound of the voices rose up and died away in the high darkness of the roof. Sometimes they would go round being waits and sing at other houses, and at farms, and we would go with them, walking back with our lantern after midnight over dark frosty fields, with stars very clear in the frost. Of course it was not always like that—sometimes it was wet and we had colds, and it was all a disappointment—but not often, and somehow I don't remember those times.

We had Christmas Trees too, generally on New Year's

Day, and the children from the village came, and some old people, and then there would be games.

My grandmother came to stay very often at Christmas. We all liked it when she came.

VIII

My own life at school was uneventful. I was not unhappy, nor unkindly treated. I think it was rather a good school, but I did not learn much, and it never mattered to me one way or another. It was time to be lived through, and that was all; and I lived through it without much trouble or distress.

I was not naughty, so far as I can remember. I did not get into scrapes or mischief. But I was not clever at all. Arithmetic I have never been able to do, or the things connected with Arithmetic, and subjects like Literature and Poetry were badly taught. I had learned much more of them from Cousin Delia and from Hugo.

The only friend I made at school was Sophia Lane Watson. She was two years younger than me, and came to school when she was thirteen, so I had been there nearly three years when she came. But I was struck by her as soon as I saw her, and we made friends in a kind of way, almost at once.

She was standing in the 'girls' hall when I saw her first. It was the first day of the summer term, and everything was in a bustle: the noise and uncomfortableness of arrivals; girls rushing about everywhere and shouting to each other, and slapping each other on the back or kissing, according to the 'set' they belonged to. How I did hate those 'first days' at school!

I had come by a different train from most of the others—I don't remember why—and drove up from the station alone. They had taken my luggage in, and I walked in by myself; and there I saw Sophia Lane Watson, standing quite still by the fireplace in the 'girls' hall.' She was quite alone, not talking to anyone, nor reading; just standing still and watching all the hurrying about, quite impassively, with a perfectly expressionless face. She did not look shy or frightened or unhappy—just quite detached—and that interested me. She was a striking-looking child too, with her very big eyes and her straight black hair, and her very white face. Her eyes always looked so dark, much darker than mine or even Hugo's; but they were not black or brown when you saw them close, only grey, sometimes almost green. She was medium height and very thin, and her hands and feet were too big; but rather beautifully made. Her clothes always looked as though they were falling off her; her skirt was always crooked, sagging down in a tail, either behind or at one side. She was certainly not pretty, though I still think she was prettier at that time than afterwards. Perhaps it was only that her queerness was more attractive in a child.

She certainly did attract me. I know I stopped then, on my way through the hall, and looked at her, and she looked at me perfectly stonily, without any change of expression. Then I went upstairs to my room and found the three other girls in it, all talking and sitting on their beds, and I had to stay and talk to them a few minutes while I took off my things; but when I came downstairs again, I went straight up to Sophia and asked her her name. She was still standing exactly as I had left her.

She answered rather slowly:

'Sophia Lane Watson.' Her voice was rather deep; a curious voice.

Then I asked her age, and she told me she was thirteen. She was not very easy to talk to, for she merely answered my questions and volunteered nothing. But I persevered, and offered to take her round the school, and show her the classrooms, and afterwards we went into the garden and walked round the playing field, and we sat together at tea.

She told me that she lived at Salchester, that her father was a Canon of the Cathedral, that she had two brothers and one sister, and that she had never been at school before.

I don't know why, but I felt curiously consoled by her having come. The utter blankness of that first day, the blocks of bread at tea, the noise and hurry and ugliness, seemed less unbearable than usual, and I had a feeling when I went to bed that evening that something important, pleasantly important, had happened.

IX

Sophia Lane Watson and I made friends. It was a rather odd friendship, never very intimate. I used to doubt sometimes if she could be intimate with anybody. She seemed to live her own life inside a sort of fortress, and although she would open the door a little way, she never opened it wide and let one really in. And for me, any friendship at school was a subsidiary thing, not comparable really to my friendship for Guy and Hugo.

But life at school was very different for me after she had come.

She used to surprise me often; sometimes she shocked me; she seemed to have thought and decided upon so many subjects which had never crossed my mind at all.

She told me about the second week of our acquaintance that she was an atheist and an anarchist. She looked at me with a sort of quiet defiance as she said it, and added:

'It is best to be quite plain about it—now you know.'

I don't think I was very sure at the time what either meant. We had never discussed religion or politics at Yearsly. That may seem odd, but it had never come our way, and I only associated anarchists with bombs; but I was not disturbed, for I was sure that I liked Sophia.

She leant me Shelley's *Essays*, and expounded Atheism and Anarchy of a very theoretic kind to me, and I was a good deal impressed. The very fact of not having defined my own beliefs made the shaking of them less severe. Afterwards of course I told Hugo what she had said, and he too read the *Necessity of Atheism* and was interested in it; but Hugo never cared very much for Shelley, not as he cared for Keats, and Shakespeare, and Campion, and *Paradise Lost*.

Sophia was at this time a Shelley devotee. She knew hundreds of lines by heart, not only the lyrics, but a great deal of the political verse as well. I remember her walking down the passage from her bath, in a blue dressing gown, saying over and over with intense feeling: 'I met Murder by the way; He had a Mask like Castlereagh,' and she told me about this time that she thought if Castlereagh were alive now she would kill him.

'Or at least I would like to try,' she added with the sudden drop into reasonableness which often surprised one.

She would talk endlessly on subjects of this sort—freedom and tyranny, and what truth was, and whether there was such a thing as goodness. I expect most of what she said was nonsense, but even so, she must have been precocious for a child of thirteen. But of her personal feelings she hardly ever spoke, nor of her home.

I thought at first she was homesick, but she was not. I don't think she liked her home any more than school. She gave me the feeling sometimes of a creature at bay, on the defensive somehow against life. She said once—I forget how the subject came up:

'I hate pretty people—my sister is pretty.'

And another time when I had been speaking about Yearsly, she looked at me seriously with her big green eyes and said:

'It is curious how you love Guy and Hugo. I should have thought you would dislike them, being brought up with them like that.'

These were the sort of things that shocked me at first, but not when I knew her better. I realized then that she did not mean them in a shocking way.

I thought how differently I should feel if I had not lived at Yearsly, if, for instance, my own mother had brought me up, and I felt very sorry for Sophia, and that made me like her more.

She was in a higher form than me, although she was younger, and I did not see much of her during the day, but in our second term we were put to sleep together, just us two in the room, and we used to talk in the mornings and evenings, and on Sundays, when we went for walks. Sophia had been ill and she was not allowed to play games. She always went for walks, and I did so too when I could, and walked with her.

It was the end of that second term that she made her sensation.

There were always recitations at the end of that term, and a prize for the best recitation. That time there was a choice of three pieces, all Shakespeare, and one was Lady Macbeth's speech.

I was considered good at this, and there were two or three others who were good. Nobody expected anything of Sophia—she was so unemotional and stiff as a rule.

And then suddenly she took us all by storm.

She stood up on the platform, looking like a ghost, and the moment she began to speak a thrill ran through us all. There were visitors there, parents and people, and they too were completely taken by surprise.

It was not like a child reciting at all. Her great deep voice rose and fell, with an odd little break in it at times. She held her hands in front of her and rubbed at the spot like some one in a dream. It was, I still believe, a marvellous bit of acting, quite on a different level from anything we were used to. When it was over there was a thunder of applause, and Miss Ellis, the head mistress, went across to Sophia and shook hands with her. The recitals were her special subject, and the visitors were all asking who Sophia was.

Sophia slipped off at the back of the platform and came back to her seat in the hall, but afterwards when the prize-giving was over people crowded up to her, girls and their parents and mistresses. There was a buzzing and a fuss, and I could see that Sophia was not liking it. Then she disappeared, and when Miss Ellis wanted to introduce her to a distinguished old man who had written about Shakespeare she couldn't be found, and Miss Ellis was annoyed. Afterwards I found her under her bed, crying bitterly on the floor. She was quite wild and wouldn't come out, and told me to go away. At last I got her to come out, and tried to find out what had upset her, but for a long time I couldn't make out. She kept saying that she could never come back to school now, she could never face the girls again.

'Why did I do it?' she wailed. 'What possessed me to do it? Now I have let them inside and I have given myself away. Oh, it is awful! And perhaps they will say something about it at home!'

I thought vaguely that she must have some plan of going on the stage, but it was not that.

'Don't you understand?' she said at last. 'It is as though

you had got up and told all that crowd just what you feel about Guy and Hugo and Cousin Delia. You couldn't live if you had done that, could you? Can't you imagine it?— Ella Price and Rosa Baylis and all of them.'

She was beside herself. I think now it was probably a reaction from excitement, and that she hardly knew what she said, but I was frightened then. I did what I could with her, and got her into bed. I think she agreed to go to bed as a means of avoiding the girls downstairs. Then I told a Miss Singleton, whom we both liked, that she was not well, and Miss Singleton came up to see her. I don't know how much she told Miss Singleton.

The next morning the school broke up, and we all went away. I wondered if Sophia would come back after all the next term. She did; but she would not speak about that evening, and she would not recite again all the time she was at school.

I told Hugo about it in the holidays, and he did not seem at all surprised.

'I quite understand her feeling like that,' he said. 'That is if it was really good, you know, not just good, but really first-rate, and it must have been from what you say. Like saying your prayers aloud, real prayers, and then finding suddenly you had done it. . . . I should like to see that Sophia.'

I asked Sophia to come to Yearsly at Easter, but she couldn't. One of her brothers had whooping cough, and she was in quarantine; and I asked her again in the summer, but for some other reason she couldn't come.

When she did come for a few days the next year, Hugo was disappointed in her. She didn't talk and seemed out of it, and Guy thought her too 'intellectual.' He was in a phase of disliking 'intellectual women.'

X

Sophia wrote a great deal of poetry. She did not show it to me till I had known her over a year. I don't know now if it was good; I thought so then. It was odd, passionate stuff, very correct in form. She wrote a good many sonnets, some obscure, rather mystical things about the universe, and some love poems, which surprised me very much. I wanted to show them to Hugo, but she would not let me.

'I don't want anyone to see them ever,' she said. 'I have only shown them to you—and I shall be sorry about that!'

At the end of her second year at school Sophia got pneumonia. She was very ill indeed, and there were special prayers for her in the school service.

Several girls cried. Ella Price came up to me afterwards, wiping her eyes.

'I shall never forgive myself,' she sobbed, 'never, if anything happens to Sophia.'

'You were always unkind to her,' I said.

Then I was sorry for Ella, for I thought how terrible it would be if Sophia did die, and she knew she had been unkind.

'I don't think you mattered very much to her,' I said.

It did not console Ella, but it was the most I could say. I was unhappy about Sophia, and it made me angry with the people who had been unkind.

Sophia got better, and when she was better I was allowed to sit with her, and I asked her one day if she had been frightened when she was so ill.

She looked at me a long time without speaking, and her eyes looked enormous.

'Not frightened of dying,' she said. 'I heard them talking once, and they said, "Not much hope now—just a chance," and I was glad.'

I thought:

'"Not much more to face." I can't face life when I am tired.'

It gave me a shiver to hear her.

'Are you really so unhappy, Sophia?' I asked.

And she said:

'Not unhappy, exactly—but I do hate life. I feel it trying to down me all the time, and sometimes I am afraid that it will in the end.'

I wondered what Cousin Delia would have made of Sophia. She would not have felt like that, I thought, if she had been with Cousin Delia.

Sophia and I remained friends, but as the time went on it was not equal. She needed me more than I needed her. I think she wanted some one to admire and love very much, and she had no one else—and of course I had.

She said to me once:

'I wonder sometimes what it would be like to be lovely like you.'

And I laughed at her and said:

'But you don't like pretty people.' But I was pleased.

She said quite seriously:

'I feel differently about it since I have known you, and besides, you're more than pretty. You're *lovely*. It's like the sun coming out of clouds when you come into a room!'

I laughed at her, but I liked her saying that, all the same. Nobody had said things like that to me before.

When I went home the next holidays I wondered if Guy and Hugo thought me pretty, and Cousin Delia. I wanted to ask them, but I couldn't.

What I enjoyed perhaps most at school was the dancing.

We had dancing lessons twice a week and practice dances on Saturday evenings.

It was like discovering a new world to me, learning to dance. We only danced with each other, of course, and with whichever partner was allotted to us, except on Saturdays, when we chose as we liked. There was one girl called Flora Hilman, whom I always danced with when I could. She was very tall, with red hair, and she danced beautifully. We hardly ever spoke to each other in between, but we danced together whenever we could, and I forgot everything else when we were dancing. I expect she did too, but she never said so and I never asked her.

I met her once after leaving school. She was walking in Kensington Gardens with a man in a top hat, and I was with Guy. We stopped when we saw each other and looked pleased. I think we both thought at first that we had lots to say to each other, and then found there was nothing at all. We said:

'How funny to meet here.'

But it wasn't funny really, as we both lived in London.

Then we said:

'How nice to see you again,' or something like that.

And she said:

'Do you ever go down to Ellsfield now?' (The School was called Ellsfield.)

And I said:

'No, do you?'

And she said:

'Yes, I do sometimes.'

Then we waited a minute or two, and Guy and the man in the top hat said something to each other, and then we said 'Good-bye.'

I have never seen her again. Somebody told me she had married a German just before the war, but I didn't believe it somehow, I don't know why.

Sophia couldn't dance at all. It was funny how she couldn't learn, and I think she was sorry about it. And she couldn't play the piano. She started to learn Russian about this time. She got a dictionary and grammar, and some Russian books, and she used to try and learn it in odd moments, in bed at night, and at times when she ought to be preparing lessons. She had a passion for Tolstoy at this time, and said she must read him in the original. She did not get time to do much at school, but she learned quite a lot by herself in the holidays.

It seems odd in a way, considering how much we were friends at that time, that we did not keep up with each other more afterwards. It was my fault, I think. I left school two years before she did, and my life was so full of other things and people that she slipped out. We wrote to each other for a time, and she kept on writing for a bit after I had stopped. It was on my mind, I know, that I had not answered her letters. I kept meaning to, and putting it off, and then I wrote and she did not answer, and we let it drop. When we met again, later, it was quite a different thing, just as one meets a stranger.

XI

When I was sixteen my mother married again and went away for good. She married a Canadian judge, with some special scheme for prison reform. He had reorganized the penal system in Manitoba, my mother said, and that interested her. They went to live in Winnipeg, and only came back at long intervals to visit England. I believe she was happy in Winnipeg. She ran evening classes and formed Women's Societies of different kinds. When I saw her next, about five years later, she seemed to me kinder than before, and more tolerant, and I think that may have been because she was happier.

Once, long after this, Cousin Delia said that she had been sorry for my mother, and that had surprised me very much. She had never seemed the sort of person one could be sorry for, but when Cousin Delia said that it made me think about it, and I wondered if she understood that nobody cared for her, none of my father's people, I mean, and I wondered if perhaps that had made her harder and more aggressive. After all, she could not help being what she was, always wanting to alter things and put people right, and of course if she was like that, it must have been disappointing for her that my father was not and that I was not. I can see too that to her, Cousin Delia might be irritating just because she was so peaceful and didn't want to upset things at all.

They never said they did not like her; they were very careful about that, except Guy and Hugo, of course; but I knew, and I knew that Cousin Delia had asked her to come to Yearsly and that she never came.

Her marriage made very little difference to me, but it was a certain relief. I felt as though a quite vague fear had been removed—a fear that some time she might assert herself and claim me, and take me away from Cousin Delia and my grandmother. Now I knew she would not.

XII

The next thing that happened was Guy's twenty-first birthday. He had been at Oxford two years by then, and Hugo was just leaving Winchester.

It was on the 15th of July, and there was a party at Yearsly.

On the day before there was a dinner to the tenants and a school treat, but on the day itself there were no official festivities, just a party of people Guy wanted, mostly staying in the house, and a dance in the evening in the hall.

Hugo and I had come back from school for it, for the school terms were not quite over. It was my first real dance, and I was very excited.

A good many people were staying in the house. There were three Oxford friends of Guy's—Ralph Freeman, John Ellis and Anthony Cowper. Ellis and Cowper had been at Winchester with him too, and stayed with us before. Ralph Freeman was new. Then there were Mary and Margaret Lacey, second cousins of Guy and Hugo on the other side, they too had stayed at Yearsly before, and Faith Vincent, the Vicar's daughter, and Claude Pincent, who was also some sort of cousin of Cousin Delia's. There were no other Laurier cousins, for my grandmother and Hugo's grandfather had no other children but our fathers.

Claude Pincent too had come before, but not often. He was older than Guy and had been at Cambridge. He was supposed to be a very brilliant young man, and we were a little bit in awe of him. He was distinguished looking, with bright, big eyes and a crest of hair. He seemed much more mature and experienced than we were, and that impressed us too.

In the afternoon we bathed in the fishing pool by the willow, and then we had tea down there by the stream. Cousin Delia and Cousin John were at the picnic, and we liked them to be there. They never spoiled the fun of what we did—even rather silly young parties like this one.

It was a perfect day, hot and almost cloudless, and the hay was not yet cut. Buttercups danced in the long grass, just as they had on that day nine years before when we heard that Hugo was going to school.

The pool was hardly big enough to swim in, but it was clear and deep and very lovely, and the dogs came too. Maurice, the deerhound, stood on the bank and watched us, but Libbet and Oscar, the spaniels, jumped in after us and swam all about. Then we lay in the long grass—we were allowed to spoil the hay for this occasion—and had tea, and laughed a great deal at silly jokes, and then we lay still and were lazy, and before we knew where we were it was time to pack up the tea things and get ready for the dance.

The Hall had been decorated since the morning. Cousin Delia and old Joseph had done it together, and I had helped them for a bit. There were big clusters of roses in silver vases—light coloured roses against the dark wood of the stairs and the panelled wall—and four white lilies in pots at the four corners, and there were sconces with pale green candles fixed up along the walls to light later on, when it got dark.

Mary and Margaret were sharing a room, and Faith Vincent, who was a special friend of theirs, had brought her dress to change in their room. I was alone in mine and I was glad. It was always the same room, looking out into the beech trees on one side, and the big light window to the north, and the shiny chintz curtains were the same that I had always had, and the little comfortable arm-chairs. There was a special jug and basin too—rather too small for general use, but pretty— very fine clear china and hand-painted flowers. Cousin Delia had put it there for me when I was little and I would not have it changed. Now there was a shining brass can of hot water waiting for me and a thick soft towel over it, and Nunky came in to help me dress.

I had a pale yellow dress, very pale yellow and very soft and plain. It was the first time I had worn a low-cut evening gown. The first time too that my hair was to be done up.

Nunky was as pleased dressing me as though she had been dressing a doll. I had yellow stockings and satin shoes too, and Cousin Delia had given me a coloured Spanish shawl, which belonged to Mary Geraldine. It was a beautiful shawl. The colours were a little faded, but still brilliant. It had a creamy background and a quaint intricate pattern of bright flowers upon it; red and pink flowers and bright green leaves.

I sat in front of the looking-glass while Nunky did my hair, and laughed at myself and her, reflected smiling at me in the glass.

My hair was not difficult to do, for it was always curly— a little bit curly, so that it stayed where it was put—and very bright golden brown. I know that it was pretty hair. It is so long ago now, that it is not silly to say so, for it isn't like that any more.

I was pleased with my hair done up. It looked much nicer, I thought, than just tied behind with a ribbon. And with the stockings and the satin slippers and the dress. I was pleased with my bare neck and arms. I had a dark blue enamel bracelet that was almost black, and a little necklace of yellow topaz, that my father had brought back from India for me when I was a baby.

Then Cousin Delia came in to see me, and she turned me round and round, and then she kissed me, smiling as though she were pleased.

'Dear heart,' she said.

I put the Spanish shawl round my shoulders: I loved its many colours and its softness and we went downstairs.

They were mostly there already, standing about in the hall. Hugo was in the furthest corner talking to Anthony Cowper and Faith Vincent. Guy was standing at the foot of the stairs with Claude. They looked up at us as we came down. Cousin Delia came first, and I followed her. The candles were not lit yet, for it was still broad daylight, but the hall seemed filled with light, as though it were illuminated—coming down into it, with its flowers, from the shadow of the stairs. They both looked up at me and smiled.

Guy said:

'That's splendid, Helen. You do look nice'—and he too looked pleased.

I laughed and went past them into the hall, and as I passed I heard Claude say to Guy:

'I say, Guy, that little cousin of yours is a beauty!'

And I felt all warm and glowing, and as though I was stepping on air. I ran across to Hugo, and he turned to look at me.

'Jolly,' he said, 'and that shawl is just right. I love that shawl.'

There was supper first, two long tables in the dining-room; and after supper more people arrived, various neighbours, and the dancing began.

The music was in the drawing-room with the doors open, and we danced in the hall. The floor was polished oak, very smooth and perfect for dancing, and there were chairs at the end for the older people who were there.

Claude came up and asked me to dance, and I said, 'Oh, the first is for Hugo'—but I danced with him afterwards, three times, and then with Guy.

Guy was the best dancer I know. It was like his riding and his singing and everything he did—a complete mastery and ease, as though it all came naturally to him with no trouble or effort at all.

Hugo was not so perfect, but I loved dancing with him, and we danced together a great deal.

Later the candles were lit, the pale green candles on the wall, but it was not dark outside, hardly twilight, and the big doors were open at each end of the hall, and people went out between the dances and walked about or sat in chairs on the lawn.

Hugo and I went out into the garden. We were hot with dancing and it was cooler outside.

There was a crescent moon, low down still over the walled garden, and a long line of pink sky where the sun had just gone down. There were stars beginning to show, pale stars in the light sky, and the air was very warm and still.

We turned towards the walled garden. Cousin Delia's roses smelt sweet as we passed them, and we stopped and wandered about on the little flagged paths among the cupids. The tune of the last waltz kept echoing through my head, and my feet seemed to be dancing while we walked.

'It is too hot to go in for a bit,' said Hugo, 'and awfully nice out here.'

And I said:

'Yes, it is nice out here too.'

The jasmine on the Jasmine Gate smelled strong in the warm air. We stopped to smell it. There was something strange and exciting in the strong scent—all the garden round seemed excited that night, still and expectant and waiting for something, and I was excited, and Hugo. He pushed open the Jasmine Gate and we walked through into the walled garden. A spray of jasmine was hanging down. It caught in my hair as we stepped under it. I put up my hand to pull it away, but I couldn't at first. Hugo undid it for me. He broke off the spray and gave it to me, and I stuck it into the front of my dress. The Spanish shawl slipped down from my shoulder and Hugo lifted it up. The music had begun in the house again. We could hear it, dimmed by the distance and the high garden wall. Up in the High Wood the owls had begun to call.

I looked up at Hugo and found him looking at me. There was something strange in his eyes that I had never seen before. I felt elated and a little frightened, and still very excited and happy. We stood and looked at each other, without speaking, and then Hugo touched my arm.

'Oh, Helen, how lovely you are!' he said suddenly. 'I never knew you were like this!'

There was an odd excitement in his voice, and his face was very white. He was breathing fast.

A thrill ran through me, and then I was afraid. I looked at Hugo and he looked at me, and I felt his fingers, warm and strange, on my bare arm.

And it seemed to me suddenly that he had become strange himself—that he was not the Hugo I knew at all. I found that I was trembling all over, and could not stop. I could not bear his fingers on my arm. I wanted to pull it away, but I did not dare.

Then Hugo stepped back and took his hand away, and it seemed as though something had snapped. It seemed as though a barrier had come down between us, and we were suddenly very far apart. Something had happened to us that I could not understand. We had become strangers to each other and to ourselves, and for the first time in our lives we were afraid of each other, and shy.

Again I had the sense of a door closing, of time passing and not to be called back. It will never be the same again, never in all our lives, I said to myself, and a sense of complete desolation came over me. It seemed to me then that the best thing in my life had gone irretrievably. We had broken something that could never be mended.

I shivered, and Hugo asked if I was cold.

I said:

'Yes, a little,' and we turned back towards the house.

Hugo felt the same as I did, or something like it.

I knew that, and he knew that I knew, but we could not

speak of what we felt. For the first time in our lives we had something to hide.

We turned back towards the house, through the Jasmine Gate, and past the rose garden. Francis, the cat, ran silently across the lawn in front of us. Two people were walking about by the statues at the end of the path. I think they were Anthony Cowper and Mary Lacey, but they did not matter. The light streamed out from the windows of the drawing-room, and in a great shaft from the open garden door. The music was stopping again as we reached it, and more couples came out, laughing, and some wiping their faces, for the night was still very warm. Hugo and I went in. We did not dance together again that evening, and the light had gone out for me.

I did not know what I had done, but I felt miserable, and somehow oddly ashamed.

The next day both Hugo and I went back to school.

We did not meet again till the end of the summer, for that August Guy and Hugo went abroad, to France and Italy.

My grandmother came to Yearsly with me, and part of the time the Lacey girls were there, but the place seemed empty and all wrong without Guy and Hugo.

They came back in September only a week before I went back to school, and two other friends of Guy's came too.

In October Hugo went up to Oxford with Guy, but I did not see them there till the next spring.

PART TWO

'For if they do these things in a green tree,
what will they do in the dry?'

—Luke xxiii. 31

I

AND now the Addingtons came into our lives. For the next few years they were part of all we did and thought. They were part of our life. It used to seem odd, during those next years, to realize we had known them so short a time. As soon as we knew them it seemed as though we had always been friends. I think that the Addingtons were about the best people I have known. They were so dear, too, and so true.

Of most people, even people I love very much, I feel that they might in certain circumstances act wrongly or from some bad motive; but with George and Mollie one felt from the beginning absolutely sure that they never would. There was a sort of solid nobility in them both that nothing could shake or alter. They were unlike each other in a great many ways. George was much cleverer than Mollie, much more amusing and more whimsical, but in this essential quality they were the same, and it was this, I think, that attracted Hugo so strongly to them first, and then Guy, and then me. I suppose we three in our different ways all rather lacked this quality. But Guy lacked it less than Hugo and me.

George had been at Winchester with Guy and Hugo, but they had hardly known him there, for he was a scholar, and they were not. It was when they met again at New College that they became friends, chiefly Hugo and George at first, and then Guy too; and Mollie was at college too in Oxford at that time.

The first time I met them was in Hugo's room at New College. He had a room that looked out on the old wall and a wonderful double cherry tree. It was a clear spring day, and the cherry tree was in full bloom.

It was a big room, and Hugo had had it redecorated. It had white walls and grey paint and no pictures at all (that was a phase that Hugo went through; later on he had pictures again). There were books in a long grey bookcase, and a plain grey carpet, and in one corner a big bronze cast of the Delphic Charioteer. The whole room was planned to suit that, and I think it did. There was a sort of plainness about it, an absence of ornamentation and extras of any sort, that was like the straight folds of the charioteer's drapery. That was Hugo's idea, as he explained it.

The curtains were bright Egyptian blue, and the only other colour was from flowers, sometimes blue, sometimes red, as the mood took him, in two tall glass vases on the chimney-piece. Hugo delighted in his room. It was the first time he had designed one for himself, for his room at Yearsly had evolved itself gradually, and was not planned out as a whole.

There were grey arm-chairs, plain to look at but very comfortable, and an oval table of dark mahogany with a blue bowl in the middle.

Later, his pianola was there too, and the room modified its severity a little, but in essentials it remained the same, Even afterwards in London his room was very like it, and I think in its later, more modified form, the room was like Hugo.

Their grandfather had left a special £100 each, to be given to Guy and Hugo on their twenty-first birthdays. Guy had bought a hunter with his; Hugo bought a pianola. He used to play on it a great deal, chiefly Mozart. About the time he was twenty-one Hugo had a passion for Mozart. He would go up to London for Mozart concerts, and sometimes got into trouble for this, and he read everything he could about him. It used to remind me of Sophia Lane Watson and her passion for Shelley. I never had passions of that sort, nor did Guy.

All this, however, was later. That day when I met the Addingtons was in his first year, and he was not yet twenty.

Old furniture and Donne, and George Addington, were his chief interests at this time.

I had come up to stay with a Mrs. Peters who had known my mother. Mr. Peters was a Don and had been coaching Guy. It was the first time I had been to Oxford, for before this I had always been at school, and it seemed to me a wonderful place. I don't know how it is that it seems so different now. Guy and Hugo had been to lunch at the Peters'. Then they took me out and showed me places, and we walked about colleges, and in New College Cloister, and I felt it a place like a dream. It always used to seem like that when I visited Guy and Hugo, and I was often there during the next few years.

Now I try sometimes to see it like that again, but I cannot. I can only remember as a fact that I once felt it so, and I wonder how it was.

Hugo had talked about George Addington at Christmas, and I longed to see him.

'He is such a splendid fellow,' he had said, 'and such a wonderful mind.'

'And such jolly good company,' said Guy.

I was rather disappointed when I first saw him. He and Mollie were waiting for us in Hugo's room when we came in. There was a big fire burning, and hot cakes standing down in covered dishes on the hob, and tea all waiting on the round polished table. Outside the sun was shining, a thin, cold sun, and it slanted in through the window and mixed with the firelight.

The china teapot with the birds on it was there on the table, and there was a feeling of warmth and comfort in the room. I believe now that it was Mollie who made it feel so comfortable, but then I only thought 'What a delightful room!'

She was doing something to the kettle when we came in. I think it had boiled over and she was setting it back again on the coals.

Her back was to us, and I saw George first. He jumped up from the grey arm-chair.

'Late again, of course, Hugo. We had almost left in a rage!'

Hugo laughed and said:

'Here is my cousin Helen, and you can't be cross with me.'

George came forward and shook hands. He was smiling, and I thought he had a pleasant face, but I had expected some one more striking and impressive, and so I was disappointed.

George was too short, and beside Guy and Hugo he looked still shorter. He had grey eyes, not dark romantic grey like Guy and Cousin Delia, but an ordinary blue grey colour, and his hair was mouse colour, rather fair than dark. He had a broad forehead and very straight eyebrows, rather close over his eyes. He was not at all what I had expected.

Of Mollie I had heard less, but I liked her as soon as she spoke. She had a pretty voice, very sweet, and like herself.

She struck me as much bigger than George. I believe she was actually about an inch taller, but she had the same forehead and level eyebrows and grey eyes. These straight brows were characteristic of them both. Her hair was fairer than his, and there was more colour in her face. It has often puzzled me to define why Mollie was not pretty. Her features were well cut and even, and her colouring very pleasant, yet she did not strike one as pretty. One got to love her face and her charming, rather boyish smile, but with both her and George you did not see at first how special they were. Some people never saw, and that used to make me angry.

She was dressed in blue that afternoon. I think it was a blue homespun. I know it seemed just the right colour in that room.

I made the tea in the coloured teapot, and we all sat round the fire and had tea.

Later Mrs. Peters came in. She had to be there as a chaperone, or Mollie would not have been allowed to come. I thought they were joking when they said this, but it was true. It seemed to me a funny idea.

II

Mollie and George Addington had no parents. Their mother had died when they were tiny children and their father when Mollie was sixteen. He had been in business in

Manchester; a cotton business of some sort, and they were brought up in a suburb of Manchester, in a big ugly red house a few miles out of the town. Mollie once showed me some photographs of their house, and it seemed to me odd that George and Mollie should come from a place like that. It was not like them at all. They were rather rich and had a motor-car long before every one did. Their father was interested in politics, and a Liberal. He used to read articles from the *Manchester Guardian* aloud to them in the evenings, and later on when they were older they used to read them to him. It was chiefly Mollie that did the reading; imports and exports and rates of exchange. I asked Mollie once if she had hated all that reading aloud, and she looked surprised.

'No—not particularly,' she said. 'It never occurred to me to hate it, and I was sorry for Father.'

Mollie went to a High School in Manchester. She went in by train with her father in the mornings, and came back alone after tea.

George used to go to a day school too at first, and then he got his Winchester scholarship and went away. Mr. Addington was quite well off, but he had said from the beginning that George should not go to a public school if he did not get a scholarship.

'And so I got it,' said George with his broad smile. 'I don't suppose I should have, except for that. Father was like that; he was grim, and he made people do things.'

Mollie looked after them both. I think she would have looked after them anyhow, but her father put her definitely in charge of the house when she was fourteen. She was given the keys of the store-cupboard and the domestic cash-box, and three months later the housekeeper was dismissed. 'I will give you three months' apprenticeship,' her father had said. 'You will do the housekeeping with Miss Hopkins at first, then under her supervision, and at the end of three months you should be competent to undertake it without help.'

He gave her eight pounds a week, and she had to account for every penny she spent. On the first of each month there was an 'audit day' when she brought her account-book into the study and handed over to her father all the receipted bills. Everything had to be paid in cash, and she might not leave one penny unaccounted for. At first there were many discrepancies. She forget to enter tram-fares; sometimes she gave pennies to beggars and forgot to put them down. Her father was patient with her, she said. He would go over the whole account, checking each item to see if the missing pennies could be traced. Sometimes they could not, and he would write '3*d.* unaccounted for' across the foot of the page. He did not punish her when this happened, but she felt it a disgrace, and sometimes she would cry about it in bed.

This did not happen often after the first year, and Mollie was a wonderfully capable person when I knew her.

Afterwards, when I tried to do accounts and couldn't, I used to wonder if I should have learnt better if I had been trained to do it by Mollie's father, but I don't suppose it would have made much difference really.

Mr. Addington was a Unitarian and a teetotaller. George and Mollie used to go to a big chapel with Morris windows, and they were put into a 'Band of Hope' when they were eight years old, and signed 'pledge cards' to say they would never drink alcoholic drinks. When she was fifteen Mollie had to teach in the Band of Hope. She had to give lessons on the effects of Alcohol on the Human Body, and her father gave her books to read about it in. All this seemed very odd to us when we first got to know the Addingtons. It was so different a world from ours, and yet the Addingtons were like us in fundamental things.

Mollie showed me her 'pledge card' once. It had a picture of St. George fighting the Dragon, by Walter Crane, on it, and some rather fine texts round the sides. It seemed to me a queer, barbarous idea, like 'unclean meat,' or some old primitive taboo.

Mollie laughed when I said so.

She said:

'I suppose it is. I should never make my own children sign anything like that, but I somehow didn't like to give it up. I feel a sort of loyalty to Father. I don't think it matters, but he did; if he was alive I think I should tell him I didn't agree any more and give him back the card. But as he is dead I can't. Perhaps that's rather silly, but after all, there's no strong reason the other way.'

George was not a teetotaller when we knew him. He had felt like Mollie for a time, he said, after their father's death, and then he definitely broke through the feeling of taboo, as something irrational to which one should not give in.

'*Magnus pater sed maior veritas*,' he said, and Hugo laughed at him, and said he was a Puritan in his negation of Puritanism.

Neither George nor Mollie had remained Unitarians. Mollie's scientific mind had overcome her loyalty here; also, as she herself told me, Mr. Addington's religion had been far less vital to him than his political and social creed.

They were both Liberals, and this seemed to me the oddest of all. To Hugo too it seemed odd, but not so much to Guy. I believe that with a different environment Guy might have been a politician. It had always been a joke against Guy that he liked to read the newspaper; not just reviews or headlines, but the solid political articles. But even he had no particular party, and it was the party that seemed so curious to Hugo and to me. To suppose that one could agree, always, on all points, with one group of people, and that one must support one party.

'How can you agree always with one group of people?' Hugo asked George one day, in a punt.

'I don't always agree on every point,' said George, 'but mainly, on the most important questions.'

'But you might agree with one party on one important point, and another on another. What would you do then?'

'That doesn't often happen, as a matter of fact. But if it does, I suppose one would go with the party one agreed with on most points. You must work together with some group if you want to get things done.'

'Yes, getting things done. That's the whole difficulty. I doubt, you see, whether this getting anything done is worth the intellectual dishonesty involved in it.'

George laughed.

'But if you see something very wrong going on, a child working in a mine, or something like that, you want to do something about it. You want to stop it.'

'No,' said Hugo after a pause. 'I am afraid I don't. I only want to run away and not look.'

George laughed again.

'I don't believe that,' he said, 'I am afraid that is "intellectual dishonesty" on your part, Hugo. You don't like to own to an ordinary good impulse.'

Then we all laughed, Hugo too. But he added presently:

'It would not be a good impulse even if I did try to stop a child working in a mine; it would only be another sort of selfishness, removing something that was disagreeable to see.'

And George rejoined:

'But I never said the Liberal Party was unselfish. I never suggested the motive that made them want to remove abuses. I only said they did want to!'

And so it would go on. I used to be interested listening to their arguments. I agreed most with Hugo, but what George said made things stand out quite differently from the way I had thought of them before. Chiefly, though, what interested me, was the fact that George and Mollie should be Liberals themselves. I had taken it for granted that political parties were silly; George and Mollie were not at all silly. That was more convincing to me than arguments on either side.

George was a few months younger that Hugo, Mollie a few months older than Guy. George and Hugo were in their first year at Oxford, Mollie and Guy in their third.

They were all together a great deal during the next two years, and the Addingtons came to stay at Yearsly in the vacations.

Once Guy and Hugo went to stay with them in Manchester, and once I did, but that house never seemed to belong to them as their rooms in London did.

When Mollie had finished at college they left the Manchester home and moved to London, to the flat in Chelsea which seemed afterwards so much a part of them and of our life in the next few years.

There had been a suggestion at one time that I should go to college. If my mother had been at home I expect I should have gone; but Cousin Delia had a slight inclination against the idea, and my grandmother also, and as I was undecided myself the balance turned against.

If I could have been there with Mollie it would have been

different, but she would have left almost as I arrived, and after she had left I saw much more of her in London; and Hugo I should hardly have seen in term time. To be there with him, and rules keeping us apart, I should have hated; and I had had enough of being in a herd of other girls.

So after Christmas I was sent abroad, to a French family first, and then a German.

I stayed five months with each and came back for the summer in between.

It was dull with those families. I had thought it would be exciting to go abroad, but it wasn't. They were kind people, but they never left me alone. I was taken about to museums and galleries and looked after all the time. It was almost less free than school.

When I came back, Mollie had left Oxford. She took only three years there, and went on with her biology in London.

I lived in term time with my grandmother again, and went to classes and lectures at Bedford College. I learned Italian and went on with my music, and Mollie came very often to Campden Hill, and I went to her in Chelsea; sometimes I would meet her at the laboratory where she worked, and we had lunch in an A.B.C.

Often, too, we went to Oxford and saw Guy and Hugo and George. We stayed in lodgings in St. John's Street, generally from Friday till Monday, and we would go long walks, all together, over Shotover sometimes and a long way on towards Otmoor, or sometimes along the Upper River past Godstow and Bablockhythe. There was a ferry there that we used to cross. It was in autumn or winter, that walk. I remember it chiefly with a red frosty sun. And in the summer we would go up the Cherwell in canoes; right up beyond the branching of the rivers, to a place where the willows met overhead and their shadows met together in the water.

III

It was on one of these picnics that I met Walter. George had invited him; it was generally George that brought new people in. He was more interested in different sorts of people than Guy and Hugo.

We were waiting in Guy's room to start for the picnic. He had rooms in Broad Street then, looking on to the Sheldonian Theatre. George came in and said:

'I've invited Sebright to come too. You don't mind, do you?'

'Well, I suppose not,' said Guy. 'He is a dull dog.'

'Who is Sebright?' asked Mollie.

'Oh, he is the star of New College,' said Guy. 'He's got all the pots this year—Ireland, Hertford, Gaisford. I don't know what all—and looks like a mouse.'

'No, not a mouse,' corrected George, 'more buttoned up than a mouse.'

'Well, a stick then—a burnt stick;' and Guy laughed.

'I like him,' said George, 'and I am rather sorry for him too. What do you think, Hugo?'

Hugo was sitting on the table. He smiled his vague absent-minded smile.

'Do you know, I don't believe I've ever thought about him,' he said, and we all laughed at Hugo.

He did not come for thirty-five minutes. That was like Walter too—just to spoil it by keeping every one waiting too long. Hugo was late very often, but no one minded it in Hugo. In Walter they did, but I suppose that was not Walter's fault.

Guy kept saying:

'I shall tell him what I think of him,' and looking out of the window.

He was in a hurry when he did come. Guy saw him first, coming across the Broad from New College Lane. I looked out too and saw him, but he was running and I could only see a figure scurrying along past the corner of the Sheldonian. Then we heard him on the stairs. He was coming upstairs very fast, and stumbled on a loose rod or something at the top. We heard a great scrabble and bump, and then he tumbled against the door and came in.

'I am sorry,' he began, 'awfully sorry I was late.'

He looked round, rather timidly, I thought—but Walter wasn't timid really. 'I had to finish some things.' He was blinking, for the sun shone straight in through the window into his eyes, and the staircase was dark.

I remember him very distinctly as he stood there; his light blue eyes and the iron-rimmed spectacles, and the greenish Norfolk jacket that didn't seem to fit anywhere, and the grey flannel trousers, baggy at the knees, and his fair hair, very straight and lanky, one lock of it flopping down over his forehead. His mouth I noticed even then, rather wide and thin-lipped; a sensitive, rather beautiful mouth, and he had beautiful hands, but that I did not notice till much later.

I felt then chiefly amused at him. He looked so funny blinking there in the sun, and I knew that Guy was very much annoyed with him, and equally well, that he would not say anything at all.

'You didn't tell me you couldn't come at half-past two,' said George mildly.

'No—I'm awfully sorry—I didn't think it would take so long; I had something to finish.'

'All right, we'll come along now,' said Guy. 'This is my cousin Miss Woodruffe, and Miss Addington.'

Walter bowed jerkily at us, and we all went downstairs and out.

IV

It is strange about that picnic; I remember so little about it. It merges in my mind into so many others. I remember that we went up the Cherwell; a long way up, past Water Eaton and under Islip Bridge, and that we had tea and supper, and came back late; but all that was the same as many other picnics, and I cannot remember anything distinctive about this one, except being in a canoe with Walter for a part of the time, and finding him hard to talk to.

It is curious to realize that it made so little impression on my mind when it made so much on his. He told me afterwards that he had hesitated about coming. He wanted to finish a bit of work that afternoon, and then George ran into him in the quad and asked him to come.

'Half-past two at Guy Laurier's rooms,' George had said, and he had answered: 'Oh, thanks awfully. I'd love to come,' and gone on to his room, thinking; 'I needn't go, after all, if I don't want to. I'll wait and see what I feel like when the time comes.'

And he had gone back to his own room and worked at Demosthenes all the morning. By lunch-time he had almost finished what he was doing. He had lunch in his own room, and then went on with the work. He heard the clock strike two, and remembered George, but he said to himself: 'I needn't decide yet. I don't think I will go.'

Then he got intent on his work, and really forgot when it was half-past. When he came to a pause it was nearly three; he looked at his watch and remembered George again.

'The Lauriers and their cousin and my sister,' George had said.

Walter was shy of girls, especially the kind of girls he imagined us to be, and he had even then a sort of prejudice against Guy and Hugo.

He says that he was irritated by their air of superiority, when he knew they had nothing to be superior about. But I believe he was attracted by them too, and annoyed with himself for being attracted. He says that he decided first that it was too late to go, and then thought, 'If I don't go, it will be because I am afraid of them, and afraid of going at the wrong time'; and that decided him the other way. As soon as he decided to go he became in a great hurry, and ran all the way down New College Lane. He said he felt a fool when he tumbled on the stairs, and he said he knew we thought him funny. That made me ashamed, for I had not supposed he would see what we thought at all. That was always happening, though, with Walter. He seemed so stupid at times, as though he didn't understand anything one was feeling or thinking at all, and then long afterwards one found out that he had understood quite a lot.

He said that he looked at me as he came into the room, and that he thought me beautiful, and different from anything he had ever seen before. Of course poor Walter had not seen many women before besides his mother and Maud, and of course I was quite different from them—and that then he wished that he had not come. He said that he felt suddenly that his clothes were all wrong, and he remembered that he had not brushed his hair before he came out, and that for the first time in his life he wished he was different from what he was, handsomer and smarter, and more like what he despised as a rule.

'I blessed George Addington,' he said afterwards, when he was talking to me about that afternoon. 'He was the only person who made me feel at ease. I forget now what he said—something quite ordinary—but I didn't feel he was sizing me up and not quite liking me, as I did with the rest of you.'

He said that he went a long way with me in a canoe and that we talked about New College and the windows in the Chapel, and that he was impressed by my knowledge of stained glass.

That too is funny, for I never knew much about glass, nor was much interested in it, and I don't remember talking about it at all.

He says that I was kind to him, not snubby or supercilious as he had expected. Why he should have expected that I can't understand. Neither Guy nor Hugo was snubby, and certainly not George.

He was afraid I should be annoyed at going in the boat with him. I don't suppose I minded which boat it was. We were all quite near together as far as I remember, and I was very happy on those picnics.

He said that he felt envious of Guy and Hugo because they were often with me, and he felt they were not good enough for me: 'Just the idle commoner type,' he called them—and that I was better than that. He knew even at the time he told me that he had been wrong about them; he got to understand something of them both in the end, but never very much. He was never fair to them, nor they to him, but they realized it more than he did.

At that time, too, he thought me much cleverer than I am.

Walter could not care for anyone whom he did not think clever, and he did care for me. He has told me how he went back to his rooms after that picnic and stood by the window in the dark, and said to himself over and over again:

'I am in love—I am in love with Helen Woodruffe,' and that he could not sleep that night, but walked about his room till early morning. It seems curious to me when he was feeling so much I should have felt so little; that I should have had no notion of what was going on in his mind.

I suppose it was like Hugo. I had just not been thinking about him.

V

Guy went down from Oxford at the end of that term. He took a First Class in History, and then started reading for the Bar.

It always annoyed Walter that Guy had got a first, for Walter felt these distinctions very important. He used to talk of people as first-class intellects or 'the sort of man who might get a Second in History,' and I know he considered Guy should belong to the second group. He said once that he didn't think much of the Oxford History School, because such obviously second-rate people could get firsts in it, and I thought he was thinking of Guy.

I never could see that it mattered very much, or meant very much. George got a first too in his examination, 'Greats,' which was the same that Walter did himself, and Hugo only a second. Walter used to say of Hugo later on that he was good material wasted; that he might have been the scholar type if he had ever been taught to work.

Hugo liked the work he did for that examination. He read a lot of Greek philosophy and got excited about it. He used to read it to me in the vacations at Yearsly and translate it as we went along. We read Plato like that one summer, lying in the hay, one particular 'pike' of hay, on the way to the Temple. It was wonderful stuff, and the idea of one's ideas and thoughts being as real as the actual world pleased both of us. I had always felt that, and so did Hugo, but I did not know that serious people thought so too.

Hugo said he would teach me Greek, and we began it that summer, and we went to see Greek plays in London; but I didn't get very far, and we gave it up after a while, and I read the translations instead.

Guy took some rooms in Clifford's Inn. He took four rooms, for Hugo was to come and live there too when he went down. Hugo meant at this time to go into the Civil Service.

There had been a great deal of discussion about Hugo's career. Cousin John had wanted him to go into the Diplomatic Service, but Hugo did not want that. He could not be always so polite, he said, and that made us all laugh, for it was a joke against Hugo that he was too polite; that he could not be rude or disagreeable to anyone, and sometimes people were annoyed with him because of it, because they thought he had agreed with them when he had not.

Then he thought he would like to be a Curator in a museum, in the South Kensington Museum if possible. But George Addington was going in for the Civil Service as soon as he had finished at Oxford, and it was his idea, I think, that Hugo should do so too.

That next Easter we were all in London: George with Mollie, and Hugo with Guy. They all came to Campden Hill Square. Grandmother made them welcome.

They came and went when they liked, and so did I. It was wonderful, I think now, how she managed with us all. We felt perfectly free, we were free, and yet I believe she knew all that was going on, and was watching us and thinking about us a great deal.

In these later years I got to know my grandmother much better. She had seemed, when one was a child, a little alarming, much farther off than Cousin Delia. I don't think she cared for children naturally, as Cousin Delia did, but now we were older she understood us more, and we her, and we found that she was not alarming at all, but very witty, and full of vitality, and interested in everything that went on.

She was much more lively than Cousin Delia, and I suppose more intellectual.

She read a great deal. Every night when she went to bed she used to read for two hours or more, every sort of book. She had read the French, Italian and English poets, but she did not care much for poetry. She had read the Fathers of the Church and the German Mystics, but she did not care for religion. What she enjoyed most, I think, were the French Encyclopædists, and the French eighteenth-century memoirs. She was, I used to think, very like an eighteenth-century great lady.

When Guy and Hugo came to meals, or George and Mollie, she talked to them quite frankly and simply as though they were contemporaries of her own, but afterwards, almost always, she would go up to her own sitting-room, she had a big sitting-room of her own at the top of the house, and leave them downstairs with me. There was no fuss about it. We never felt hurt that she did not want us, nor yet that she was hurt at our not wanting her. There was no beating about the bush with Grandmother.

'Aunt Gerry is wonderful,' Guy once said. 'It is like talking to a man when you talk to her, not to an old lady.'

She was fonder of Guy than of Hugo. I sometimes thought her a little impatient with Hugo, but I think she loved him too in her own undemonstrative way. George and Mollie pleased her very much.

'They are refreshing,' she said the first time they had come to the house. 'They do me good'; and after a pause while she was polishing her spectacles she put them on, and added, looking at me: 'I did not know Hugo had so much good sense.'

She meant, I knew, as to choose such sensible friends, and also a little to tease me, for she thought me too uncritical of Hugo. So I only laughed and said: 'Perhaps it was they who had the good sense,' and she laughed too and said: 'Perhaps it was.'

I had defended Hugo at first when she criticized him. That had amused her, and she did it more, but she never was unkind about him. She never said things that really hurt either him or me.

VI

It was that Easter that Hugo met Paulina Connell. He saw her first in *The Tempest*. She was playing Miranda, and she did it very well.

We were all there. Guy and George and Mollie and I. We all enjoyed the performance, and we all thought Miranda charming, but Hugo was bowled over.

'Isn't it lovely? isn't it lovely?' he kept saying. 'I think that Miranda is quite perfect. She is just what Miranda should be.'

We knew that that was high praise from Hugo, for *The Tempest* was one of his favourite plays at this time.

We went back to Guy's rooms in Clifford's Inn and had coffee and biscuits, and George began to chaff Hugo about his enthusiasm for Miranda, but Hugo was serious.

'I want to see her,' he said. 'I must get to know her.

How beauteous Mankind is! Oh brave new world

That has such people in't!

Didn't she do that divinely?'

'I shouldn't get to know her if I were you, Hugo,' said George. 'She will probably be a disillusionment. Let her remain the "stuff that dreams are made of."'

Mollie was laughing and I laughed too, but I didn't like it. It gave me an odd little pain to watch Hugo as he talked about her and then I felt ashamed of myself.

Hugo did get to know Paulina. He found that Anthony Cowper knew some one who knew her, and Anthony Cowper's friend took Hugo and him to call one Sunday afternoon.

Hugo told us all about it when they came back. She was just as lovely in private life, he said. She lived with her mother in a flat in Battersea. Her father was dead and she had one brother, called Victor, who was a professional singer. Hugo did not see him, for he was touring somewhere. Mr. Connell had been in business, Mrs. Connell said, but it was an army family—"'military people, you know, and well connected."'

It was Anthony Cowper who reported the conversation. Hugo blushed a little and laughed.

'So hard on dear Paulina,' Mrs. Connell had said to Anthony, 'to have to go on the stage—not that it was a penance at all to her, for if ever a girl had a passion for her art it was Paulina; but of course you understand, Mr. Cowper, it is not the sort of profession her father's family would approve at all. My family is different, you see. We are all artists—artists to the finger-tips—and you understand, Mr. Cowper, to an artist social distinctions do not exist. But I do feel it hard for Paulina. . . . Yes, of course, her father's relations do *not* take the interest in her which one might have expected.'

Anthony Cowper was a mimic, and he made us laugh very much when he described the interview with Mrs. Connell; and now and again he turned to Hugo and said: 'It was just like that, Hugo, wasn't it?' and Hugo admitted with good humour that it was.

'She was rather a terror,' he agreed. 'But Paulina was quite different, and she didn't like it much, I thought.'

Hugo gave a tea-party in Guy's rooms before he went back to Oxford. He invited us all to meet Paulina, and Mrs. Connell came too.

'I had to ask her too,' he explained, 'for she said she did not allow Paulina to go out alone.'

Paulina was beautiful; that was true. She was very fair, with bright, golden hair, very straight and smooth and shining, and serious blue eyes. She had red lips, curved and rather like a Rossetti saint. She was dressed in white, with white furs, and she did not talk very much. She sat looking beautiful and statuesque, and made rather solemn remarks from time to time.

'It is only in the true Socialist State that art will be duly recognized,' she said, and at another time: 'True art has no need for subterfuge.'

What she meant I didn't know, for I only caught scraps of the conversation. Guy and Anthony Cowper were talking to her—but I felt convinced somehow that she didn't really know what she meant herself that she was repeating things she had learnt from somebody else, and that annoyed me, for I had never liked that sort of person.

She always talked about Art. Once she said:

'I live for my Art. A true artist must'; and it sounded silly. A 'true artist' would never have said it, I felt sure.

She was talking to Guy when she said that, and Guy was very funny with her. He looked serious too, and said:

'Really. How interesting. I suppose it is awfully hard work to be a true artist.'

And she answered in a sombre sort of way:

'A crucifixion at times, but one cannot escape one's destiny.'

'Oh no; one can't,' agreed Guy. 'Awfully hard luck, isn't it?'

Guy saw me watching them and his eyes twinkled. He had a trick of raising one eyebrow, the left, when he was amused.

Mrs. Connell said to Hugo:

'Paulina is so sensitive—the artistic temperament all through. Modern life is very hard for the artist.'

Hugo murmured something sympathetic. He wanted to talk to Paulina.

Mollie crossed the room and talked to Mrs. Connell. I saw Mrs. Connell pouring out a long confidence, and Mollie nodding her head from time to time.

George came over to me.

'Are you impressed, Helen?' he asked with his wide smile. 'Does the goddess thrill you?'

I said:

'No, I am afraid she doesn't. I liked her better at a distance.'

'Poor old Hugo,' said George. 'He is a dear goose, you know—but I don't think we need worry.'

I felt extraordinarily grateful to George for saying that. It seemed somehow to make it all right. I had been afraid all day, and before that day; an uncomfortable, unformulated fear that something had been going to happen to Hugo. I had not defined my feeling, and it had in an odd way become less, since Paulina came to tea, and I had seen her myself. What George said comforted me much more. It was like waking up from bad dreams. I felt suddenly very fond of George, fonder than usual.

After tea, when the Connells had gone, I walked back with George and Mollie to their flat.

'I am rather sorry for that girl,' said Mollie.

'Yes, the mother is a terror,' agreed George, answering, as he often did, what Mollie had felt and not said.

'Is Hugo as bewitched as ever, do you think?' Mollie asked, and George shrugged his shoulders and looked at me.

'Helen and I have decided not to worry yet,' he said.

She gave Hugo a big photograph of herself, with the white furs close up round her face, and a big hat pulled low over her eyes. There was a scrawling signature across it. Hugo kept it in his bedroom on his dressing-table. Guy told Mollie about it, and said:

'I don't like it, Mollie. If he had stuck it in his sitting-room I wouldn't have minded it so much.'

And Mollie said:

'But Hugo wouldn't put even his wife out in public—his wife's photograph, I mean.'

And I remembered how he wouldn't have Cousin Delia's photograph out in his study at school. He took it with him every term, and kept it in a box, 'because it was precious.'

And I thought:

'Well, he doesn't put Paulina in a box; that is something.'

He wrote a lot of poetry at this time, and did not show it all to me as he used to. George saw it and said it was good.

We went to the Commemoration Ball that year, and Hugo asked us to bring Paulina.

Cousin Delia came, and we stayed at an hotel. Guy came up too, and Anthony Cowper.

Hugo danced with Paulina a great deal. He danced with me too, of course, but it was not like it used to be. Paulina looked very lovely. She wore a pale blue gown with sequins embroidered on it, that shimmered and rippled when she moved, and her hair shone like corn in the sun.

I sat with Cousin Delia for a bit and watched them dancing, and I wondered what she was thinking.

I wanted to say:

'Paulina is very pretty, don't you think?' and see what she would say. But I couldn't. Cousin Delia would always know what you were really meaning if you tried to say something else.

Once she touched my hand.

'I like that dress of yours, dear heart,' she said. 'Did Mollie help you to choose it?'

Cousin Delia was very fond of Mollie, and Mollie loved her. We were all glad about that.

Guy and Mollie came up to us. I thought how pretty Mollie looked that night, more as she ought to look always, and I thought I would rather look like Mollie than Paulina, in spite of everything.

Hugo brought Paulina to Campden Hill that summer. Grandmother did not like her.

'No, my dear Hugo,' she said afterwards. 'Not a suitable young woman, in my opinion. Unintelligent and pretentious. I advise you to leave her alone.'

Hugo blushed and smiled.

'I am sorry, Aunt Gerry,' he said. 'I am sorry you don't like her.'

'It may have been a mistake to say what I did,' she said afterwards to me, 'but I don't think so. *Épris*, I think—distinctly *épris*—but not *inamorato*.'

VII

Hugo went abroad that summer with Guy and George. Anthony Cowper joined them in the Tyrol, and they walked down into Italy. They visited Verona and Bologna, and then the Umbrian towns. Hugo became interested in the early Umbrian painters. He came back very full of them. He had a copy of one, a very primitive Byzantine-looking Madonna, pale gold and white and grey, which he hung up in his room. That was the first break in his regime of no pictures at all.

We were all at Yearsly at the end of September. Mollie and I had been in Ireland. We went by ourselves to the West Coast, and bathed and walked, and came back to Yearsly in September.

Guy had to go back to London to his law work soon after, and Hugo went with him for a bit. He saw Paulina in London. Mollie and I knew that; so did Cousin Delia. I wished sometimes I could have talked to him about Paulina quite naturally, as we should have talked once, but things had got different with him and me. We were not close and harmonious as we used to be, and it was that that I minded more than anything else.

VIII

That was Hugo's last year at Oxford. He belonged to

Literary Societies and read essays to them. He enjoyed himself very much, I think. He seemed so full of interest in so many things that I wondered at him sometimes—and wondered what he would do in the end.

His enthusiasm for Paulina died down again. Exactly when it died, or why, I do not know, but I felt it go, and so did the others.

It was Guy who first spoke of it, when we were at Yearsly that Christmas. We were sitting in the old schoolroom, round the fire. He was sucking at his pipe, and he took it out to fill.

'Hugo has recovered,' he said. 'The Paulina episode has passed.' George grunted.

'Time too,' he said, and it almost sounded to me as though he were annoyed with Hugo. 'Hugo takes a long time to grow up,' he said. Guy laughed.

'You talk as though you were fifty, George,' he said.

'I am fifty,' George answered, 'compared to Hugo. That is partly,' he added blandly, 'why I am less charming.'

'Only partly,' rejoined Guy, stuffing down his pipe.

Guy and George always smoked pipes. Hugo did not. He started at one time, but gave it up.

'He'll smoke a pipe when he's grown up,' said George.

'We shall be dead when he's grown up,' said Guy.

'I think Hugo is just as grown up as any of you,' said Mollie. 'I don't think he will ever be different.'

'Should we like it if he was different?' I said.

George looked slowly round at me.

'Well, no,' he said. 'I think Helen is right. We grumble at Hugo sometimes, but we shouldn't like him different,'

IX

Hugo and George went in for their examinations. George got a first and Hugo a second.

Walter was in for the same examination; I remember seeing his name in the list.

After that they were in London for the Civil Service Examination.

George did well in that too, but Hugo did not. His name

was a long way down in the list, and they said he might not get a post at all. Cousin John was worried about it.

'I don't want him to get into some side show,' he said. 'He had better give it up and try for something else.'

But Hugo said he would like to wait and see. He furnished the two rooms that Guy had kept for him.

He had his Delphic Charioteer, and his Umbrian Madonna, and the blue curtains and the grey chairs. It was very like his room in Oxford had been. That autumn was a happier time. We were all together again.

George got a post in the Treasury before Christmas, and he set up house with Mollie in Cheyne Walk. They had the two top floors of a house, far along where the river is wide, near the four chimneys. Mollie worked in her laboratory in the mornings, and sometimes after lunch as well. She was writing a thesis on enzymes. It seemed funny always to me that Mollie should do that sort of thing, but she liked it, and it never seemed to use up her soul as I have seen it do since, with other people.

Mollie cared really far more about George and about Guy than she did for all her science, and about me and Hugo too, and she did not pretend not to.

'I do the biology too,' she said, 'because it interests me and I have plenty of time. If I had not plenty of time I should not do it.'

'The perfect dilettante,' Walter called her, when I told him that. 'How much value will her biology be, treated like that?'

And I said:

'I don't know about the biology, but she is of value. She is one of the most perfectly balanced people I know.'

And Walter did not deny it, for he liked Mollie.

X

Hugo joined a society of New Poets. They used to meet and read poetry aloud in a room behind Leicester Square. Hugo was interested in metres. He used to spend days in the British Museum reading old Renaissance poets who did tricks with metres, and he started to translate the Greek Anthology. Some of his verses, were, I think, very beautiful, and George thought so too. But he wanted to do more than that. He had not found He had not yet what he wanted to do.

In February he had an offer of work in the Inland Revenue. He refused it, and gave up the idea of the Civil Service. He thought again at this time of a post in a museum, and began to qualify for that.

I was learning dancing now, with a Russian lady called Ivanovna, who had been in the Russian ballet. I loved those lessons, and they filled in the time when Mollie was at work. I should like to have done some definite work too, but I did not know what to do, and I was happy just waiting and being alive.

That spring and summer we were very gay, and our party had grown larger now, for Anthony Cowper had work in London too, at the Chancery Bar, and Ralph Freeman was in the Foreign Office, and we all enjoyed ourselves. We danced a great deal. We all liked dancing.

And Ralph Freeman had a sister Daphne who used to come too, when we liked; and we went to theatres, almost always in the pit, and to races in Anthony Cowper's car. Sometimes I rode with Guy in the Park before breakfast, and sometimes we went down to Richmond and had supper on the river in punts.

Often we went to Yearsly for the week-end, and Yearsly was always the same, and Cousin Delia always the same.

I think of that summer often when I am in London in June; the scent of limes and chestnut trees, and dust, and the fresh green of the trees, and the watering carts in the streets, and people coming out of houses in new clothes, pretty summer clothes, light-hearted people as we were then. Hugo had a lavender-coloured tie that summer, and George used to chaff him about it; and Guy had a light grey suit; George said it was too light a grey. Walter used to say that they must have spent a great deal of money on clothes, but I don't think they did. Their clothes amused them, among other things. So did my clothes and Mollie's, and we saw no harm in that. I see no harm even now.

It was like the old days at Yearsly in one way. We lived

in the present. We did not look ahead much or wonder what was going to happen. The days passed so quickly, one behind the other. It was the long hot summer of 1911. Life was very full and very sweet.

XI

And then Sophia Lane Watson came back. It seems odd now to think of that time without her, and then her coming back. She had mattered so much to me before, and now again in a different way, and in between she had not mattered at all.

It began in that Poetry Shop near Leicester Square. I was there with Hugo, looking at books, and I found a book on the shelf of new publications. *Verses*, by Sophia Watson. I was looking at the verses without thinking of her, for Sophia Watson seemed different somehow from Lane Watson, and then as I read the verses they reminded me of her. They reminded me of the poetry she used to write at school, and I suddenly wondered if it could be the same. I showed the book to Hugo, and he started to read it, and then he went on and on.

There was a great shaft of sunlight with dust in it—motes of dust floating in it; it shone through the little window high up at the back of the shop and across the foreign books in paper covers that were there, and on to Hugo, and I watched him as he read and felt pleased I had shown him the book, for he always found the new books as a rule.

'By Jove,' he said at length. 'This is jolly stuff. Do you say you know the woman? Sophia Watson? I don't remember her.'

'She was at Ellsfield—at school you know. Don't you remember, she came to Yearsly once? She was a great friend of mine then—at least I think this must be the same.' Hugo puckered his brows.

'Oh, a little dark thing. I believe I remember her. Was that her name?'

'I wonder where she is now,' I said. 'I think I shall write to her again.' I felt suddenly that I should like to see her.

Hugo bought the book, and I wrote to her and addressed

the letter care of her publishers.

It was over a week before I had an answer. Then it was an answer very like her.

'Dear Helen,—

'Thank you for your letter. It was kind of you to write. I am glad you liked my poems. I don't know if they are good. I am living in London now and this is my address.

'Yours sincerely,

'Sophia Watson.'

It was like a child's letter, so stiff and abrupt, and it made me laugh. I invited her to tea at Campden Hill, and Hugo and Mollie to meet her.

She was very like what she had been as a child, but I think less striking. Her hair was up, of course, and did not look so much and so black, and it mattered more now she was grown up that she was so badly dressed.

She was wearing a cotton dress that afternoon—a lilac check that might have been quite nice, but it was all washed out and hung down behind in a tail, as her skirts used to do at school, and she had a green straw hat that did not go with it at all, and grey stockings and brown shoes.

She was very stiff and polite when she came in. Grandmother spoke to her first; she remembered her coming to lunch when we were little, and she had known her father long ago, she said. She smiled at me, but gravely, in a distant sort of way.

She said:

'It is a long time since we have met, but I should have known you again.'

'And I you,' I said. 'I am sure I should.'

Grandmother laughed at us.

'What, six years, is it, or five? I should hope you would remember.'

I laughed too. I said:

'Six years is a great deal at our time of life.'

Sophia smiled. 'It seems a very long time,' she said.

Hugo was watching her, but he did not say much. He never spoke to people about their poetry or pictures or things they did, unless he knew them well.

It was impertinent, he used to say—like talking about

their feelings for their husbands or wives.

George said that was a mistake—that out of every ten authors nine at least liked to talk about their own works.

I never wrote myself, or painted, and I don't know which is true in general, but I am sure that with Sophia, Hugo was quite right.

She seemed to unfreeze after a bit, when she saw we were not going to talk about her book.

She was living by herself, she said, in rooms near Sloane Square.

'Not far from us,' said Mollie. 'You must come and see us. Do come and see us.'

Sophia said she would like to come, and Mollie gave her their address.

'Come to supper on Thursday,' she said. 'Can you? Just my brother and me.'

And Sophia said she would.

'A funny, quiet, little person,' said Grandmother when she had gone. 'Not at all like her father, as I remember him.'

'Oh, not quiet—wild,' said Hugo. 'Like a wild animal in a cage.'

'I think she was very shy,' said Mollie, 'but I liked her.'

'She was wild when she was at school,' I said. 'Wild underneath, I mean'; and I wondered how Hugo had seen so much in so short a time. But that was like Hugo.

XII

After that we saw a good deal of Sophia. She liked Mollie, and Mollie liked her. It surprised me rather, but I was glad. They were so unlike each other that they did not clash, and Mollie looked after Sophia, and treated her rather as a child. She was living in rooms alone, in a street off the King's Road. We thought she had run away from home, but she never told us so.

She did not speak about her home to Mollie or me.

I believe she did to Hugo.

She was writing a play, but she did not speak about that either. But she talked a lot when she got more used to us very much as she used to talk at school, about impersonal things. I felt her inhuman, and too odd; it had not mattered so much when she was a child; but she was attractive still, in her own queer way. You couldn't help wondering what she was thinking about, and wanting to know. George and Hugo liked talking to her, but not Guy.

He said:

'She is too clever for me, I can't live up to it.'

But Guy said that very easily—it was almost a pose in Guy.

Hugo understood her from the first. It was extraordinary how his mind seemed to interpret hers. I don't know how else to describe it. But it was very often like that, as though she were speaking a foreign language and only Hugo understood. You would not have expected that at first, for they were so different, Hugo so gracious and lovable and gentle, and Sophia so fierce and buttoned up. And Hugo was not tolerant and easy-going like Mollie; he was easily jarred upon and irritated if people and things were 'Wrong'—but Sophia never jarred upon him, even when she seemed rude and ungracious, and she had a curious influence upon him, in his most special things.

He began to read Russian novels, which he had not liked before, and he went with her to odd meetings of Russian Anarchists, 'Friends of Freedom' they were called. She tried at one time to persuade him to go to Russia and help the Revolution. Guy was worried about it, and so was I; we thought Hugo might really go; but George said no, he wouldn't, and George, of course, was right.

It sometimes surprises me to think how often George was right; instinctively, too, we asked for George's opinion, and were satisfied by it to a great extent; funny George, with his wide, humorous mouth; dear George, with his steady eyes. I don't know which side of him was best.

XIII

I don't believe now that Hugo was in love with Sophia. His relation to her was an intellectual one. He was fond of her, and very intimate with her in a certain way, and she did have a great influence in his life, yet in one way he was more like an elder brother. We all treated him rather as though he were a dear, precious child, even I, who was younger than him, felt always as though I must protect him and defend him from something. He protected her, and although he read the books she recommended and went to the meetings she liked, she seemed to look up to him and depend on him in a different way from us.

I did not see all this at the time. I see it more clearly now; I am less prejudiced, and less entangled, and much less afraid.

It is fear, I think, that spoils everything. If one was never afraid one would make no mistakes. George said that once, and I think again that George was right.

I tried very hard to be fair to Sophia, to look at her impartially and judge her suitable or not. I felt sure that Hugo would marry her, and I wanted to be glad, but I could not. I don't suppose I could have been satisfied with any one for him; I loved him too much. If it had been Mollie I should have felt different about it. But Mollie was for Guy—that was settled.

Sophia was not beautiful enough for Hugo, nor comfortable enough. I could not imagine her in a home of her own, and Hugo coming back to her in the evening and being happy. He would not want always to read Turgueniev, and books about people who were hanged. There was a book called *The Seven that Were Hanged*: Sophia gave it to me for my birthday, and I hated it. She understood one side of Hugo, better perhaps than I did, but there was another side, the more personal side, that she would never understand.

And then I would be angry with myself and miserable.

I went for long walks by myself at this time. It was the autumn now. We had been at Yearsly and come back. Sophia had come too for a week. She had fitted in better than I expected, and I thought that Cousin Delia liked her.

Now it was October.

'Very soon, now, they will be engaged,' I thought, and wished almost that it would be soon.

I went for a walk in Kensington Gardens and tried to think it out. The gardeners were sweeping up the leaves—

yellow leaves of lime trees and planes.

'It is my own fault,' I kept saying to myself. 'I have spoilt it all myself.'

My relation to Hugo had been perfect once—a beautiful, almost a holy thing. He had been my brother and something more, for there was a freedom, an element of choice, which would not have been there if we were really brother and sister; and now it was as though I had made claims upon him that I had hardly realized myself. I felt hurt by him and injured, though he had done me no injury. 'It is not his fault,' I thought, 'that he wants other people besides me, and I want only him. That is quite natural. It is only my feeling like this that is wrong'; and I felt ashamed and unhappy.

XIV

Hugo asked me to be kind to Sophia. It had not occurred to me that I was not.

He said:

'She likes you so much, and you used to like her.'

He had come to dinner at Campden Hill. I could see that he was excited and happy, he talked so much at dinner, and his eyes shone. Grandmother noticed it too, for I saw her watching him, and she asked him, when the coffee came, what he had been doing that day.

He said:

'I went for a walk with Sophia Watson in Richmond Park.'

Grandmother said:

'Her father's name was *Lane* Watson.'

'Yes, I know, but she thinks that sounds pretentious. She says their name was really only Watson to begin with. She hates fuss.'

'It is generally simpler to have the same name as one's parents until one is married,'

'I don't think Sophia's parents can be very nice people. They have not been kind to her.'

'Ah,' said Grandmother slowly. 'That is a different matter.'

'The trees were beautiful in Richmond Park, so bright and red and gold. I suppose they have more colour when the summer has been hot. The leaves were coming down all round us, like rain, in the wind. It was very windy.'

Grandmother said:

'Oh.'

She looked at Hugo over her spectacles, and Hugo flushed.

'I wish you could have been there,' he said rather lamely. 'It was awfully nice.'

Grandmother laughed; she said:

'You had better bring the young woman to see me, Hugo, I liked her much better than the other one—Miss . . . Connell, wasn't it, with the fair hair, but—take your time.'

Hugo murmured something inarticulate; he was peeling a pear and I could not see his face, but I knew he was saying it wasn't like that at all.

Coffee came in, and after the coffee grandmother went upstairs. She had not looked at me at all, and I was glad.

We went into the drawing-room, Hugo and I, and sat down by the fire. At least I sat down and Hugo stood up with his back to the fire. He took a cigarette from the jade box on the chimney-piece, and then he began to talk. The room was rather dark, for Grandmother would not have electric light, and there was only one lamp on the table behind.

He said:

'Aunt Gerry is a dear, I am awfully fond of her. But she does get the wrong end of the stick sometimes. I suppose in her generation it would have been like that.'

I said:

'Yes, I suppose so.'

Hugo looked down at me and then away.

'It isn't a question of "taking time" at all, and of course Sophia is quite different from Paulina. One couldn't think of them in the same sort of way at all.'

I said:

'No, they aren't at all alike.'

My cigarette had gone out. I asked Hugo for the matches. He gave them to me and went on:

He said:

'I liked just looking at Paulina. Didn't you? She was beautiful to look at, and she did speak her lines awfully well too, but of course—well, she hadn't got a *mind* like Sophia. Sophia is so frightfully interesting. It is like exploring in an unknown sea. . . .' He laughed, a little apologetically. 'You never know what Sophia will think or feel about a thing, but it is always real, what she thinks or feels.'

I said:

'Yes, I think it is,' and he looked pleased, 'Of course you were interested in her at school,' he said. 'I remember that—you used to talk to me about her a lot, and I think you really described her rather well. But I don't know how it was—she didn't interest me a bit that first time I saw her, when you brought her to Yearsly.'

I said:

'No, I was disappointed then that neither you nor Guy seemed to care for her much.'

'Guy doesn't appreciate her now, and I can understand that. She is not at her best with him. She is shy, and he doesn't get any further.'

I said nothing, and he went on.

'I don't think people realize how shy she is. They think she is disagreeable and ungracious sometimes, and they don't understand that she is just frightened of them. Do you know, Helen,' he looked straight at me, and gave a little laugh, 'she is even afraid of you! She admires you awfully, and would like you to like her, but she thinks you don't. I told her, of course, that that was nonsense—that I was sure you liked her, and I told her that you used to talk a lot about her when you were at school.'

'What did she say?'

'Oh, she said that that was quite different. "People change and outgrow each other," she said, and then she said that even then she had cared for you much more than you cared for her. She thinks you find her dull and dowdy. You do like her, don't you, Helen?'

He asked it almost wistfully, and suddenly I wanted to cry. If I could have spoken quite frankly about Sophia, as though she did not affect me personally at all, it would have been all different; if I could have asked him straight out what he felt about her; if we could have talked to each other simply and without reserves, as we used to once, I think our lives might have been very different afterwards; but we couldn't. He was trying to, I think, but I couldn't respond. I was fighting against something in myself, and it was almost as though I was fighting against him. I did not want him to know my thoughts and my feelings as he used to know them; and I could not talk to him about Sophia.

I said:

'Yes, I do like her, quite, but we haven't an awful lot in common. I don't think I am intellectual enough for her.'

Hugo ignored that. He said:

'I should like you to be kind to her, Mollie is awfully kind to her, and she is very grateful to Mollie, but'—and he paused a moment—'Mollie isn't you.'

'I don't see what I can do for her that you and Mollie can't do much better. What do you want me to do?' Hugo fidgeted with the jade box on the chimney-piece.

'Oh, I don't know exactly—anything just to show her you like her. She minds about her clothes. Couldn't you advise her about her clothes? She admires yours so much.'

And then I was angry. I wanted to say, 'I am damned if I will.' But I only did say, 'I tried once to teach her to dance. It was no good.' That was all I said, but Hugo knew I was angry. I could see that from the way he looked at me, and when he looked at me like that it was harder still not to cry. He looked hurt and puzzled, like a child who is spoken to crossly and doesn't know what it has done wrong.

I was ashamed of myself again, and very unhappy.

XV

One day I was with Mollie in her flat, and we were dressing to go out. We were in her bedroom brushing our hair, and I remembered that dance at Yearsly on Guy's twenty-first birthday, and old Nunky brushing my hair. I had been so pleased with my hair that night, and so had she, and now suddenly I hated it.

I said:

'I do wish my hair was different, I am so tired of it like this,'

Mollie said:

'Your hair is lovely, Helen. I always envy you the way it curls.'

I said:

'It is so dull, just brown and ordinary. I wish it was bright yellow, or black and straight.'

Mollie looked round at me; she was brushing her own hair.

'You poor pretty thing,' she said, and threw her arms round my neck. 'Oh, Helen, I'm so sorry for you, but don't mind—it will be all right.'

Then I began to cry, and she comforted me. We never said what was the matter, but of course we both knew.

XVI

It was about a fortnight later that I went to Hugo's room in Clifford's Inn and found him out.

We were going to Richmond that afternoon, the Addingtons and Hugo and I, for a walk. I was to pick up Hugo first, and then we were to go on to the Addingtons in Chelsea.

When I got there, Hugo was out. Guy opened the door, and I thought he looked sorry.

He said:

'He went off with Sophia to a Strindberg play. Did he know you were going to come?'

I said:

'Yes, he knew—but I suppose he forgot. It doesn't matter.'

We both stood still for a minute. I wanted to say something else, but I couldn't think of anything to say.

Guy said:

'Come along in.'

And I said:

'No, I can't. George and Mollie will be waiting.'

I wanted to say: 'Don't tell Hugo I came,' but I couldn't say it.

Guy said:

'I'll tell Hugo you came, I'll blow him up.'

'Oh, I shouldn't bother. It's all right.'

Guy said:

'I wish I could come, but I've got to finish this stuff.'

He nodded his head towards his room and the table spread with papers. It was a joke with us now that Guy was working hard.

I said:

'I wish you could. Come next Saturday.'

He said:

'Yes, next Saturday I can. But we'll meet before that.'

'Oh yes, lots of times. Good-bye.'

I turned down the stairs. I was glad to get away. It hurt me that Hugo should have gone out and forgotten—it had never happened before.

When I got to the Addingtons' flat, Mollie was upstairs. George was reading by the fire, with his back to the door. He looked round and took his pipe out of his mouth.

'Hullo,' he said. 'Where's Hugo?'

'Hugo had gone out to a play with Sophia.'

I pulled off my gloves and sat down in the other chair.

'Strindberg,' I said. 'I don't like Strindberg.'

George bent forward, and tapped his pipe out on the hob.

'Nor do I,' he said.

I had chilblains on my fingers. It was cold that afternoon, and raw, and they tingled and hurt. It was partly the chilblains that made me feel so wretched. I stretched my hands out to the fire.

George filled his pipe slowly, and lit it. The flame flickered up and down against his face as he drew it in. He grunted and threw the match away.

He said:

'Hugo is a fool.'

I said:

'I don't know. He has a right to like it if he likes.'

George puffed away in silence for a time.

There was some of Mollie's restfulness about George. It was good to have him in the room when one was troubled.

'I am losing patience with Hugo,' he said at last. 'It is

time he grew up.'

I wanted to defend Hugo even from him. It was not Strindberg we were talking about. We both knew that.

I said:

'I think it is a mistake to say that. One can't choose for other people. Hugo knows what he wants.'

'No,' said George shortly. 'He doesn't. That's the trouble.'

He glanced up at me, and away again into the fire.

'We must be patient with Hugo,' he said in a different tone. 'He takes a long time to understand things sometimes, but he does understand in the end.'

'I think perhaps he understands too much,' I said, and wished I had not said it.

XVII

And then, that Christmas, I met Walter again.

We were on a walking tour along the Roman Wall, Guy and Hugo and the Addingtons and Sophia and I. We had begun at Hexham, and we walked along the wall towards Carlisle. It was on the fourth day that we met Walter, in the camp at Howstead.

It was a windy day, very cold and clear and bright, and we reached the camp about the middle of the day. We had sandwiches with us, and we sat down to eat them at the Northern Gate, looking out over the waste space of fell towards Scotland.

Suddenly I saw Walter. He had come up from behind somewhere, and was standing beside me.

'Hullo,' said George. 'Where have you come from, Sebright?'

He said:

'How do you do, Miss Woodruffe?'

I felt, that time, that he was looking at me, and that he was glad to see me.

He said:

'I have waited three years for this.'

Mollie said:

'It's a wonderful place.'

He meant that he had waited to see me. He told me afterwards that he had meant it, and I knew before he told me. I knew, I think, when he said it, up there on the hill, and the odd thing is that I wasn't surprised.

He sat down beside me on the stones of the Northern Gate.

He said:

'The barbarians were down there. It looks like it, doesn't it? And there were Southern soldiers up here. They must have hated it.'

He took us round the camp afterwards and explained to us what the places were—where they washed their clothes and where they cooked. It seemed to me very interesting, what he told us, and there were inscriptions on some of the stones that he showed us too.

'Sebright is a dab at inscriptions,' George said to Hugo.

'He got some honour in Berlin for a thing on inscriptions.'

I thought that he made it very vivid, the life in that Roman camp, and I had never felt much interest in Rome before. Sophia was interested too, and George—but not Hugo. Hugo used to say sometimes that he had a blind spot in his mind for history; but I was vexed with him this time for not being interested. He was polite, of course—he was always polite; but I, who knew him well, could see that he was bored.

Sophia began talking to Walter; she did not seem shy of him at all.

'They must have been hard, enduring sort of people, she said. Up here at the end of the world—it is like the end of the world,' she went on half to herself, 'looking out on to that . . . I like the Romans.'

Walter looked pleased—but he was talking to me, and I knew it and was glad.

I don't know even now how much the difference was in him and how much in me. He seemed to me very different this time, from that afternoon at Oxford three years before. He seemed to me now to have more life and more assurance, as though he felt himself here on his own ground. But perhaps

I was more ready to notice him now. There had been no room for him at all in my mind before.

When we had finished looking at the camp Guy said we must go on. We were to sleep at Gilsland that night if we could, and the evenings were short.

Walter had come that way the day before, and slept at a farm near by, but he said now that he would walk back with us. He did not say 'if you don't mind' or 'may I?' as one somehow expected him to say. He just said:

'I will go with you. I know this wall pretty well.'

We walked along the top of the wall for a long way, up hills and down, always at the edge of the cliff, with the barbarian country below. Then the others said they would take the lower track, farther down across the fell, but I wouldn't. I kept along the top of the wall, and Walter came with me.

Once Hugo called me.

'It is much easier along here,' he said. 'You had much better come down.'

And I said:

'I won't come down. I am going into the barbarian country.'

And I laughed at him, and then I jumped down on the other side of the wall and ran down along the slope of the hill. It was not so steep in this place—towards a little lake with trees beside it, down in the flat wild country.

'Do you want to see the barbarians?' Walter asked, and I said:

'Yes, but they are all gone.'

Walter said:

'They are not gone, only civilized. Do you ever wish you could get away from civilized people, and culture and books and all that sort of thing?'

And I said:

'No, I have never wished that. I have never thought about it.'

He said:

'Perhaps you haven't been oppressed by it, as I have. Routines and curricula and examinations—always doing what you have got to do and never what you want.'

I said:

'No, I generally do what I want—or at any rate I *don't* do what I *don't* want.' And I thought of Cousin Delia and Yearsly, and how seldom the question had arisen.

Walter said:

'That is better. That is much better. That is partly what I felt about you!'

He said it with a sudden vehemence and then stopped short. I looked at him and he was looking at me. I felt suddenly uneasy, and an odd ridiculous feeling came over me that I was really outside a safe wall, in a strange country, and I wanted to go back.

I said:

'We will go back now, or we shall be lost. It will be too steep further on.'

Walter said:

'It is too steep now. We must go on now we are here.'

And I felt as though we were walking in a dream, as though everything that he said and that I said were symbolic and fraught with a deeper meaning than we knew. It was an odd exciting feeling and made me a little bit afraid.

We found a track along the fell, and walked on it, and Walter began to talk about his work on the Roman inscriptions in Britain. He told me too that he had been appointed to a lectureship in Archæology in London University.

'I shall be coming to live in London after Easter,' he said, and then, 'I hope I shall see you there.'

I said:

'Yes, surely. We are all in London now.'

He said:

'I know.'

We came at last to a place where the wall was lower and broken down, and we climbed back and over it into the Roman country. The others were waiting for us—sitting on big stones.

We stopped at Greenhead for the night, for it was getting dark already.

Walter stopped with us and went back the next day.

XVIII

Walter came to see me at Campden Hill Square.

Grandmother was in the drawing-room when he came in.

When I came downstairs I found them having tea.

Grandmother said:

'Here is Mr. Sebright, my dear. He has been telling me about his studies in Roman Britain.'

It was like my grandmother not to be surprised. She had never heard of Walter, I am sure, for we had none of us thought or spoken of him before, and since that walk at Christmas, I had thought of him a good deal, and not wanted to speak.

Grandmother liked 'antiquities.' When she was a girl she had visited a great many museums; with her father first, who thought it was good for her, and then with her husband, who liked museums himself.

She used to say that it was a sign of our generation not to like museums, and a bad sign. Some things about us she considered good. I could see that she was pleased with Walter.

'Mr. Sebright tells me that the inscribed rocks at Chester are not really so interesting as those at Corbridge,' she said.

Walter was standing up to shake hands with me.

I knew again that he had been waiting for me, and wanting to see me very much.

Grandmother went on talking to him about the inscriptions at Corbridge.

It did not interest me at all what they were saying, but I felt excited at Walter's being there. It was now that I noticed his hands, what beautiful hands they were, as he handed me my tea and bread and butter, and I watched his face as he was talking to Grandmother. He did not seem to me absurd now, as he had at first.

Afterwards he was talking about something in the British Museum—bas-reliefs, I think, with some inscriptions on them—and I said I didn't know the British Museum. I had only been there once, with Hugo, to look at Greek vases, and

he said:

'Oh, but the Greek vases are very dull. It is the early things you should see—little pieces of things that mean nothing by themselves, but when you piece them together tell you about whole nations you didn't know. You ought to see the Mycenaean fragments and the Hittite things. Won't you come one day and let me show them to you?'

I said I should love to see them; and even while I was saying so I wondered why I said it, for I did not care for fragments of things at all, and I did not like the Museum the one time I was there.

'Will you come next Thursday?' Walter asked. 'I shall be there all day Thursday. If you could come in the afternoon— any time in the afternoon—I shall be there. I could show you lots of things, and then,' he added, more shyly, 'we could have tea.'

Grandmother laughed. She said:

'If you make an archæologist of Helen I will take off my hat to you.'

I said:

'I will come at half-past three.'

I did not mind Grandmother's laughing. She did not laugh in a way one would mind.

When Walter had gone away I wondered if I had been silly. Why had I said I would go and look at inscriptions? I felt uncomfortable about it, and not at ease with myself.

XIX

I went to the British Museum on Thursday. Walter was waiting for me on the steps, and there was another man with him. The other man was called Furze. He was a professor at some University in Wales. He was older than Walter, but not very much older. He had a very kind face, and a funny way of ducking down his head. I liked him and was glad he was there too. He had been working with Walter all the morning in the Assyrian Room, it seemed, and now he came round with us for a bit, till it was time for him to catch his train.

He did not talk much; Walter did the talking. I thought

he knew quite as much about the things as Walter, but he was not so excited about them.

We looked at some Assyrian bas-reliefs of people hunting lions. They were more interesting than I had expected, and rather beautiful too, some of them—rather beautiful clean lines—but Walter said even these were too late, and we went on to cases of rougher broken things, and he explained what they once had been—pots and ovens and tiles and all sorts of household stuff.

'You will get back to your "Urdummheit,"' Mr. Furze said, smiling at Walter, '*I* think these pots were not very well made.'

Walter tossed his head. He seemed self-confident here, as he had been at Howsteads; not a bit shy or nervous, as he was at Oxford.

'Who cares if they were well made? This is not an Arts and Crafts Exhibition. Of course Praxiteles made pretty ornaments, if you want that.'

'Well, I still maintain that if you make a pot at all, it is better to make a beautiful pot than a misshapen one.'

It was evidently an old argument. I could see that.

I agreed with Mr. Furze.

'I do get so sick of beauty,' Walter said. 'Beauty is quite beside the point.'

And then he laughed, for he saw Mr. Furze was laughing.

'What do you think, Miss Woodruffe?' he asked.

And I said:

'Oh, I am afraid I like beautiful pots best, if there have got to be pots at all.'

He looked at me oddly, with a troubled, perplexed expression.

'I expect you think me a Philistine,' he said. 'I am too, I suppose. All these shapes and designs and proportions that people keep talking about—they just mean nothing to me. They seem to me so *dull*—like rows of pretty faces with no souls.'

'When old age shall this generation waste
Thou shalt remain in midst of other woe,'
I said, and Walter wrinkled his forehead.

'What is that?' he asked. 'I ought to know it, I expect,

but I don't. Poetry is another of the fringes for me. I've never had time for it.'

I was sorry I had used the quotation, for he looked vexed, and I had not meant to vex him.

I said:

'It's the Ode to a Grecian Urn. That's what made me think of it—talking about urns.'

Walter grunted, and I realized that he did not know the Grecian Urn, but I couldn't say, 'It's by Keats.'

Mr. Furze interposed.

'Sebright is quite incorrigible,' he said. 'He doesn't like Grecian Urns, and he doesn't like poetry. He will certainly not read a poem about a Grecian Urn.'

Walter shrugged his shoulders and gave a little laugh, and I felt it had not mattered after all.

Soon after that Mr. Furze had to catch his train. I was sorry when he went away.

There was a tensity in the air when we were alone, and I felt somehow as though I were there on false pretences. Walter took me to a big stone in a square frame.

'This is the Rosetta Stone,' he said. 'I think this is one of the most exciting things here.'

And he told me that there were three different languages on it, and three different scripts, and that had been the key to discovering a whole new civilization. People had worked out another language—Ancient Egyptian, he said it was—letter by letter, sign by sign, through comparing one side of the stone with the other, for the same legend was written on all three.

I could see that that was rather an exciting thing to do.

'You know,' he said suddenly. 'I saw this stone first when I was ten years old. I had read about it in a book called *The Wonders of Antiquity*, and I came to see it with my mother, and it seemed to me even then the best thing in the world to work out new languages from old inscriptions, and discover new worlds like that—much better than discovering new things in this world. I have wanted to do it ever since, and now, partly, I can work at that; but I have to do Roman inscriptions too, because that was for a thesis to start with, to get my D.Litt., and I have to for the History school also. So I have got launched into Roman Britain, but what I really want to get at is the proto-Hittite script from Zenjirli and Sakjegöze and those things—those undeciphered hieroglyphs, you know.'

I did not know what the proto-Hittite script was then; it seems curious now to think of a time when I had not heard of it, but I thought I understood what he meant about discovering new worlds that way.

I asked:

'Do you feel you can find out quite a lot about the people who wrote those inscriptions? Do they get quite real to you in the end?'

He said:

'No, not like that. I don't want them real like that. It is more to me like fitting pieces into a puzzle—thousands of tiny pieces, and a very big puzzle—and if they do fit, if even quite a small piece of the puzzle gets done, you know it's right. That is one of the satisfactory things, it can't be just better or worse, it must be right or wrong. Do you see what I mean at all?'

His voice changed; he asked the last question almost shyly. I think he did not expect people quite to understand.

I thought I did, and it interested me. This was a new world to me too; a cold intellectual world that I did not know at all; and I was in a mood to explore.

Afterwards we went out to tea in an A.B.C. near the Museum. At tea he was different again, more like he had been on the picnic. He was shyer and spoke more jerkily, and I felt much more that he admired me. The A.B.C. was crowded and rather noisy, and the marble top of the table was smudged with coffee that had been spilt. It seemed to me very odd to be sitting there with Walter. I seemed to be looking on from a long way off, and wondering how I came to be there.

After tea we got on to a bus. I said I could go home alone, but Walter would come with me. We did not talk very much on the bus. It was beginning to rain, and we pulled up the mackintosh cover from the seat in front.

He said good-bye to me on the steps of Campden Hill Square, and I thanked him for 'a very interesting afternoon.'

He waited on the step.

'May I come again?' he asked. 'May I take you out again?'

He asked it in his funny, jerky way, as though it mattered to him very much. I could not answer him at once. I felt somehow, irrationally, that my answer was very important.

I said:

'You know; I don't agree with you at all about Beauty and Poetry—and—all that sort of thing. I think perhaps I let you think this afternoon that I did agree.'

It sounded foolish even as I said it, and it was not even what I wanted to say.

He said very quietly:

'I know that. You are the other side of life—all that I have not got, and don't understand. I know I am one-sided. I would like to be different if I could.'

My heart began to thump. I had not realized that he would talk like that, yet. I was not ready. I wanted to go inside and shut the door, but I couldn't shut the door while he stood there. The rain was falling faster now, and as I moved my head a little stream of water ran off the brim of my hat, down my neck.

I said:

'I suppose everybody would like to be different if they could. I should like to have black hair, quite black and straight'; and I tried to laugh. 'But we can't be different really, ever.'

He said:

'Not completely different, of course; but we can alter. People do alter. They can develop new sides in themselves without losing what they have got.'

I said:

'It is too wet to talk any more now. Good-bye.'

He said:

'I may come again, mayn't I?'

I said:

'Of course, if you like.' I tried to answer lightly, to make what we were saying seem of no consequence.

I fumbled with my latch-key at the door. At last it opened, and a shaft of light shot out on to the steps. He turned away then and went down the steps, slowly at first and then faster. He turned down the Square to the north, towards Holland Park Road, and I went into the house. The hall was light and warm, and I shut the front door behind me with relief. Upstairs in my bedroom there was a fire. I took off my shoes and stockings and my wet coat, and then I sat down on the hearth-rug and cried for Hugo. He had never seemed so far away before.

XX

I did not speak to Mollie about Walter at first, nor to Hugo. It was almost a week before I saw Hugo again and then we were all together, and Sophia was there too. We were going to a concert, a Mozart concert at the Queen's Hall. We did not go to dances so often since Sophia came, because she couldn't dance. I danced with George and Guy sometimes, Mollie and I, without Hugo; but of course that was not the same thing.

The concert was lovely. It made us all happy. I felt that I had been horrid to Sophia, and that I would be nicer.

We went back to Hugo's rooms and had coffee. It looked very pleasant, Hugo's room that night, with the fire flickering on the low ceiling and the blue curtains and the charioteer.

Hugo said:

'That music does one good. People could not be bad-tempered or fussed or worried if they heard some Mozart played every day before they got up.'

Guy hummed an Aria from Don Giovanni, a bit we had heard.

'That is about the most perfect thing of all,' he said.

Mollie was pouring out the coffee; she always did that part.

'I think sometimes,' said Sophia, 'that music is all wrong, and poetry too, and all that we call art. I wonder sometimes if it isn't all a kind of dope that we make for ourselves because we can't face life; and it seems all pointless then.'

I said:

'How odd that you should say that. It is almost what Mr.

Sebright said.'

'Sebright?' said George. 'When did he talk about it?'

'I went to the British Museum with him the other day.' I tried to say it nonchalantly, but I felt self-conscious, and that vexed me, for why shouldn't I go with him? 'He says Greek vases are like faces without souls.'

'So they are,' said George. .

Hugo said:

'No, they are not at all like that. They are more like souls without faces—impersonal and rather cold. Why did you go there?' he asked abruptly.

And I said:

'Because he asked me to. It was very interesting there.'

'I don't suppose he would care for vases,' said Hugo, 'or statues. He would like just objects of interest. Did you like them?'

I felt then that I could not discuss Walter, nor repeat what he had said, even what he had said while Mr. Furze was there. I felt suddenly that they were all hostile, my own dear people, and that Walter had somehow put his trust in me.

I said:

'I did when he explained them to me.'

Guy said:

'I should not have expected him to explain very well.'

'Who is Mr. Sebright?' asked Sophia. 'Was that the man we met at the Roman Camp?'

'Yes,' said Mollie. 'He is an archæologist.'

'Epigraphist,' corrected George.

Sophia said:

'I liked him. He was a wild man.'

Guy said:

'Oh, not at all wild. Quite a model young man—no vices and a credit to his college.'

Sophia said:

'I didn't mean wild in that way. More fanatical—or ruthless—I meant—as though he would be burned alive for something quite foolish—or burn other people.'

Sophia understood him better than the others, I thought, and I liked Sophia for it.

'We might see Sebright some time,' said George. 'He is

here now, isn't he, at the Grey College?'

XXI

After that the Addingtons invited Walter to their flat. He came several times, and generally I was there. Sometimes Guy or Hugo came too, and once Sophia. Ralph Freeman was abroad at the time in Vienna, and Anthony Cowper had also been abroad.

Mollie talked to Walter about his work at Grey College and his pupils and the courses they were taking. Mollie could talk to people about that sort of thing. She did not find it boring, if it made the conversation easier. That was partly why people liked Mollie.

But he did not talk to her as he had to me, about the proto-Hittite script, and the Rosetta Stone. That side of his work was nearer, I felt, to him than the classes and lectures, and it was somehow a sort of secret between him and me.

I used to watch Walter when he was talking to Mollie or to George, and I used to wish he looked different from what he did.

I could not bear the black steel spectacles he wore, and I wished he would not speak so jerkily, nor come into a room as though he were afraid.

He was worst, always, when Guy and Hugo were there. He seemed ludicrous then somehow, like a caricature of himself. He would say provocative things in a nervous voice, and I could see that he irritated Guy.

He came for me again at Campden Hill Square, as he had said he would. Once he took me to a lecture on excavations in Syria. It was a dull lecture, but it seemed somehow an adventure to be there with him. It was like walking on a volcano, for I did not know his mind. I did not know what he would think or say next, as I did with Guy and Hugo, and with George.

Another time we went for a walk by the Serpentine, and he told me how he used to go for walks there when he was a little boy, on Sundays with his mother. He had lived near Earl's Court all his life. He still lived there, with his mother.

His father had been a clergyman at some church round there, and had died when he was five. He had a half-sister much older than himself, who was headmistress at a school. He had been at St. Paul's himself.

He was devoted to his mother.

'She gave all her life to me when my father died,' he said. 'She was with me always and did whatever I did. I can't think how children grow up with ordinary mothers, when I think what mine was to me.

'We were poor, of course,' he said. 'We were always poor. But I am glad of that. It made us closer together. In a household with lots of servants, children cannot be close to their mothers, as I was to mine.'

I thought of Cousin Delia, and disagreed. But I did not interrupt him. Walter was never easy to interrupt.

'I owe a great deal to my sister too,' he said. 'She helped with my education. My mother would not have known about that, but Maud saw that I was well prepared, and that I worked hard. I don't think I was idle by nature, but I am grateful to Maud.'

He did not ask me about my childhood. He did not seem to like it when I spoke of Yearsly. He talked mostly about himself. He was ambitious, he told me that, and determined to do great things with his proto-Hittite script.

And all that attracted me in an odd, contrary way. It was so unlike Hugo—and I thought of Walter as strong because Hugo was weak, and determined because Hugo was undetermined. I was trying hard during these weeks to think less well of Hugo. It seems a long time now, that time with Walter before we were engaged. It seems strange now, in a way, that Hugo did nothing—but when I think of the dates I know it was not long at all. It was at the end of February that Walter came first to Campden Hill, and he asked me to marry him on the 10th of April.

We had met, I suppose, a dozen times, not more. We did not know each other at all.

He came to me in the drawing-room at Campden Hill Square. He had not said that he was coming, and I was not expecting him.

The room was full of tulips from Yearsly, for Cousin

Delia sent them to us every week, and the parcel had just come. It was a warm sunny day, and the sun streamed in through the window at the end of the room. I was sitting on the window-seat, and the window was open. I had been putting the tulips in water. They were done now. I was gathering up the ends. There was string and brown paper, and a note from Cousin Delia as well, and the little stalks and ends of leaves from the tulips.

I was thinking of Yearsly, and Cousin Delia, and not of Walter at all. I was thinking that I would go down to Yearsly for a bit; that I would write to Cousin Delia that evening and tell her I was coming. I had not been there lately even for week-ends. I would go alone now, without Hugo or Guy, and be there with Cousin Delia.

And then the door opened and the parlourmaid came in and said:

'Mr. Sebright to see you, Miss.'

It was a red-haired parlourmaid called Hannah. She had not been with us very long, and she married a policeman soon afterwards, soon after I was married.

Walter came in, and she shut the door. It took me a little time to collect my thoughts—they had been so far from him—and then I looked at him, and I knew why he had come.

He came into the middle of the room, and stood there. I asked him to sit down, but he didn't listen.

He said:

'I have come to ask you to marry me. I have meant to always, since the first day that I saw you—at Oxford, in those rooms in the Broad.

'I don't see the good of waiting any longer. You are different from me, I know that. You are beautiful and bright, like a flower, and I love you for that. I love you for being what you are. I am a dull fellow in many ways. I know that too. But I could be different with you.' He said it in a jerky, monotonous voice, as though he had learnt it by heart—and he did not look at me while he said it.

His eyes were fixed on the floor, about a foot in front of me, and his hands were clasped behind him. My eyes followed his, instinctively, and I saw a leaf there—a little leaf that I had forgotten to pick up. I couldn't pick it up now.

I had known this was coming sooner or later, but I was not ready. It was as though I was paralysed and struck dumb—I could not say anything at all.

And then he looked up suddenly and our eyes met. His were all alight—those pale blue eyes of his behind the steel spectacles. I had never seen them like this before, and his voice shook now when he spoke.

'I don't suppose it is any use,' he said. 'I never thought it was. But I had to tell you—it can't hurt you to be told.'

I said:

'I am sorry.'

He said:

'Don't be sorry. There is nothing to be sorry about. I am glad I met you. My life was very empty before I met you. It can never be so empty again.'

And I felt suddenly:

'What is this I am doing? What am I pushing away?' I felt that it was wonderful to be wanted like that—and that Hugo did not want me—and I said: 'Forgive me. I will marry you if you want me.'

It was funny, I think, that I said, 'Forgive me.' I didn't know then why I said it—I just heard myself saying it.

Walter came up to me and kissed me. He did it awkwardly—very stiffly, as if he did not know how—and I thought how Hugo did not kiss me on the night of Guy's party, at Yearsly by the Jasmine Gate. And I knew as he was kissing me that I had made a mistake.

I felt very cold, and I shivered—perhaps because I had shivered with Hugo at the Jasmine Gate. But that had been different, quite.

Walter said:

'Don't be afraid, my precious. I will try to be what you want.'

And I thought:

'Does he understand after all? How much does he understand?'

XXII

I went the next day to tell Mollie. It was a Saturday, I remember, and it had rained; all the streets were wet.

Walter had stayed with me all the evening before, and I asked him not to come the next day. I felt that I must have a day in peace, without him, or anyone.

I sat in my room all the morning, and tried to read. In the afternoon I went out and walked about.

The trees were all green now, but it was not warm. Clouds had come up in the night, and the sky was still grey.

I meant to go to Mollie in time for tea; I was on the Embankment by half-past four, but I did not go in; I went to a tea shop instead, a little restaurant, not far from Mollie's flat, where we had had lunch together very often before. I sat a long time over my tea. I shrank somehow from seeing Mollie and George; he would be there too on a Saturday afternoon. They might be out of course, but I did not think so, for it had been arranged before, or half arranged, that I should go there this afternoon.

I went out again, on to the Embankment; I walked along by the river, westward, past the Addingtons' windows, towards the power station. The sun was beginning to go down, and the sky was all pink now, behind the four chimneys; the broad stretch of river where it bends, beyond Battersea Bridge, was pink too; a mist was coming up, with the tide, I suppose, from the sea, and the colours were dimmed and obscured by the greyness of the mist. A man came along with a stick, and lit the lamps, one lamp, and then two, and then three; it was quite light still, and the lamps looked small and rather foolish; I wondered why they lit the lamps so soon.

There was an old man selling flowers by the corner of Battersea Bridge; I had never seen him there before; he looked a very poor old man; I bought a bunch of narcissi from him; it cost a shilling.

I thought:

'That is expensive, for a bunch of narcissi.'

I thought:

'It is no good; I must go in and tell them; it is too late to go back; I must tell them now what I have done.'

I knocked on the door, and rang the bell. The woman from below opened it; she often did, and I went up.

There was a knocker on the door of Mollie's room; it was the first door one came to in their part of the house. I knocked on the door with the knocker and walked in.

They were sitting beside the fire, George in his armchair, and Mollie on a cushion on the floor. There was tea on the table, pushed back again against the wall; they had finished tea, and were reading; the grey cat was with them, on the hearth-rug.

It was comfortable, and familiar, and homely. There were blue curtains in this room too, but there were patterns on them, blue and white, and the cushions on the chairs were red; it was a homelier room than Hugo's, and the chairs came mostly from their old home in Manchester, ordinary sort of chairs, not straight deep shapes like his. There was a Persian carpet that had been in Manchester too, the ordinary blue and red sort of carpet, a pinkish red like the cushions; Hugo said they did not match it quite, and Mollie said she would change them, but she never did; and we got to like the cushions that did not quite match, and we would not have liked to have them changed.

'We thought you were not coming,' said Mollie, looking up from her book. George pulled up another chair for me.

I threw the bunch of narcissi into Mollie's lap:

'A peace offering,' I said. 'I meant to come sooner; I started out quite early after lunch.'

'You've had tea?' asked Mollie, and I said, yes, had.

George had his pipe; he always had; he took it out of his mouth, and held out his book.

'Have you read it?' he asked. 'Awfully good!'

I looked at the book; it was Aksakov's *Memories of Childhood*; I had not read it; I turned over the pages, and read bits of it, here and there. I said:

'I came to tell you, really, that I am engaged to Walter Sebright.'

I did not look at either of them, only at the book.

'What?' said George, sitting up sharply.

Mollie said:

'Oh, Helen!'

They were both looking at me; I knew it and pretended not to see. I felt as though I were going to cry, and was determined not to.

'Do you mean that, Helen?' Mollie asked very gently.

I said:

'Yes; are you surprised?'

She said:

'Yes; very much surprised; I didn't expect it at all!'

I looked at George, but his face was turned away; he was staring at the fire, bending forwards, away from me.

I said:

'Won't you congratulate me, either of you?' and my voice sounded odd, and jerky, even to myself, 'Won't you give me your good wishes?'

'Yes . . . oh surely, all good wishes . . .' Mollie said, 'but . . .' She hesitated and I saw her look at George. . . .

'If you are going back now, I will go with you,' George said abruptly.

He knew, of course, that I had not meant to go back then, for I had only just come. Mollie looked at him again, surprised, I thought, and anxious.

I nearly said: 'I am not going back!'

But I wanted to get away, and somehow, too, I had to do what George wanted.

I said:

'Yes, I am going back now; but you needn't come.'

He got up from his chair and went to get his hat it was hanging up on the landing, outside the door. I stood up too. Mollie took both my hands in hers.

She said:

'I wish you happiness with all my heart, you do know that, my dear!'

I nodded; I felt I could not speak without crying, and I did not want to cry.

George was waiting for me outside, at the top of the stairs; he waited for me to pass and then followed me down.

We crossed the road to the pavement by the river, and turned Eastward, towards the bridges and the trams. We passed the two bridges, and Oakley Street, where my bus for Kensington would run; we did not, either of us, think about that. We were walking very quickly, along the river; the lamps were all lit now, broad streaks of light lay out in front of each, across the wet pavement and the road.

'It isn't true, what you said just now?' George asked at last.

I said:

'Yes; why should it not be true?'

'I can't believe it is true!'

'You mean that no one would want to marry me?'

'No,' he said quietly, 'I don't mean that.'

We walked along without speaking; we were nearly at Chelsea Bridge now.

George stopped walking, and turned round:

'Does Hugo know?' he asked.

I said:

'No. I haven't seen Hugo.'

He leaned his elbows on the stone parapet and looked straight in front of him, across the river.

'You know, Helen,' he said, 'you must not do this; you can't understand what you are doing; you haven't thought.'

I said:

'I am tired of thinking'

'I know it is not my business; you can say it is nothing to do with me; but it is; Hugo . . . and you are the best friends I have; I can't stand by and see you . . . and Hugo messing up your lives . . .'

His voice was very low; I had never heard George's voice like this.

I thought:

'How he loves Hugo! Why do we love him so?'

I said:

'I thought you liked Sophia?'

He said:

'I do like her.'

'And you like Walter Sebright too; you said you did.'

'I do,' he said, 'I like him too, but not for you.'

I said:

'That is for me to judge.'

He said:

'No, not now; you don't know what you are doing. You are unhappy and angry, and . . . oh Helen, why do we beat about the bush? You and Hugo love each other far too well to marry other people? You know that . . . I know it . . . and Hugo knows it too!'

I said:

'I don't think Hugo does.'

'He does . . . . I know he does. Give him time, Helen. He will never care for anyone as he does for you.'

I said:

'He leaves it to you, to say!'

'Can't you wait a little while? Six months, or three months even . . . ? That is not very long to wait . . .'

I said:

'I am sick of waiting. I don't know even, that I want Hugo, now.'

George was silent; I knew how hard it must be for him to say these things, and I wanted to hurt him. There were sea gulls walking in the mud, at the edge of the river. They rose up in a cloud in front of us, calling and flapping their wings.

I said:

'It is good of you to consider Hugo so much, but I don't think he would be grateful to you.'

I said it in a hard, horrible voice.

George clasped his hands together; he clasped and unclasped his fingers, and said nothing at all.

I said:

'I suppose you think I should wait for ever, on the chance of Hugo's wanting me some day? You don't mind what happens to me?'

I can't bear now to think how I spoke to George; it was as though a devil was in me. I did not mean what I said, and I knew that I did not mean it; I would have waited for Hugo always, if I had thought he would want me ever; but I did not think so. That was not George's fault.

George said:

'I did not mean that, Helen. You know, surely, that I did not. Do you think I should have said all this, if I did not mind what happened to you?

'It is not fair to Sebright,' he said abruptly, 'to marry him like this.'

I said:

'That is his affair, and mine; you had better leave it alone.'

We walked on again; past Chelsea Bridge, and along Grosvenor Road. There was no parapet here, only railings, and the river showed through the iron bars, with the lamplight on it. Across the water, where the wharfs and warehouses are, there were more lights, and a noise of hammering. A train went past with lighted windows, across the railway bridge. I did not ask George to leave me; I did not want him to go. Twice I looked round at him.

'Why does he mind so much?' I wondered. 'It is wonderful to mind so much about other people.'

I said once:

'It is very dark for April.'

He said:

'Yes, it is getting late.'

Lorries went past us, a train of lorries, with iron girders on them. There was a Salvation Army meeting at the corner of a street.

I said:

'I should like to be religious.'

George said:

'So should I.'

I wished already, that I had been kinder to George. I knew how hard it must have been for him to say all that to me. I was grateful to him for caring about it at all.

We had left the river now, and were walking through streets with more warehouses and yards. We came out soon to Westminster, and crossed the wide space in front of the Houses of Parliament. We stood and waited for a bus.

George said:

'Forgive me, Helen. I am afraid I have made it worse. I am sorry, if I have.'

I wanted to say:

'Forgive me, George. I love you for what you said. It was dear and brave of you to say it. It was like you, George.'

But there were people all round, near us, and my bus was

coming, round the corner, and across to where we stood.

I only said:

'It's all right; you haven't a bit. Good-bye.'

I held out my hand, and George took it.

Then I climbed up on to my bus, and went up the steps to the top. I turned round to wave to him again, but he did not see me. He was standing quite still, where I had left him, staring in front of him at the road.

XXIII

I did not write to Hugo. George told him, and Guy wrote to me at once.

'Congratulations and good wishes,' he said; that was all.

Cousin Delia asked me to bring Walter down to see her I said I would, the next week-end.

Hugo wrote later:

'Helen dear, I hope you will be happy. I hope you have chosen right. Other people cannot judge for you, not even we, who have known you best.'

I thought:

'He does not mind. He does not like Walter, but he does not mind.'

Walter took me to see his mother. She looked old to be his mother; much older than Cousin Delia. She had light blue eyes like his, and fair hair. Her hair was not so grey as Cousin Delia's, but her face was much more lined. She was small, and like a bird, with quick, nervous movements. She was dressed in purple; a purple silk bodice, with a high collar, up round her chin. She was very neat and slim, and her face was pink, like a soft apple.

She lived in a high house, with steep, dark stairs. There were Indian things in the room; weapons, and powder horns, and inlaid tables. Walter's grandfather had been in India; he was an Indian merchant who traded in rice. There were water-colours on the walls, of cottages, and churches in green trees; old-fashioned, rather charming pictures, but the room was dark all the same; the curtains were dark and heavy, and there was too much furniture; I felt very much a stranger in that room.

Mrs. Sebright kissed me in a fluttering, half-frightened way.

'My dear, I am so glad to meet you,' she said. 'Walter has talked to me often about you. I should like to have seen you before.'

She made me sit down in a big chair; it had a chintz cover with purplish flowers on it; faded, dull sort of flowers.

'I must look at you,' she said, 'you must let me look at you, my dear!'

She put on her spectacles, and looked at me. It was natural that she should want to look, but I felt embarrassed.

'Yes, you are very pretty, very pretty indeed! Walter told me so. Walter is always right.'

She gave a little nervous laugh.

'We must make friends now,' she said; 'you see, it seems so strange to me, that I do not know you at all. Walter has been such a good son to me, such a devoted son, and good sons make good husbands, so they say. . . . I am sure my Walter will. You are a fortunate young lady, my dear, though I say it, and I am sure you will do your best to deserve him.'

I said I hoped I should. I liked her for thinking so much of Walter; she was so naive, and so single-hearted; the attitude of my friends would have been inconceivable to her.

And I thought:

'She knows him much better than they do, after all.'

She said:

'You must tell me all about yourself. Your parents are dead, I believe?'

I told her that my father was dead, and my mother had married again.

'Poor dear, poor dear, so you were all alone?'

I told her about Cousin Delia and Yearsly.

I said:

'I was with her long before, after my father died.'

'Ah, yes; and you had cousins there, to play with, I believe?'

I said:

'Yes; two cousins—Guy and Hugo.'

'They must be almost like brothers to you now?'

I said:

'Yes; almost.'

'Walter knows them, I think? He knew them at Oxford.'

I said:

'He does not know them very well.'

'They would not be quite Walter's type, perhaps . . . you see, Walter is so clever, he does not care much for people who are not . . . but he will, of course, my dear, later on, if they are your cousins. He has a most affectionate nature, and I am sure they are very nice young men!'

I suppose I did not respond, for she added quickly:

'I did not mean, of course, that your cousins were stupid, Walter has never said such a thing to me, oh, not at all, but I thought from what he told me that they were . . . just . . . not quite like Walter . . . he has, of course, a quite exceptional brain.'

I said:

'Oh no; my cousins are not like Walter; but I love them very much; I hope he will be friends with them, more, later on.'

I did not mind what Mrs. Sebright said; I did not mind what Walter had told her about them.

I thought:

'She feels about Walter as I do about Hugo; I am glad that some one feels about him like that.'

Walter came in then. He had left me alone with his mother for a talk. He stood beside her with his hand on her shoulder, and looked at me.

'Wasn't I right, Mother?' he asked softly. 'Isn't she all I said?'

He looked flushed and happy; his eyes were shining; I wished he would not wear those black steel spectacles.

Grandmother went to call on Mrs. Sebright. Grandmother was the only person who seemed really pleased at the engagement.

She said:

'I like your young man. He has brains and character. You might have done worse. You won't be well off, not at all well off; but that does not matter; we all value money too highly, and you will have enough when I die,'

I don't know what she said to Mrs. Sebright, or Mrs. Sebright to her, but she was not displeased.

She said:

'A good woman, I think, but a fool; he must get his brains from his father. Stupid women often have clever sons; perhaps the clever men marry them. She will not trouble you, Helen, she won't interfere, but you must be kind to her, and attentive.'

I said that I would try. I was grateful to Grandmother for being pleased at all.

XXIV

Guy and Hugo were not at Yearsly that week-end; they were sorry they could not come, Cousin Delia said.

She welcomed Walter, giving him both her hands, and looked at him hard, as his mother had looked at me; but she did not ask him questions. Some people said that Cousin Delia was hard to talk to, for she never asked you the ordinary things; she did not ask people how their relations were, as some women always do. She took people as they were, and left them alone; and she talked, when she did talk, about anything that was in her mind, or yours, at the moment.

She showed Walter some gems, Greek gems, in the library; he told her about them, their dates, and where they were made. He did not say they were decadent, or 'too late,' as I expected. He was polite to Cousin Delia, and treated her with respect.

He said:

'She is not at all like her sons.'

I said:

'Oh, Walter, I think her so like them both.'

He did not get on very well with Cousin John; that did not surprise me; Cousin John might seem dull to anyone who did not know him well.

I took him to Joseph and Mathew, and the Elliots at the farm. He was awkward with them all, and did not know what to say. They shook hands with us, and wished us joy, but they were not hearty, and as we turned away, I heard Elliot say to his wife:

'I aye thought it would have been Mr. Hugo!'

I don't think Walter heard what he said.

I took Walter to the Temple, and into the High Wood. He made love to me and kissed me, and called me pretty names; I would not have thought he could say the things he did, and I was glad he did; but I did not show him the Happy Tree, nor the Frog Pond, nor the Jasmine Gate.

XXV

Cousin Delia came to see me in my bed, as she used to when I was little.

She said:

'Dear Heart, are you happy?'

I said:

'I don't know, Cousin Delia. Ought I to be?'

She said:

'I don't know. I wasn't; but some people are. It is better to be happy.'

I said:

'Yes. I know it would be better.'

She stood beside my bed, and looked across it at the window, and the branches of the trees. There was a moon outside and we could see the branches; I had pulled the curtain back.

She said:

'Poor Hugo; I am thinking of my Hugo.'

I said:

'You need not be sorry for him.'

She looked down at me.

She said:

'No? Need I not?'

I said:

'No. Be sorry for me; and Walter.'

She said:

'Walter has got what he wants. Not many people get that.'

I said:

'No, not many people; I know that; and I don't think Walter really has.'

She said:

'Dear Heart, don't be impatient; don't decide too soon.'

I said:

'I have decided.'

She bent down and kissed my forehead.

She said:

'I like your Walter; and he is very happy.'

XXVI

Walter took me to see his sister Maud. She was the headmistress of a school at Lessingham; a County Secondary School.

We travelled by train for nearly two hours; we were to spend the night with Maud, at the school.

We sat opposite to each other in the train; we had two corner seats.

I thought:

'It will be like this when I am married to Walter. We shall travel together always. How funny that will be!'

Walter had bought me newspapers at the station. He bought a lot of them and put them on the seat beside me; there was *Vogue*, and *Colour*, and the *Daily Mirror*; and I laughed.

I said:

'I should not have thought you would buy papers like this. Have you ever bought any of these before?'

Walter laughed too.

He said:

'No, of course not; I have never had any one to buy them for, before.'

He had no newspaper himself; he did not read them; he had told me that before. He took out a German book, *Der Hittitische Kult*, and began to read it, but soon he put it down. I was looking at him, and now he looked at me.

He said:

'Not even that, when you are here. I wonder if you know how much that means?'

He leaned across, and took my hands in his.

He said:

'Perhaps, you will make me human. Perhaps I shall be quite different when I am married to you.'

I bent forward too and kissed his forehead; I felt curiously moved.

I thought:

'Perhaps, he really needs me; perhaps I have something to give him that he really wants . . . beyond mere falling in love.'

I felt that there were depths in him I had not fathomed.

I thought:

'Can I do it? Am I what he thinks me?'

And then I thought:

'Perhaps I shall love him more than any one, in time.'

People got into the train at the next station. Walter talked to me about his sister Maud.

He said:

'I hope so much you will like her'; and I felt behind his words, the hope, more doubtful, that she might like me.

He said:

'She is a very remarkable woman; she took a i.i. at Cambridge, you know, that is not common for women, and she did it all herself. She was only seventeen when my father died. She was at school then, of course, and insisted on staying on. My mother would have taken her away, I think, and gone to live in the country, but Maud was right. She said it was better for us all, to keep her on at school, and at college too; she would earn more in the end, and of course she was right. She paid her own way with scholarships, all the way up, just as I did afterwards, and she helped with me too. She kept me up to the mark, and my mother too. My mother was inclined to spoil me. She thought I was delicate and that the work at St. Paul's was too much for me, but Maud insisted on my working hard, and again, I am sure she was right. She is not so gentle as my mother, of course, nor so affectionate, but I admire her very much, and I am grateful to her.'

I said:

'I don't expect she will approve of me!'

Walter hesitated.

'Not quite, at first, perhaps, but you mustn't mind that. She does judge people on their merits, really, in the end, though sometimes she is prejudiced at first.'

I was afraid that I should not like Maud, and I was sure that she would not like me.

XXVII

Maud was waiting for us in her 'Private Room.' We came to it through long corridors with notices on the walls, and a place with pegs, and rows and rows of hats and coats. There was a smell of disinfectant, and ink, and books. It was different from the smell at Ellsfield, but reminded me partly of that.

The 'Private Room' was pleasanter. There was a big window with green serge curtains, and a table with a green serge cover, and lots of books on it. There were daffodils on the table in a green, 'art pottery' jug, and reproductions of pictures by Watts on the walls, in broad, dark oak frames.

Maud came forward to meet us. She was tall and fair; she seemed much taller and more powerful than Walter; she looked healthier, and more athletic. Her hair was parted in the middle, and pushed forward, very neatly, with little combs behind each ear. She was wearing a very clean, well ironed, white silk shirt, with a dark blue tie, a tie-pin, and a long, navy blue serge skirt; she had pince-nez, rimless ones, fastened by a fine, black cord.

She smiled in a bright, business-like way, as though she were accustomed to smiling.

'My dear Walter, how do you do? How do you do, Helen?'

She kissed us both, brightly too, and led us back to the tea-table, which was waiting by the hearth-rug. There was no fire, though the day was rather cold; the kettle was boiling on a brass spirit lamp, on the table.

'Your train must have been late,' she said, as she made the tea. 'I expected you a quarter of an hour ago. Fortunately, to-day is my "free day," and I have an hour and a half, quite free, after tea.'

She made us feel that it was our fault that the train was late, but that she forgave us.

Walter murmured an apology, and she smiled again:

'It is of no consequence, none whatever. I have kept myself entirely at your disposal this afternoon. I had to take the chair at a staff meeting between three and four; we have a staff-committee now, you know, Walter, to decide on internal questions of policy in the school, slight variations in curriculum, and so forth, as far as our governing body will permit: it meets on Saturday afternoon. I find it a useful experiment. I find that it encourages keenness in the staff, more especially the younger members, if they feel they have some say in the management of the school. I have, of course, a casting vote myself, but I seldom use it. It is surprising to find how often we are unanimous, or practically so. Sugar, Helen and milk?'

She gave me sugar and milk, without waiting for my reply, and handed me the cup.

'Let me see,' she went on, 'where were you at school? Walter did tell me, I believe.'

I said:

'Ellsfield, in Surrey; Miss Ellis's school.'

'Ah yes, of course! They do not take the Higher Certificate there, I think? There was some discussion about it at the last Headmistresses' Conference. Miss Ellis takes, shall we say, an independent line?'

I said:

'I don't think they did many examinations. I believe Miss Ellis didn't approve of them.'

'Quite, quite; and not many of the girls would go on to the Universities, I suppose?'

'Some did, I think; oh, several did. You could go if you liked.'

Maud smiled.

'No compulsory abstention,' she said, 'but not unduly encouraged, I suppose. Of course here we have quite the opposite idea. We train our girls to regard a University training as the natural culmination of their education. Under present conditions they cannot always afford it, but it is surprising how many can, when once the girl and her family are made to feel it the natural and proper thing. There ought to be more scholarships, of course, for Oxford and Cambridge are too expensive for most girls of the class who come to us, but the Provincial Universities are now excellent. A number of our girls go to Birmingham and more still to the University College here.'

I said:

'It must be very convenient to have a college here.'

'Yes, a good departure, quite good. Standard not very high yet, but that will come. I thoroughly approve of this movement for increasing the number of University Colleges in Provincial towns. By the way, Walter,' she went on, 'I want to speak to you about that last regulation of the Board of Faculties and Arts, about the P.Q.T. External Examinations, you know the one I mean, 1346; I think it is on the new schedule.'

She took up a bunch of papers from the table beside her and began to look through them.

'Here it is,' she said, and began to read it aloud.

It was something about the qualifications necessary for anyone going in for some particular examination; it conveyed nothing, of course, to me. Walter said something about its not making much difference, and she interrupted him:

'I entirely disagree with you, Walter. Take the case, for instance, of a girl in the Vth Form who had already passed 3y and 6b in the Higher Certificate; her position would be quite anomalous!'

'But do many girls pass 3y and 6b, and nothing else?'

'Not many, but some do. In any case it ought to be made quite clear; would such a girl be eligible, or not?'

'You see,' she said, turning to me, 'so many of our girls take the London University External degree, and as Walter is now a Member of the University, I always apply to him in my difficulties.'

Walter said:

'I am afraid I can't be any use to you over this, Maud. I really have nothing to do with the External Examinations. You had better apply to the Secretary of the Board of Faculties, direct.'

There was irritation in his voice; he held out his cup.

'May I have some more tea?' he asked.

'Certainly, certainly. I did not see that you had finished; and, Helen, let me give you some more. You did say milk and sugar, I think. Walter, please give Helen some cake. Yes, I think I had better apply to the Board of Faculties direct. It is always best to go to the Fountain Head. But you must support me on the Board, if the question is raised. Helen must excuse us talking so much shop,' and she turned brightly to me: 'We Academic people have so much shop to talk, and so little opportunity.'

Walter said:

'I find plenty of opportunity!'

'Ah, but you are at the Fountain Head! That is one of the advantages of University life over that of a school. It has that advantage, undoubtedly. But what is Helen most interested in? We must make friends, mustn't we? Now that we are to be sisters-in-law!'

Walter said:

'Helen is interested in a great many things. Literature and pictures, and music . . . aren't you, Helen?'

I felt like a child, being discussed and drawn out by grown-up people.

I said:

'Yes. I am interested in that sort of thing, chiefly, I suppose.'

'I see,' said Maud, artistic. 'Well, that is a very important side of life. I always teach my girls to appreciate Art. We have lectures on Art, every alternate week, in the Winter terms, with lantern slides; and literature too; three of our girls took A.A. in the English Literature paper of the L.L.U.'

'Helen is a great dancer too!'

Maud gave a little laugh.

'The lighter side,' she said, 'that we can hardly call Art!'

I wondered why Walter had said it. I thought he might have known that Maud would not count dancing 'Art.'

'It can be Art,' said Walter doggedly. 'Have you seen the Russian Ballet?'

I was surprised that Walter should have seen it himself.

Maud laughed again, her quick, business-like laugh.

'I am afraid I have no time for Ballets,' she said:

'Helen will not find much time to dance when she is married, I am afraid. I am afraid Academic life will seem a little strange to you at first. We are poor, dull people you know, my dear, but we have our good points, if you take us as you find us! And now, would you like a walk round? We have extended the playing field since you were here last, Walter, and there are some new books in the Classical Library.'

Walter and I were not alone all the evening. There were prayers for the boarders, and supper in a big dining hall, only two tables, at the end in use, for the day girls were not there.

In the morning we went to church with Maud and two other mistresses, and the boarders.

We were alone for a little, in Maud's room, before lunch.

'When did you go to the Russian Ballet?' I asked.

And Walter said:

'When you said you liked dancing; in the tea-shop near the British Museum. I went the next evening.'

I took his hand.

I said:

'That was dear of you. Did you like it?'

He said:

'I don't know if I liked it really. Not very much, perhaps, but I liked to know what you liked . . .'

He hesitated, and smiled shyly.

'I thought it made me understand you better.'

I felt, somehow, nearer to Walter after that visit. I felt that there was an understanding between us in relation to Maud. He did not say it and I did not say it, but I felt that he was on my side, and not on hers; that he was resisting what she stood for, and defending me.

I had dreaded the meeting with Maud, and now it was over I did not mind her; I was not afraid of her: it did not seem to me that she would count.

XXVIII

We were to be married in July, as soon as Walter's term ended. Grandmother had arranged that, I think, with Walter.

Cousin Delia said:

'Wait a little. Wait till the Autumn, or even Christmas.'

Mrs. Sebright said July seemed rather soon.

Walter said:

'Why wait, now it is settled?'

I let them arrange it as they liked. I felt all the time quite passive, as though things happened, and decisions were made, quite separately from me; it was not my business to interfere; I just watched.

And I thought:

'Now this is happening, now that. Now she is engaged to be married. Now she is looking for a house. Now they are getting clothes for her. Now, sheets. Soon there will be a wedding in a church. And what then?'

It was as though I were watching it all from a long way off.

We found a house in Hampstead; number seven, Edinburgh Terrace. It was a stucco house, semi-detached, with a garden back and front, and a high flight of steps up to the front door. There was a stucco wall between the road and the garden in front, and a straight path that sloped up from the gate to the front door, so that the house itself looked high up, higher than it really was. There were lilac bushes at the side of the house, where the back door was, and a trellis gate that led through to the garden behind. There was a verandah at the back, with iron steps leading down to the back garden. The gardens were oblong strips of grass, neglected for some time. The whole terrace had been built, I should think, about 1850; it was old-fashioned, and a little dilapidated; much more attractive, I thought, than more modern houses, and Walter thought it cheap.

I wanted to have the outside of it painted; it had been painted a sort of cream colour once, and I wanted it white, and the windows and door bright green. It was the sort of house that ought to be white and green.

Walter said he thought it would do as it was. We could decorate it inside, and then see how much money we had left. We had five hundred pounds to spend on decorating and furniture; Mrs. Sebright said that would be ample; Grandmother said we must do the best we could with that, and that she would make up the extras. I could see that she did not think it would be enough.

Cousin Delia came to see the house. She stood on the steps and looked at the front garden.

She said:

'You should grow roses here; red roses, I think. Richmond, or General Macarthur; and a pond in the middle, perhaps.'

I said:

'Will roses grow in London?'

She said:

'Oh surely they will! Do you think they won't?'

Cousin Delia seemed always a little lost when she came to London; a little bit as though she were walking in a dream.

She said:

'It would be dreadful, of course, if the roses would not grow.'

I showed her the rooms inside; upstairs and down; She said:

'It is a nice little house. You shall have the "Little chair," from Yearsly. It would go well, I think, in that drawing-room. Your chairs must be small, for these rooms.'

She said that the paint on the stairs would not do. It was dark brown paint, and very ugly, but Walter thought we should leave it.

She said:

'It is all wrong, that brown paint, you must have it taken off.'

Mrs. Sebright said we must have the drains relaid. I had thought we might leave the drains.

Maud came up from Lessingham to see the house. She said we should have the paint inside green.

She said:

'It saves work; white paint gives far more trouble.'

But I did not want green paint inside.

In the bedroom, she said:

'You can have a nice fumed oak suite, in here. There are excellent fumed oak suites at the Army and Navy Stores. I have furnished the bedrooms in our teachers' hostel with their suites. Well made, and in very good taste.'

Walter said:

'Helen does not like fumed oak.'

'Oh really! I thought every one liked fumed oak now. What does Helen like?'

They always talked of me as though I was not there.

Walter said:

'She likes old furniture. Old mahogany and . . . and walnut.'

Maud laughed:

'Oh, of course,' she said, 'we should all like old walnut best, I imagine. I am afraid Helen will find that a professor's salary will hardly allow of furnishing in that style!'

She smiled at me, in what I think she meant to be an encouraging way.

She said:

'Helen will soon learn, I am sure. A poor professor's wife can hardly expect to live in the way she has been accustomed to; even clothes, for instance, the cost of clothes will have to be considered,' and she glanced at mine, 'but I feel sure that Helen will soon learn. We must all help her'; and she smiled again.

I began to hate Maud. I wondered if she wanted to make it all seem horrid.

I said:

'We can have packing-cases with chintz frills. Sophia Lane Watson has those in her room and they look very nice. I would rather have that than fumed oak.'

'Rather too, what shall we say? . . . Bohemian, perhaps, to live in packing-cases. I am sure you will have ample for your needs, if it is laid out carefully, with foresight, and consideration.'

Mrs. Sebright gave us a sideboard; it was a big mahogany sideboard that had belonged to Walter's grandfather.

It was ugly and took up a great deal of room; and she gave us a portrait of his grandfather too, the India merchant; Walter was not at all like him. I could not say I did not want them, but they spoiled the rooms.

I thought:

'It is only the dining-room, after all; we shall not sit in it very much.'

George and Hugo came to see the house when it was almost finished. Mostly they liked it, but Hugo said:

'Oh, must you have that sideboard?'

And I saw George nudge his elbow, to stop him speaking about it.

I said:

'I rather like it. It belonged to Walter's grandfather, who was a merchant in India. It is interesting to have it, I think.'

Hugo said:

'Oh, yes . . . yes, of course! If there is a reason for it, that is quite different!'

He looked at the portrait of the grandfather, a big portrait in oils, badly painted, but he said nothing about it.

He said:

'That room upstairs is awfully nice! that drawing-room, with the steps down to the garden, and I am sure you can make the garden awfully nice.'

I had hardly seen Hugo, since I had been engaged; only once or twice, at parties; at Campden Hill Square, and at Mollie's. I did not want to see him much just then.

He gave me an alabaster bowl; old white alabaster; I think it was Chinese. I put it on the drawing-room chimney-piece, in the middle, and straight silver candlesticks, from George and Mollie, on either side. Walter thought it looked rather bare. He thought it would have been more convenient to put a clock there, but he didn't mind about things like that.

We had old walnut furniture in the drawing-room, after all, for Cousin Delia and Cousin John gave me a walnut cabinet, a beautiful thing, like one at Yearsly, and Grandmother gave me a writing-desk, Queen Anne walnut too.

XXIX

Cousin Delia came with me to buy sheets.

It was June now, and the house was nearly ready. We were to be married on the third of July.

She bought a great many sheets, and bath towels, and

pillow-cases. We were sitting facing each other, beside the counter, on two high chairs; and then, quite suddenly, when we had nearly finished, I felt that I could not marry Walter; I felt terrified at what I was doing; I felt as though I was caught in a trap.

I don't quite know what did it, but I think it was the sheets. Cousin Delia was feeling them in her fingers, and she told me to feel them. They were very fine and soft, and I liked the feeling of them, and then I thought of them on a bed, and me in bed, and Walter; and I realized that he would sleep with me, and be as close to me as that; I had not, somehow, thought of that before, and I felt it was impossible; I could not go to bed with Walter.

I said:

'Cousin Delia, I don't think I want any sheets.'

Cousin Delia looked at me, and I think she knew what I was feeling, for she did not ask me why. She waited a minute or two, and then, when the shopman came back, she said, quite quietly:

'I think we will leave the sheets for to-day. Send me the bath towels and the face towels; that will be enough. We can send them back afterwards, if we want to,' she said to me, and she took me into the tea-room which was in that shop.

We sat in two basket chairs, very low, with cushions in them, in a corner, away from the door. There were little white cloths with green shamrocks round the edge on the tables, and a band was playing, a string band, with women in green uniforms playing. A waitress came round with a big tray of cakes, very gorgeous cakes, that you took with a fork.

I kept saying to myself:

'It can't be true. I can't be going to marry him, really, in two weeks. This cannot be going to happen to me, this horrible thing!'

I wished that the band would stop playing and let me think.

I looked at Cousin Delia; she was looking at me. She put out her hand and let it rest on mine.

'Dear Heart,' she said very gently, 'it is not too late. Don't do this, unless you are sure.'

I said:

'I want to think. I don't know what I am doing. I didn't until just now.'

XXX

I went to Walter that evening after dinner. I went out alone, and to his house. I asked to see him, and was afraid I should see his mother, but she was upstairs, in the drawing-room, and he came down alone.

He came into the dining-room; there was a smell of fish there, but the dinner was cleared away. There was gas alight in the room, over the table; the maid had lit it when she showed me in; it had lit with a loud report, like a gun.

He came up to me and took my hands.

'What is it?' he asked me quickly. 'What has happened?'

I said:

'It is all a mistake. I cannot marry you. I am sorry.'

He said:

'Why not?'

I said:

'What do you mean?'

'It is all my fault. It is not fair to you either. I don't love you enough or in the right way, at all.'

He said:

'You will love me in time. I know you will. I know you don't yet; not as I love you.'

I said:

'I am afraid not. That is why I have come. I ought not to have let it go on so long. Somehow, I did not understand. I don't think I shall marry any one, ever at all. I don't think I ever could!'

And then I cried; it was stupid; it was the last moment in the world to cry, but a sob came in my throat, and then another, and I sobbed out loud, and Walter took me in his arms and comforted me.

And it was over. I had meant to be cold and firm, and I could not. I felt so frightened; frightened of life, and of myself, and he was very kind. He seemed much older than me, and much wiser; he seemed just then all I wanted him to be.

He took me back to Campden Hill Square, and said good-bye to me on the step as he had said it that evening in March, that seemed now, long ago.

He said:

'It will be better when we are married. Only two weeks more to wait now.'

And I knew then that it was bound to come; that I must go through with it; and I did not know whether it was a mistake or not.

XXXI

We were married on the third of July, at St. Mary Abbots Church.

Those two weeks of waiting were terrible, but they passed, as everything does, in the end.

I thought:

'Twelve   days . . .' then: 'Eleven   days . . .' then: 'Ten . . .' and   then: 'Four   days . . . three   days . . . two days . . .'

I thought:

'It must feel like this if one is diving from a high bridge, from a railway bridge, down into a river.'

—I don't know why I thought of a railway bridge, but I did—'It must feel like this, while one is waiting to jump.'

And I thought:

'It must feel like this if one is going to be hung; counting the days, and knowing, quite for certain, that something terrific will happen to you in the end.'

And then I thought:

'It has happened to other people; to Cousin Delia, and to Grandmother, and to people I pass every day, in the street.'

And I thought:

'If they have gone through with it, I can.'

Nunky came up with Cousin Delia, to dress me for the wedding. I had a white satin dress, like all brides' dresses, and a veil that had been Mary Geraldine's wedding veil, and roses from Yearsly, golden and white.

There was a red carpet, and a great many people. Guy and Hugo were there, and Mollie and George, and Anthony Cowper, and Ralph Freeman, and his sister, and Sophia, and the Lacey girls, and Faith Vincent, and vague cousins of mine, and cousins of Walter's, and Mrs. Sebright, of course, and Maud; and there were two uncles of Walter's; one was a schoolmaster in the North of England, and one, a solicitor in the West; they came to London on purpose for the wedding, and I liked them, particularly the schoolmaster; and there were people that had to be asked, friends of Grandmother's, and friends of Mrs. Sebright's.

Cousin John gave me away, and Mr. Furze was the best man, and Mr. Vincent, from Yearsly, came up on purpose to help with the service.

My relations sat on one side of the church, and Walter's on the other; there were more of mine.

There was a good deal of music. Guy had chosen a chorale that they sang at the end; but Mrs. Sebright chose the hymns. None of that seemed to matter very much; and afterwards there was a party and a cake, at Campden Hill Square.

Walter was dressed in a tail coat; he looked quite different; it made it seem queerer, somehow, and more like a dream.

I walked up the aisle of the church with Cousin John while the choir sang 'Oh Perfect Love, All Human Thought Transcending'; and Walter and Mr. Furze were waiting for us at the top. I had never been to a wedding before, and only twice to this church when the banns were being read and Grandmother said we had better go. It seemed odd to see Mr. Vincent there; he belonged so much to Yearsly, and the little old church with so few people in it, but he smiled at me, and I was glad.

Then he said the things about Holy Matrimony, and asked us the questions, and we answered, first Walter and then I, and then there were prayers and hymns, and the vicar of the parish preached a sermon, and then there was the chorale that Guy had chosen—a Bach chorale that he used to sing with the waits sometimes at Christmas; I liked to hear that again, and I was glad that Guy had wanted to choose it.

Then we went into the vestry and signed our names, and other people came too, and signed their names. Cousin John and Guy signed, and Walter's two uncles, and they were all talking.

And I thought:

'Now I am married. There is no escape now.'

And there seemed to be a great singing noise in the church, though really it was quiet; a sort of noise like the sea on a beach, or wind in trees.

Outside the vestry, Hugo was waiting. He said good-bye to me there, for he did not come on to the party. He stopped me in the shadow of the aisle, as I came out with Walter, and said Good-bye.

He said:

'Dear, God bless you. Be happy.'

And he took my hand; and then he went away; he seemed somehow to drift away, in the shadow, at the side; and we walked down the middle of the church to the door.

There was a motor-car outside, and we got into it. We were alone in the motor, driving back to Campden Hill Square, and Walter kissed me, very seriously, and we sat very still. I think he was a little frightened too, now it was done.

The drawing-room at Campden Hill Square was full of people, and the dining-room too; there was food in the dining-room, a wedding cake, and ices, and claret cup, and things like a supper at a dance; and every one came up and shook hands with Walter and me, and talked to us; and Walter was introduced to my relations, and I was introduced to his; and there was a great noise of people talking all round, like there is at an evening party; it was like an evening party, though it was only twelve o'clock.

Mr. Furze came and spoke to me too.

He said:

'It is not very long since our first meeting, in the British Museum. That was a very different scene!'

I said:

'Yes; different; but it seems to me a long time ago.'

He said:

'Four months, not quite four months, A great deal can happen in four months.'

He smiled at me, but he looked sad, I thought, and I wondered why.

XXXII

After a time they called me away, upstairs, and took off my wedding gown and dressed me in other new clothes, a brown coat and skirt, and a hat with a long feather, and a fur neck thing; all these were new too; I had been to shops with Cousin Delia to buy them.

And then we got into the same motor that had brought us from the church. Some one had lent it, but I can't remember who, and Cousin John shut the door of the motor with a bang, and people shouted and waved to us, and Anthony Cowper threw some rice, and some one else confetti. Some of the confetti got into my umbrella, I don't know how; it fell out a long time after, on the platform, when I opened the umbrella; that was on the journey back, after our honeymoon was over.

We drove to Euston, for we were going up to Carlisle the first night, and then on to the farmhouse on the Roman Wall, where Walter had been staying when we met him there.

It was a long journey; too long, perhaps, and people were in the carriage until Crewe.

The funny thing is, that I don't remember that journey distinctly. I remember getting into the train at Euston and getting out at Carlisle, but in between it is a sort of blur; I only remember looking out of the window, at the rails, running along beside us, and thinking:

'I might throw myself out on to those. That would be a way out of it still.'

But I knew I would not throw myself out really. That was nearly at the end of the journey, after passing Preston, and the place where the railway runs near to the sea.

It was evening when we reached Carlisle, but quite light, for it was summer and the days were longer there than in the South.

We got into another motor and drove to the hotel. A room had been engaged for us at that hotel, and the motor had been ordered; everything seemed to happen automatically, as though we were puppets, and somebody else was moving us by strings; at least, I felt like that; I don't know if Walter did. I suppose it was he who had arranged these things, or he and Grandmother together.

People at the hotel came out to meet us; a sort of concierge man in uniform, and the proprietress of the hotel, who was fat and smiling, with black hair. They took us upstairs, and another man came after with the luggage. They took us along a passage, to a big room with a wardrobe in it. Bedrooms do have wardrobes in them as a rule, I know, my own bedroom has, but this wardrobe was different; it was so big that it seemed to dominate the room, it was a sort of triple wardrobe; it had two doors with looking-glasses at each end, and a long plain part in the middle, and the doors came open too easily, so that they swung out, and you saw yourself reflected somewhere, wherever you walked in that room. I did not want to see myself. I did not like that big wardrobe.

There was a big bed too; bright red mahogany like the wardrobe, with very thick, shining posts, and red curtains at the back. There were heavy red curtains at the windows, with big mahogany curtain rods and rings, and lace curtains inside. It was a bow window-looking out into the street, but it was not a noisy street.

The proprietress said it was her 'Best bedroom.'

'We keep it for these occasions,' she said, smiling.

She meant to be kind, I could see. She thought how nice it was to be just married; I could see that she thought that. I suppose that she had been married a great many years, longer even, than I have now.

She said:

'Dinner will be served whenever you wish; in the dining-room, or a private room if you prefer it?'

And I said quickly:

'In the dining-room, please.'

I didn't want to be alone with Walter.

Then she went out, and a maid came in with hot water, and I poured it out and washed; and there was the wedding ring on my finger; I could see it through the water and the soapsuds in the basin, when I held my hand right down.

Walter was standing behind me; he saw the ring too.

He said:

'My hand now,' and took hold of my wrist, and I laughed, and drew my hand away, and I dried it quickly on the towel, and told him to go downstairs, and I would come.

I wanted to brush my hair, and clean my face, and I was shy of Walter being there.

I thought:

'How shall I ever take off my clothes, with Walter in the room? Will he stay downstairs? Will he understand that I want him to stay downstairs?'

After dinner, we went out for a walk. That was much better than staying indoors. We walked about the streets, and looked at the Castle, and the road to Scotland; and Walter talked about the Romans, and the Picts and the Scots.

It did not get dark till nearly ten o'clock, and then we had to go in.

As I went upstairs I thought:

'Other people have been through this. Grandmother, and Cousin Delia, and even the proprietress of this hotel. They do not tell us about it, because they can't. I shall not be able to tell my daughter.'

XXXIII

Next day, we went on to Howsteads, to the farmhouse; we went early and had lunch at the farm. They were pleasant people there, and they seemed to like Walter. I was glad to be there.

We stayed six weeks at that farmhouse. We spent the days out of doors, going long walks over the Fells, with sandwiches and books in a rucksack, and not coming in, very often, till it was dark.

Walter had brought Gibbon with him, and he read it aloud to me, lying out on the Fellside, with the sound of plovers calling, and sheep cropping, and sometimes a stream rippling over stones, and we were happy. It was a new world to me, and a new life. It was all quite different from my old life at home, and the country here was not Hugo's country, and the books we read were not Hugo's books.

And I thought:

'I shall learn to know Walter's world as well as I knew Hugo's; his is a bigger, stronger world; it needs more knowing.'

I found Gibbon interesting, and Walter explained it well. Once he was annoyed with me because I said that *Love among the Ruins* made me feel 'past greatness' more than Gibbon, but he was not seriously annoyed. I said I would read *Love among the Ruins* in exchange for his reading Gibbon, and when I had read it he said that anyhow the last line was sense, and he kissed me, and we did not argue about it any more.

When we came back to London, we were almost used to each other.

I thought:

'How funny it is that I was so shy of Walter. I am so close to him now. It is wonderful to be so close to anyone.'

XXXIV

Mrs. Sebright had engaged maids for us; a cook and house-parlourmaid. The cook was called Sarah, the house-parlourmaid Louise. She was younger than the cook, and pretty, but Mrs. Sebright said she was not so good a servant.

The house was all ready for us. Mrs. Sebright had ordered in food, and she was waiting there to receive us. She was like a little bird, fluttering from room to room; showing us little things she had done; muslin curtains tacked up behind wash-stands, rubber knobs on the floors to prevent doors banging backwards, and so on; she did so hope I would not mind, she said.

I did not mind, of course. I thought how nice it all was; I thought:

'How delightful to have a house of one's own!'

I thought how kind Mrs. Sebright was, and how easy it would be to get on with her.

I thought:

'I will never let her feel in the way. I will never let her feel that I have taken Walter away from her.'

And so we settled down in our own home, and enjoyed it. Walter began work again. His University work did not begin till October, but besides that, he was writing a book on proto-Hittite scripts. He was only at the beginning of the book, the very beginning, and it would take many years to finish, he said, but it would be the only book on that subject, or at least on that aspect of the subject.

He had a study upstairs, looking out on the garden behind. He was very pleased with the study; he said it was so quiet, and there was good wall space for books.

He would work there all the morning, while I did housekeeping and gardening. I found the housekeeping great fun. I bought cookery books, and made Sarah try new recipes, French and Italian ones that I found in books. She did not mind trying, though they did not always turn out very well. She treated me as though I were a child whom she was humouring; she made me feel always, that she knew much more about it all than I did, but then, that was quite true, and I did not mind.

I used to go marketing with a basket; there was a little group of shops, down the hill, two streets away; sometimes I used to go there, and sometimes further afield. It was interesting to me to discover the prices of things, for I had never heard prices discussed, and knew nothing about them. I did not know that chicken cost more than rabbit. At Yearsly, we had both fairly often, and both were supplied at home; it never seemed to make any difference which we had, and at Campden Hill Square, it was much the same; chickens and game and rabbits came from Yearsly, and I never heard Grandmother speak about the price of food.

Sometimes now they sent hampers to me, and that was nice, but I enjoyed more to buy my own food. It seems odd now to think that one ever could enjoy it.

The first trouble was when Maud came to lunch, on the 1st of October, and I had bought a pheasant. It was expensive; I was surprised to find how expensive it was, but we always had pheasants at Yearsly on the 1st of October; Cousin John always went out to shoot them in the morning, and Guy with him as a rule, and some were sent to Grandmother; these, of course, she did not get till the next day. I would have had some too, if I had waited, for Cousin John sent some to me too that year; I might have known he would, but I did not think of that at all; I only wanted a nice lunch for Maud, and in the shop I saw pheasants, and I remembered it was the first, and I thought:

'That will be just the thing for Maud! I must try and please Maud, for Walter's sake.'

The pheasant cost fifteen shillings, and I bought it, and Maud was not pleased at all. She remarked on it at once.

She said:

'Pheasant already! I did not think they were in season yet!'

And I said:

'It is the first to-day.'

She said:

'The first?'

'The 1st of October. I don't know how they got them in the shop so early, though.'

She said:

'My dear child, you don't mean to say you bought a pheasant the first day they came in?'

And I said:

'Yes; I saw it in the shop, and I remembered it was the first. Guy will have gone down to Yearsly to-day; he always does.'

Then Maud asked me what it had cost, and I told her fifteen shillings, and she took in a deep breath, and looked at Walter, and Walter looked uncomfortable. Maud asked him whether he made me a housekeeping allowance and he said he didn't, and then Maud asked me how much I spent on my housekeeping every week, and I said I did not know.

And then Maud said I must keep accounts. She said it was most important.

After lunch, she began to show me how to do them. She had an elaborate method, 'double entry' she called it, which was supposed to show quite clearly if one had made a mistake. I tried to understand it and to use it, but it was really no use to me, for when the sum came out wrong, which was very often, I could not understand at all how to make it come right. Afterwards, I asked Mollie to show me her way, and that was better. There was much less system in Mollie's accounts than in Maud's, and I understood them much better. Now, I have still to do accounts, for Walter likes me to, and in all these years I have grown accustomed to it, but they do not come right very often, even now; I have never learned to be efficient, as Mollie learned with her father; you cannot develop what is not there at all; Walter does not realize that; I do, now.

That was an unhappy afternoon. Maud went on and on. She seemed to think that it was an arithmetic lesson, and that I was a stupid child. I always was stupid at arithmetic, I know, but she made it worse, and all the time, I resented her interfering. I felt angry, and rebellious, and not really ashamed of myself, as she seemed to expect me to be.

I kept saying to myself:

'I must not quarrel with Walter's sister. I must be polite to her. I am sure she means to be kind.'

But I was not sure, really. I felt always that underneath there was a fight going on, between Maud and me, for Walter. It was not quite a personal fight; she stood for one side of life, one attitude towards life, and I for the opposite, and Walter was wavering between.

It was true, of course, that I had been silly to buy the pheasant, I realized that, and it was true, too, that I was stupid over accounts, and did not know how to manage, and organize, and yet I felt underneath that there were some things I knew and Maud did not, some things I could understand, that Maud never would, only my things did not seem to count when Maud was there.

She did not go away till after tea.

Generally, Walter and I went out in the afternoon. He worked in the morning, and again after tea, but he had kept the afternoon free, so far, and we used to go out and walk on Hampstead Heath, or sometimes have a ride on the top of a bus. Walter had not been much on the tops of buses; he went by Underground because it was quicker, and he was always in a hurry to be where he was going. It had never occurred to him that the actual process of going, should be enjoyed, not, he said, till he met me. Hugo always went on the tops of buses, and I had got the habit, I suppose, from him. He would sometimes spend a whole afternoon on the top of a bus; getting on at random, and going wherever the bus went, to the very end. He used to see things from the tops of buses; he used to watch the people and the streets; different sorts of people, and different sorts of streets, and different sorts of houses. He used to get quite excited sometimes about people he saw like that. Walter never looked at people or things he passed; he could read a book in the Underground, he said, and not on a bus, besides its being quicker.

It was a joke between us at first, and so sometimes to please me he would come on a bus, in those first weeks of ours. But this afternoon we did not go out at all because of Maud, and it mattered more because it was the last day before Walter's term began; after that he would not be free in the afternoons. I don't suppose this had occurred to Maud; but I don't think it would have made any difference if it had.

Walter went up to the study while Maud was teaching me; he looked worried and cross, but whether he was cross with her or with me, I did not know. He was cross at tea too, and afterwards, when Maud went away, he did not go with her to the tube, as he used to when his mother came to see us, but he did not come back to me either. He went upstairs again and worked in his study till dinner time.

The next morning, some pheasants came from Yearsly from Cousin John, and I was afraid to have them cooked for dinner; I was afraid they would remind Walter of the day before, and the trouble there had been. I gave one to the charwoman, to take home, for that was the day she came, and I sent the other to the children's hospital in Chelsea, near Mollie's flat.

Sarah was annoyed with me that time; she said it was waste to give pheasant to Mrs. Simms, and I told her a lie, and said Walter did not like it; and then I went up to my room and cried.

Maud had made everything horrid. I have never known anyone like Maud for doing that.

XXXV

It was soon after this that I first knew I was going to have a baby. I went to see a doctor called Mrs. Chilcote, whose name I had seen on a brass plate at right angles to our road. She was a nice person; efficient I think, but like Mollie, not like Maud. She was kind to me afterwards very often. Then I went out on the heath and sat down on a seat under a tree; it was a birch tree and the little yellow leaves fluttered down from the tiny branches and I tried to think what it meant. It seemed to me then too wonderful almost to be true. I would have a son, I felt sure of that, and he would be all that I was not, and that Walter was not, nor Hugo; it seems funny now to remember that I thought all that; it did not strike me as improbable at all that my son should be perfect and all I could wish him to be, and I thought of my own relation to him—how I would be a perfect mother to him, as Cousin Delia had been to Guy and Hugo, as she had been even to me; that too did not seem difficult or unlikely to me. I thought:

'I will never misunderstand him, nor be cross, nor wish him different from what he is.'

Other mothers made those mistakes, I knew, but I would not; and I thought of my son and worshipped him, shutting my eyes on the seat under the birch tree.

When Walter came home and I told him he kissed me and said he was glad, but he did not seem very much interested.

There had been some hitch at his College that afternoon. One of his lectures had been announced at the wrong time and he had not been there; he was thinking about that.

I minded his not caring more, but not badly.

I thought:

'He will care when it is there.'

And I was so happy myself, so full of happiness, that nothing else could matter very much.

Next day I went down into Oxford Street to shop, and I looked at the people in the bus, and thought:

'Which of these women have had children? How many of them have known this wonderful thing?'

Most of them probably had known it and yet they looked quite ordinary, quite dull and unexcited, and thinking of dull little things. I felt then that I could never be the same again, that I could not even look the same as I had a few months ago.

I thought:

'How could anything else count at all if one has a child?'

And I was afraid crossing the streets that I should be run over, afraid when I was in the bus that it would upset, because this wonder was too great and this happiness.

XXXVI

I used to make the coffee for breakfast myself; Walter liked it better when I made it and that pleased me, for I had never made coffee before and I felt proud now, that I should do it well. It had to stand for fifteen minutes after it was made, so I had to be downstairs earlier than Walter; that too was fun, I thought. It gave me a sense of competence to be down in the dining-room with the coffee all ready before he came.

Now, sometimes, I felt very ill in the mornings, and it was an effort to get up. Once when I got downstairs I turned faint and sick and had to sit down in the chair, and Mrs. Simms, the charwoman, came in and brought me a cup of tea. I can't remember why she came there so early, or why it was she who brought the tea, but it was.

'Poor dear,' she said. 'I know how you feels. Take a cup o' tea, mum, that'll do you good.'

I drank the tea and she talked to me and told me how many children she had had; eight, I think it was, and five of them dead and how ill she had been with every one of them; but Simms had been good to her, she said,—Simms was her husband, of course. He would bring her a cup of tea in the mornings before she got up. 'It's the putting your feet to the ground that does it. I know that,' she said.

And I thought:

'How funny it is that Mrs. Simms should know what I feel like, and Walter doesn't.'

And I thought:

'How funny it would be if Walter brought me up cups of tea.'

At home we had had tea in the mornings even when we felt quite well, and I had supposed that we would still here, but Maud had stopped that. She said it was an unnecessary expense.

'Especially,' she said, 'if it is China tea.'

I did not like Indian tea.

Mrs. Simms made the coffee that morning. It was not so good as when I made it; I noticed the difference, but Walter did not. I was sorry he did not; I wondered if he had only said he liked mine best, to please me, if he had really never noticed it different at all.

I felt very ill, those next months, and although I was so happy, I cried quite often at silly things. It was very odd to me to feel like this, for I had never been ill in my life except when I was seven and had measles. Ordinarily I felt so well and full of life. I did not expect to be tired at the end of the day; now I felt very tired, and as though the life had gone out of me.

Maud said:

'You must not let Helen become invalidish, Walter. She ought to realize that having a child is not an illness at all.'

Walter said:

'That depends, I suppose, on whether she feels ill.'

Maud said:

'Not in the least; that is merely subjective; a great many women give way in these things, especially women of Helen's type. It is most important that she should lead a normal and active life.'

Walter said:

'My dear Maud, you know nothing about it.'

I was not there, but he told me about it afterwards, and I loved him for being rude to Maud.

She seemed to come and visit us very often, but I suppose it was not very often really.

Mrs. Sebright came every Wednesday to dinner, and every Sunday we went to lunch with Grandmother in Campden Hill Square.

Hugo had gone abroad, he had gone as private secretary

or attaché on a Royal Commission in India, and would be away nearly a year. He had gone already before we came back to London, and I had not seen him since the wedding.

It surprised me rather to find how little I missed him; he seemed to belong to another life, a different kind of existence that was quite past now. That had been playing at life; I was living now. Yet sometimes I thought:

'I should like to tell Hugo about it. I should like to tell him how wonderful this is.'

He would understand, I was sure of that.

Guy came to dinner with us once or twice, but it was not a success. He and Walter did not get on at all, and somehow each showed his worst side to the other; I was sorry about it.

'We had better leave it alone for the present,' I thought, 'later on they will fit in better.'

The Addingtons came oftener to see us. George and Mollie could, I think, get on with anybody. Walter could not dislike them and they quite liked him. I was glad to see them always, but it was different even with them; they seemed much further off than they used to be, like pleasant strangers, outside one's life, instead of inside. I did not want to talk to Mollie intimately as we used to talk. 'She is not married,' I thought. 'She is not going to have a child. I cannot talk to her about the vital things'; and outside things seemed unimportant to me at this time.

Sophia Lane Watson came to lunch. She talked to Walter about Babylon, and he said she was 'an intelligent girl,' and liked her. I wondered how she knew about Babylon; she seemed to know a good deal, but one never did know with Sophia what she knew, and what she didn't; it was all in streaks.

I wondered if she missed Hugo, and why he had gone away. You could not tell anything from her; she looked just the same as always, white, and non-committal, and self-possessed; at least not exactly self-possessed; you could never be sure with Sophia whether she was hiding her feelings or just not there in her mind at all; sometimes it seemed like that, as though she was mentally and emotionally a long way off, and only her lips speaking to you.

I felt her more interesting now. I did not feel hostile to

her, as I had when Hugo was there. I did not think now, somehow, that he would marry her.

Her play was finished now. It was going to be acted. The Drama Society were going to do it. She did not seem excited about it at all. She did not want to talk about it.

I thought:

'I must see more of Sophia.'

I felt sorry for her somehow, and attracted by her as I had been at school, but I did not see much of her. She came once more to lunch, and I went to tea with her, and then I think she went away for a time; I can't remember quite, and after that it was the War.

XXXVII

Walter had very few friends. There were elderly ladies, friends of his mother's who called on us, and two cousins who lived at Southsea, and sometimes came up for the day.

I did not care for the Southsea cousins; they were effusive and rather stupid, and seemed somehow to be pretending, always, to be different from what they were.

Some of the old ladies were rather nice; there was a Miss Mix, who had blue Persian cats. She gave us a kitten. She was very small, much smaller than Mrs. Sebright, and more lively. She had a sense of fun, and seemed to find her life rather funny, though she lived all alone with her cats in a flat near Earl's Court, and was very poor.

Then there was Mrs. Allsopp, big and fat, and more earnest. She worked for the same church as Mrs. Sebright, and she had a girls' club connected with the church. She tried to 'interest' me in the girls' club and was 'very disappointed' that I would not come and help with it.

And there were two Miss Fergusons who wrote books on Italy and talked about Art, but foolishly, I thought, as if they did not really know what it meant at all.

Miss Mix was much the nicest.

Then there were Walter's colleagues at the University.

Several of them lived at Hampstead, and their wives came to call on me. They were quite kind and quite friendly, but dull, I thought. They talked about University affairs which I did not know about; not like Maud, but more as dutiful wives, who were bound to be interested in examinations and students because their husbands were.

They asked me how I saw my husband's pupils, and I said I did not see them.

Walter had never suggested my seeing his pupils. He did not care about them very much I think; he cared far more for the stuff he taught than the people he taught it to; but they said I ought to see them.

Sunday lunch was best, they said, or Sunday tea in the Oxford fashion. I did not even know that it was the Oxford fashion, but I invited some of the students to lunch and tea on Saturday; I rather liked them. They were shy and awkward, not like the young men at Oxford that I had met. I thought they were more interesting than the Oxford young men, but one did not get much further with them, and Walter did not seem very anxious to go on. He saw quite enough of them through the week, he said.

He had two friends at Oxford, 'dons' at Oxford, who came sometimes to see us. They had been at our wedding.

They counted as Walter's friends, those two, and Mr. Furze, but they were much more remote sort of friends than mine had been. When they met they talked about their work and nothing else; it seemed to me that they had nothing else to talk about, but perhaps that was not true.

Mr. Furze was different. Freddy Furze he was, but Walter never called him Freddy. He was more like my own people, at least more nearly like; I felt too that he liked me, and that we could have talked and got to know each other quite well if we had had the chance; but the chance did not quite come, for he lived at Cardiff, and only came to stay with us twice, for about a week.

He had been engaged to a girl who was drowned, Walter told me; Walter had not known the girl, but she was odd and unsatisfactory, he believed, 'not Furze's sort, I should think,' he said; and I had an idea, I don't know why, that, perhaps, I reminded him of her. Maud would certainly have called me 'odd and unsatisfactory.' And he was so kind to me; I wondered how she had been drowned, and all about her, but

I could not ask him, and Walter did not know.

I thought we would see more of him; I hoped so; but that first year went past so quickly, and then the War came, and it was too late.

XXXVIII

Walter put away his iron-rimmed spectacles. I had made him promise he would, before we were married. He had rimless pince-nez now, which I liked much better. He had promised me also that he would learn to dance. He had never learned; he had never wanted to learn, he said, but now he did want to, to dance with me. Now for a time I could not dance, and he said he would wait to learn. When the baby was born, he would learn. Then we would both dance.

'You know,' he said, 'I shall be a duffer at it; perhaps you will not like to dance with me.'

And I kissed him, and said I would.

I would rather dance with him, I said, than with Hugo; that was what he wanted me to say, I knew, and I believed it when I said it.

In the meantime he tried to teach me Greek. I told him how Hugo had begun once, but we had not got on very far. He said he could teach me better than Hugo.

'Then we could read things together,' he said, 'and you could help me a great deal too, if you would. You could look up things for me in the Museum. You might even learn Syriac, you know; that would be a great help.'

I thought I should like to help him in his work. I tried very hard to learn Greek, but the lessons were more difficult than they had been with Hugo, and Walter got annoyed if I made mistakes. I was afraid of annoying him, and that made me afraid of the lessons.

'Shall we try the Syriac first?' I suggested one day, but Walter would not.

'Greek first,' he said, 'was essential'; and so we went on.

In the evenings he took me sometimes to lectures. He belonged to several Archæological Societies who gave lantern lectures in the evening. Walter considered the theatre a luxury. That seemed odd to me at first, but I did not mind, for I was happy, and I wanted to please Walter; I wanted to fit in with his way of life and to leave my own behind me; but one cannot do that, ever, quite successfully, I believe.

XXXIX

Hugo came back from India in June.

He came to see me one morning, soon after he got back.

I was upstairs, tidying a cupboard. I had an overall on, and was dusty. When Louise came to tell me that he was there, I was surprised, for I did not know he had come home. I wondered if I was pleased to see him or not; I did not know; I went downstairs to the dining-room. The drawing-room was being turned out, and we could not go in there.

We sat down on each side of the dining-room table. There were wild roses, in a glass vase on the table, and the water in the vase was cloudy. I had meant to change the water that morning, and had forgotten. I hoped Hugo would not notice the water; I thought he would. I wished we had not to be in the dining-room where the sideboard was, that Hugo did not like. I did not know what to say to Hugo; he seemed so far away; so long ago.

Hugo said:

'I came back on Tuesday.'

I said:

'Oh, I did not know you were back.'

I said:

'Was it interesting in India?'

Hugo said:

'Yes, it was very interesting. The colours are wonderful there. You can't imagine what the colours are like.'

I said:

'Like Holman Hunt, are they?'

He said:

'Almost; the purples, not the green, so much.'

I said:

'That must be jolly.'

Hugo said:

'Yes.'

Then he said:

'It is funny to visit you like this, married.'

I laughed. I kept laughing a little, foolishly, I felt.

I said:

'I was married before you went away.'

He said:

'Yes, but hardly; now you are quite used to it, I suppose?'

I said:

'Yes.'

He wanted to know if I was happy. I knew he wanted to, and I wanted to tell him that I was, but we seemed too awkward, somehow, to talk in that way, seriously; it was as though we were afraid. He only laughed a little, and said:

'And how do you like it?'

And I said:

'Very much, thank you.'

And then we both laughed.

I wanted to tell him about my baby; that I was going to have one very soon now, though I suppose he knew; but I could not speak about that either. It was odd, and painful, the way we could not talk.

I thought:

'It is because we have not met for so long, and so much has happened in between, at least to me.'

I thought:

'It will be different when we get used to each other again. We will soon.'

I said:

'Walter is out. He will be awfully sorry to miss you.'

'Yes. Oh—I am awfully sorry to miss him. I am going down to Yearsly to-morrow. I suppose you and Walter couldn't come for the week-end? It would be nice if you could.'

And I said:

'It would be awfully nice, but I am afraid we can't. Walter's mother is coming to supper, and besides he has some work to do in the morning.'

I said it quickly. We could have put off Mrs. Sebright, I knew that really, but I did not want to go, and Walter would not want to go either. We had been twice for week-ends to Yearsly; it did not do, somehow, with Walter. He did not fit in, though Cousin Delia was the same as she had always been.

I think Hugo knew too, for he only said:

'I was afraid you would not be able to. Well, we will meet again soon. I shall be back in a week or so.'

He stood up to go, and we shook hands.

'It is nice to see you again,' he said.

And I said:

'It was nice of you to come.'

The dining-room was downstairs in the basement. We went up to the front door.

He went down the front steps and the garden path and out of the gate. He turned at the gate and waved his hat, and I waved my hand to him in turn.

Then I went in and shut the door.

XL

Eleanor was born on the 30th of June.

I could see the poplar tree in the garden through the window. The leaves of the poplar fluttered and shimmered, and I watched them from my bed. There have always been trees in my life, always, somehow, at times that were important to me.

And I thought:

'Other people have been through this before, thousands and millions of people, always, from the beginning of the world. If they could bear it, I can. Cousin Delia,' I thought, 'and Grandmother and Mrs. Simms and the women in the bus.'

And later I thought:

'I can never have any more children! I can never face this again.'

And then they told me it was a girl; and I could not believe it; it seemed such waste; I had wanted a son so much; I had been so sure it was a son; and now it seemed that he had not been real at all; I could not bear it, and I cried.

When I saw her, I did not mind so much, she was just a

baby, and I loved babies.

Walter did not mind the baby being a girl. He wanted it to be called Eleanor after his mother. He was worried and irritable at this time; he did not like the monthly nurse, nor the household being upset. The meals were not punctual, he said, specially breakfast, and if breakfast was late, it upset his morning's work.

He was busy with his book just then; he had made, he thought, a new discovery about his script and that made him irritable.

'I don't know what I shall do if that baby cries in the morning,' he said; 'it will drive me frantic.'

She had cried in the garden in her pram; she was only a week old.

I asked the nurse to put the pram round the other side of the house. She had put it there, she said, so as not to disturb me.

Walter kept coming to me about things that went wrong.

The laundry had torn his shirt, and he could not find his sleeve-links; it was odd how he seemed to depend on me, as though he were a child almost; I had hardly realized how much before, and I was glad in a way.

'It shows I am some use to him,' I thought, 'in spite of the pheasant and the accounts'; and yet sometimes I was sad about it too.

Mrs. Simms had said to me once:

'My Simms was a standby to me; you never would believe what a standby 'e was.'

And I wished sometimes that Walter were like Simms.

XLI

People came to see me and Eleanor.

Mrs. Sebright came nearly every day; and Miss Mix and Mrs. Allsopp, and of course Maud. Grandmother came too, and Cousin Delia. I was glad to see them, especially Cousin Delia. I had not seen her for such a long time.

'Dear,' she said. 'How happy you are! Is the world perfect now?'

And I said:

'Very nearly perfect, Cousin Delia.'

Cousin Delia was lovely with a baby, so quiet and so sure.

I said:

'Will it seem quite ordinary to me soon, Cousin Delia?'

And she said:

'I don't know; to me it never has; to me when Guy and Hugo are there, it is still almost like this. It has never got "ordinary" at all.'

I said:

'Were you very glad they were sons?'

And she said:

'Yes; I was glad. I wanted a daughter too, but you were like having a daughter.'

I said:

'Cousin Delia, I do so wish I had been really your daughter.'

She looked out of the window.

'I used to think it was better as it was,' she said, 'but after all it did not make any difference, did it, in the end?'

I said:

'It did make a difference, I think.'

She said:

'Yes; but not in the way I meant. I used to think that you and Hugo would be married one day. It is foolish to make plans.'

I said:

'I don't think you made plans in a way that mattered. I don't think you ever made a mistake.'

She looked round at me, surprised. I was surprised at myself. I had never tried to tell Cousin Delia how I felt about her, and now, suddenly, I wished I could; and I went on:

'I think you are the most perfect person in the world.'

She said:

'Dear Heart, thank you: I wish it were true'; and she kissed me.

Then she talked about Yearsly, and Cousin John, and the garden.

Cousin Delia brought roses with her, and all the room

was sweet when she had gone. I wished she could have stayed longer. I wished she would come again. I wished I could go back with her to Yearsly. I felt like a child left alone at school.

PART THREE

'For there is hope of a tree, if it be cut down,
That it will flourish again. . .
But man dieth and wasteth away; yea, man
Giveth up the ghost, and where is he?'

—*Job* xiv. 7

I

ON the date that the Archduke was assassinated, we were dining at Campden Hill Square. Guy and Hugo were there, and George and Mollie, and Ralph Freeman, who was back from Vienna now, in the Foreign Office again.

It was a party like old times, and I liked it. I was so happy to be about again and to have my baby; for Eleanor was incredibly precious to me at that time.

I was glad to see them all again, and I felt somehow that I had come back to life; that I wanted to do so much that I had not been able to do during the last months.

There was a new pleasure in moving, and in eating, and in being alive.

'They will all be there,' I said to Walter, as we were getting ready to go. 'We have not been all together like that since we were married, for Hugo went away so soon.'

Walter smiled, but I knew he was not pleased. He was tying his black tie, and he always tied his ties badly. He disliked dressing for dinner, and never did so, if he could avoid it.

'You must like them,' I said. 'Please try to like them. You see I do so much.'

And he looked suddenly sorry, and stopped pulling at his

tie.

'Yes, you do. I know that, and I ought not to mind,' he said, 'but I can't help it. They make me feel a fool, those friends of yours, and I am *not* a fool, and I am always afraid that you will think of me as they do, when they are there. I suppose I am jealous of them.'

And he gave a laugh.

I said:

'You need not be; it is different, and I want them to like you too; they will, if you are nicer to them.'

He said:

'You are mine now, not theirs. I need not be afraid of them now.'

I laughed, but I said:

'You old goose, you will be late, if you don't get dressed; Grandmother does not like people to be late.'

And I tied his tie for him; I nearly always did in the end.

II

George and Hugo were in the drawing-room with Grandmother when we arrived. They were talking about Dostoievski. Grandmother did not like the Russian novelists.

'My dear, a lunatic asylum,' she said once. 'It may be very true to life, of a sort, as you say, but I do not enjoy the society of lunatics.'

Hugo was saying:

'We are all like that really, Aunt Gerry, only we don't realize it, incredibly weak, and uncertain, and yet sometimes a bit heroic, only we don't like to think we are like that, so we don't think it.'

'I certainly do not think it, Hugo. I hope that you are not like that, and I know that I am not.'

She laughed, and turning to us, held out her hands.

'Here she is!' she said, as though they had been speaking about me. I realized that evening how much she cared for me, and felt grateful to her. I bent down and kissed her, and shook hands with George and Hugo. I did not feel shy of Hugo now; it seemed, here in this room, just as it used to be.

George gave me his chair, and we all sat down.

'How is my great-granddaughter?' asked Grandmother, and I said she was very well.

George said:

'I can't imagine you with a daughter.'

Then Guy and Mollie came in together. They looked happy, and I thought:

'They will be married soon,' and I was glad.

Mollie said:

'We have run all the way from Notting Hill Gate, we thought we should be late.'

Guy said:

'Ralph is later. A diplomat should know better.'

'Does Ralph count as a diplomat now?' asked Mollie.

Guy said:

'Yes, of the fifteenth class, I believe.'

And every one laughed, for it was a joke against Ralph Freeman that he was very punctilious.

Then he came in.

He apologized to Grandmother. He said he had been kept at the Office; there was anxiety over the murder of Franz Ferdinand.

'Franz Ferdinand,' repeated Hugo, 'who on earth is he?'

'The Austrian Archduke. Francis Joseph's heir, you know. Haven't you seen the paper?'

Guy said:

'I saw something about it. Herzegovina, wasn't it?'

'Yes, and Austria is sure to suspect Serbian influence.'

George said:

'Trouble in the Balkans. Do you remember Old Moore's prediction?'

Mollie said:

'That was last year.'

George said:

'Every year.'

Grandmother said:

'I read about it this morning. The young man and his wife were both shot in their carriage—a very horrid affair.'

Ralph said:

'My chief takes an exceedingly grave view of the

situation.'

The dinner was ready and we went into the dining-room. When we had all sat down, Ralph began again.

'You see,' he said to Grandmother, 'the tension between Vienna and Belgrade has been growing more acute every year. It was amazing to hear the Austrians talk, when I was out there. They would believe anything of the Serbs.'

'No doubt the crime was political,' Grandmother observed. 'It is something to be truly thankful for that we have outgrown political crimes in this country; they are always futile.'

'This may be worse than futile,' said Ralph. He was looking serious and excited, and we felt amused; Ralph was always proud of his inside information.

'Well, yes, worse than futile for the dozen poor devils who are put to death because of it,' said George. 'They have not got the man who threw the bomb, I see. There will have to be a demonstration.'

'They are saying at the Office that it may mean War.'

'War? between Austria—Hungary and Serbia?'

'That would be short and decisive. I should think.'

Guy wrinkled his forehead.

'You forget Serbia's relation to Russia,' Ralph put in; 'we might very easily have war between Russia and Austria over this.'

Mollie said:

'It all seems very remote.'

Grandmother said:

'In Eastern Europe they are always fighting. I remember so many wars—Russo-Turkish, Bulgaro-Turkish, Russo-Japanese, Græco-Turkish and the Balkan Wars. One cannot feel as distressed, as no doubt one ought. If the Russians are all like Hugo's friends they should not prove very formidable to Austrian troops. I used to know a good many Austrian officers—very charming people.'

We all had an impulse to rag Ralph Freeman. He took himself and his news so seriously, it made us want to take it lightly.

Hugo said:

'Russian Ballet versus Hungarian Band. Much more

"life force" in the Ballet.'

'It is all very well to joke,' protested Ralph, 'but this may be the beginning of a European War.'

'How often have we heard that, Ralph?' asked Guy. 'Everything may be the beginning of a European War—Dogger Bank, Agadir, Morocco—but fortunately, it does not begin.'

'Sophia belongs to a society which shows European War to be impossible,' said Mollie. 'Economically impossible, in a modern world like ours, because of international trade, credit, and so on, and international banking. I went to some of the meetings with her once.'

'I wish it were impossible,' said Ralph portentously, and we all felt sure that he was very glad it was not impossible.

'Russia and France,' said George abruptly, 'Austria and Germany—My God!' Then he laughed. 'It is fantastic,' he said. 'Why, *we* have an entente with France and Russia!'

'Exactly,' said Ralph.

I said:

'You are talking like the Navy League, George.'

'I know,' said George. 'I suddenly thought, Supposing the damned fools were right.'

Walter said:

'It is quite inconceivable, I think, that Great Britain should be involved in a European War.'

He spoke with a note of exasperation in his voice, as though every one were being silly. I thought they could not all be silly, for they were saying different things.

'It is inconceivable we could keep out,' said Guy, 'if France and Germany were at War.'

'Come, come,' said Grandmother, 'don't try to make my flesh creep, young people. I think we can trust the Austrians to settle up their own affair; it was all in their own country after all.'

She turned to Walter, who was on her other side, and asked him how his book was getting on; and after that we talked about plays, the Vedrenne Barker Season at the Savoy and Rheinhardt's production of Œdipus. I had seen none of them, nor Walter of course, for we seldom went to plays, but all the others had, and I liked to hear about them.

After dinner we had coffee in the drawing-room; then Grandmother went to her memoirs, in her sitting-room upstairs, and we played Demon Pounce with two card tables joined together and five packs of cards. We called it Prawn Eye, and we often used to play it.

Guy generally won, and sometimes George; Hugo and Walter were the worst. Hugo laughed and looked across at Walter.

'You and I are competing for the Donkey prize,' he said.

Walter tried to laugh too, but he looked worried; I could see that he thought it a silly game, and that spoilt the fun for me.

I had to go home early to feed Eleanor. The others stayed on to play longer. I ran upstairs to Grandmother to say 'good night.' She was sitting by the fire, for she always had a fire in her room, with her book on her knee and her spectacles on the table by her side. She was not reading, and she looked very tired. I realized, with a sudden shock, that she was old.

She started when I came in, and then smiled.

'I have come to say "good night," Grandmother,' I said.

She put both her hands on my shoulders, as I stooped down.

She said:

'Dear child, bless you. I am happy about you.'

I said:

'I am happy too, Grandmother.'

I waited; I wanted to say more, but I did not know what to say. I felt then that she was old, and perhaps lonely. It had not occurred to me before that my marriage had left her all alone. I wondered what it would be like to be old.

I thought:

'We shall all be old some day, Guy and Hugo, and George, and Mollie and Walter, and I; how strange that is; quite certainly some day we shall be old.'

But it was not real to me even then.

'Can I do anything for you, Grandmother?' I asked. 'Can I get you another book?'

'No, dear, no; I shall go to bed soon. Are the other young people still there?'

I said, yes, they were going on with their game.

'Say "good night" to them for me,' she said; 'they need not come up'; and she kissed me 'Good night.'

I went downstairs slowly.

Walter was waiting in the hall.

There was a taxi at the door to take us home; Grandmother had arranged that. She would pay for it, she had said.

I ran back to the drawing-room to say 'Good-bye.'

Hugo came with me into the hall, and George came out on to the steps.

'When shall we meet again?' he said. 'Are you going away soon?'

I said:

'Next week we are going, up to the Wall again. We shall be back in September.'

George said:

'Good-bye, then, till September.'

He was smiling his wide, delightful smile.

I said:

'What a nice evening it has been.'

George said:

'Yes. Hasn't it been jolly?'

Yet something in his face made me wonder.

I thought:

'Is George not happy? Can something be worrying George?'

I never saw him again.

III

Walter was annoyed about the taxi; he felt it a waste of money, when we might have gone in the tube, and he did not like Grandmother to pay it, for he liked to pay everything himself. I knew very well by now when Walter was annoyed; I could tell by the way he sat, by the way he fidgeted with his hands, even when he said nothing at all.

He said nothing this time, and I said nothing. I felt very tired now, and then, I was frightened. It was as though I had been asleep, and dreaming, and contented, and now suddenly

I had woken up; as though everything had become intense, and alive, and somehow emotional. I felt as though tremendous things were happening, all round us, everywhere; as though we were a tiny island in a great space.

I put out my hand and touched Walter's arm; it was dark in the taxi and I could hardly see him.

'Walter,' I said, 'do you feel as if something dreadful were going to happen?'

He turned sharply.

'No,' he said. 'What do you mean? What should happen?'

I said:

'Oh, I don't know exactly; I suppose it is silly; I feel as though this couldn't last, as though something were going to break.'

'It is that silly talk about a war that has upset you,' he said. 'People ought not to talk like that.'

I said:

'No; I wasn't thinking about a war; I had forgotten that; but I feel afraid of something, I don't know what. I believe George felt it too.'

He said:

'Nonsense, you are tired, that is all; it is awfully tiring going out in the evening; I am tired too.'

He put his arm round me and drew me close to him. I wanted to feel near to him, but I did not; I felt a long way off.

Two days later, we went up to Northumberland, to the farm-house on the Roman Wall, where we had stayed before.

We had a great deal of luggage, a cot and a pram, and a baby's bath. I felt very proud of travelling with those things, but Walter did not like it.

'It is awful,' he said, 'this family luggage. I suppose it will be like this now—for years!'

I minded that. It seemed to me sometimes that he resented Eleanor, that he would almost rather she were not there; I had hoped he would be pleased with her, as I was.

At the farm it was better; Walter liked being there; he went for long walks again, as we had done on our honeymoon. I could not go with him now, when he went a very long way, but I was happy at home with my baby.

IV

It seems like a dream now, that beginning of war; like something remembered very long ago, much longer ago than it really is. I cannot even remember, at what moment we realized, Walter and I, that war was coming, a war that would involve our country, I mean; that it would involve us personally, as individuals, we did not realize at that time at all; that came much later, gradually and painfully, step by step.

We were, of course, far away in the physical sense; six miles away from the nearest village of any size, with a post only three times a week. We saw nobody who understood what was happening better than ourselves, and we read the newspaper when it came so little. Walter had always an aversion for newspapers, I never quite knew why, and I was so absorbed in Eleanor, and the new life with her, that the outer world seemed to have slipped right away, when we got into the train at Euston.

The stages in these weeks that one now knows were turning points in the catastrophe escaped us then with a completeness that seems amazing.

The Austrian Ultimatum to Serbia, when it came, meant nothing at all. I remember Walter reading it aloud at breakfast, in the farm parlour; even now the smell of hot coffee and bacon brings that morning back to me, which is odd, considering how little we realized its importance.

The paper had come the evening before, but we had not opened it. Walter liked a paper at breakfast, not at other times. He opened it and read it carelessly, not caring much what he found there. He said:

'There seems to be a dustup in the Balkans after all, over that man being killed. Here is an Austrian Ultimatum to Serbia,' and he read a few lines of it aloud.

'Extraordinary,' he said, 'isn't it? going on like that at this time of day. It seems to belong to the eighteenth century or perhaps the seventeenth.'

And I said:

'I suppose they are a century or two behind us over there.'

And we did not bother about it any more. We went a long walk that day and came back rather tired, and hungry; and in the afternoon it rained, and we could not read our Gibbon out of doors, as we had meant to. I remember that we followed what happened in the newspaper with a certain interest; it gave one something to look for among the rather dull collection of Parliamentary Debates and Home affairs, but it was an impersonal interest.

I remember one day thinking about it, and being shocked with myself for minding it so little. That must have been some days later, when Russia and Germany seemed to be coming in. I went up on the hill behind the house, by myself, and sat down on the grass, and tried to realize what was happening. I remember trying to picture the Russian soldiers, and the Austrian soldiers, and to think what it meant; those hundreds and thousands of people leaving their homes, and going to fight.

'Hundreds of them will be killed,' I thought, 'perhaps thousands, and yet I don't really mind; it doesn't really affect me, just because I don't know them, and they live in countries that I don't know'; and it seemed to me dreadful that one's sympathy should be so limited.

And then another time, I did realize it for a bit; that was after the German mobilization, when the French reservists were called up; we had read the paper when it came that day, in the evening after dinner, and somehow by that time, it had begun to seem terrible; we had begun, I think, though very dimly, to feel the trouble closing in all round.

We lay a long time awake that night, Walter and I, not speaking to each other. The night was hot and oppressive, the darkness seemed to press upon us like a weight.

I thought of the French and German homes where people were lying in bed, awake too, and thinking about the next day, when the men must go out to the army; and it became suddenly real to me; perhaps because I had been in France and Germany, and knew some French and German people, and understood that they were just people like us.

And that made the others seem more real too, and I felt

the immensity of what was happening; I realized, dimly, the masses of people in Austria and in Russia too.

And then a sense of unreality came over me. I felt myself a long way off, looking on, as though I were disembodied; I seemed to hear a great throbbing, very far away, a strange pulsating sound, as though it were the heart of all the world; I suppose it was really my own heart. I thought of birds in a storm, of clouds gathering, of the lines in 'In Memoriam' about the rooks, of the Dynasts and the Pities and Powers; and an acute, quite impersonal sense of loss and desolation came over me.

Walter said suddenly:

'This may be the end of Europe, of European civilization.'

I said:

'I was thinking about the people saying Good-bye; sleeping together like us, only for the last time, people just like us, and I thought, "Supposing it was you and me?"'

Walter said:

'I know.'.

He held me tight, and I pressed close up to him. The beating of his heart throbbed through me again, like the pulse of the world. And all I had, seemed dearer than ever before, as I realized that it could be lost.

I said:

'Oh, Walter, do they love as we do? Do you think, many of them do?'

And he answered very softly:

'Yes. Hundreds of thousands of them do.'

V

The next morning Walter walked over to Alston for more news. He brought back more papers, but nothing definite besides. The people in the town were talking about war, he said, telegrams were put up outside the Town Hall. Two days later he went over to Alston again. The exact moments at which it became credible, probable, inevitable, that England would fight too, I cannot remember at all.

The postman, who brought the post on Monday, stopped me at the gate with news of the Advance into Belgium.

'Two million Germans on the march,' he said. He smiled a twisted sort of smile, and added, 'And I'm in the front line.'

It took me several moments to realize that he meant that he was a reservist.

I never saw him again.

When the British Declaration of War came, it made hardly a sensation. We had known it must come for so many hours, and hours during these days were like months.

VI

We went back to London at the end of August. We had talked of going for over a week before, but there seemed to be no trains. The reservists were called up everywhere; the shepherd from the farm was called up, and the cowman. They were in what was called 'The Wagon Reserve.'

Walter said at first that we must go back to London at once, then that we had no right to crowd up trains, when all space was needed for troops.

In London, the excitement of war was everywhere; marching men, army wagons, lorries, bugle calls, persistent, repeated, practised over and over again. There was an open space not far from our house; it had been a playing field for a school, and recruits were drilling there all the day long; sharp loud sounds of the sergeants' orders, more bugle calls, marching men, and more marching men; the pathetic sentimental marching songs, the dark blue uniforms and convict-like caps of Kitchener's Army; everything passed through the untraceable stages from strangeness to familiarity, and the war news mingled in a confused, disjointed way with the daily sights and sounds.

The Belgian resistance; Liège; the fall of Liège; the first accounts of German atrocities; the occupation of Brussels; the burning of Louvain; fighting in the streets of Charleroi, where the dead bodies pressed each other too closely to fall down, and the ranks of the dead stood upright; that in particular brought the horror of it home to me, I know.

Stories of crucifixion, of bayoneted women, of children with their hands cut off; and the first inrush of Belgian refugees. How the days passed, merged into one another, obliterated one another, I do not know; the incredible changed somehow imperceptibly into the accepted, the taken for granted, state of existence. I was caught for a time by the general excitement, and so was Walter. He bought war maps and pinned them to the doors, marking the progress of the armies each morning and evening with little coloured flags on pins.

Mr. Harland, a colleague of Walter's who lived in Hampstead too, used to come in and talk to Walter. He kept a chart with coloured maps as well.

Then came dismay at the retreat from Mons; suddenly one day as he was tracing out the line of 'position in the rear,' Walter stood still, and they stared at each other.

'By Jove!' said Mr. Harland.

And Walter said, 'Good Lord!'

'Will they get to Paris?'

'Will they break through?'

I sat and watched them, and the new consternation was as unreal to me as the War itself had been at first.

Life went on for me, in a way, unbroken by the catastrophic events all round. My own life seemed to reassert itself from the general earthquake; my baby was as adorable, as absorbing as ever, and I enjoyed being back in my own home.

I remembered the South African War; it had been very sad, very terrible; my uncle Everard had been killed in it, he had been a soldier, but it was always remote; I could not believe Walter and Mr. Harland when they talked of an invasion of England, bombardment by air, cutting off of the food supplies.

I wondered often during those first weeks what Guy and Hugo were thinking of it all. They were at Yearsly, I believed, and George and Mollie; they had been going down there too. Ralph had been right, after all, that evening at Grandmother's, and we had all laughed at him. It seemed odd already, that we had not understood what that Archduke's murder would bring.

Guy had paid some attention, and George; George most, I thought. I wondered very much what George would be thinking now.

My grandmother had been at Bath; she had gone to see a cousin who lived at Bath. She did not come back till late in September. I went to see her then and she told me that Guy and Hugo had volunteered.

VII

I was bewildered at first; I could not understand at all. I had seen the posters calling for recruits; I had seen the recruits drilling; but that too had seemed in its way remote; it had not occurred to me somehow that people of my own might go. I remember being glad, in the first days of all, that I had no one in the army. It had once been thought of for Guy, and I thought, 'what a good thing Guy is not a soldier'; and then I felt ashamed at my own selfishness, for other people were soldiers, who mattered really as much.

And now I thought, it seems dreadful to say it, but I thought,

'How silly of Guy and Hugo!'

And I thought:

'That is just the side of them that Walter doesn't like—fantastic—out of touch with reality.'

And I thought:

'It is play acting, a little bit, and I always denied they did that. It would be much better if Hugo got a sensible job at last, and if Guy stuck to his law; he was getting on very well.'

I was not anxious about them. I did not believe they would ever be sent out to fight. They were only in training now; they were in camp somewhere, Grandmother had said, Hugo in Essex, and Guy on Salisbury plain. I knew it took months to train soldiers, and they were officers; that took several years; the War would be over before they were ready to go out; that made it so silly. But I was disturbed and unhappy all the same.

When I got home I told Walter. I expected him to say too that it was foolish but he didn't.

He was sitting at his writing-table in the study. He gave a sort of groan and buried his face in his hands.

'We shall all have to go before it is done,' he said, and then abruptly:

'I don't suppose I shall finish my book now—that is all wasted.'

My heart seemed to stand still. I felt as though I was in a nightmare suddenly trying to wake up; or as though I had woken up, very early, in the dark, and thought of death; a helpless desperate feeling, as though the earth were slipping away, as though one were going to fall into infinite space . . . and then I recovered; normality came back, and I was sure that Walter too was hysterical and unhinged.

I tried to laugh.

'You are an old goose, Walter,' I said, and I put my arm round him and kissed the top of his head.

He did not look up. He was looking straight in front of him.

He said:

'I was thinking before you came in of the Germans who will be killed; of the German scholars. They are doing work which no one else has ever done. If German scholarship is stamped out, scholarship throughout Europe will die. My work is useless, if the Germans are killed.'

I said:

'But the Germans are conscripts——'

It answered my own thought, not his, and I knew that, as soon as I had said it.

'We may all be conscripts too, before we are done,' he answered. 'It will not matter much by then.'

I asked:

'Do you think Guy and Hugo were quite right to go?'

And he nodded.

The next day I heard from Mollie that George had got a Commission in the Lancashire Fusiliers, and about a week later Freddy Furze joined a Welsh Regiment.

VIII

I wrote to Cousin Delia, and to Hugo, and to Guy. I meant to write to George too, but there was an interruption, I forget now what it was, and I put it off, and put it off again, and did not write at all in the end.

Cousin Delia answered me first.

'Yes, they are both gone,' she said, 'they had to go; there was, of course, no choice. Guy will find something he has wanted, I believe. I am more afraid for Hugo,' and then she gave me their addresses (though I had got them already from Grandmother) and said she would like to see me soon; nothing about the War, or what she felt about it all; that was like Cousin Delia too.

'We have offered the house as a hospital, if they want it,' she said. 'I don't know if they will . . .'

Guy's letter, too, was like himself.

'Dear Helen,' he wrote,—

'Many thanks for yours. Yes, here we are really in for it at last, or so it seems. I am having no end of a time at present. My men are simply topping; makes one proud of one's country, and all that sort of thing, to see what its "men in the street" are like. Funny too, to be doing the thing in earnest now, after playing at it so often. We ought to get out fairly soon, as our battalion was nominally on a war footing before, but you never know. The beastly show may be over before we actually get there; I should be sorry to miss it all now I've got so far.'

'Poor old Hugo doesn't seem to be enjoying himself much, but I shouldn't be surprised if he got out before us all the same. The best chance is to be drafted out into the regular battalions, I believe. You know George is down at Aldershot. I haven't heard from him since he got there . . .'

Hugo did not write for ten days; then it was a long letter.

'Dear Helen,—

'I was glad to get your letter. I have wondered how the War took you. I am glad that you have stayed sane, and that you prefer your baby to the world. That is as it ought to be after all.

'We have most of us lost our heads, and what will come of it all I don't know. I feel a fraud drilling my wretched platoon, inspecting their kit, seeing if they have tooth-brushes, that they have polished their buttons, and mine too. I wonder what it is all for, what it will all lead to. We say "for King and Country"; we tell the poor beggars that, and they are as keen as mustard, most of them, like children playing at a game; only it is more than that, for they feel elated somehow, and raised out of themselves, at least some of them do—I did at first too, thought about being killed, and felt heroic. I don't now; danger seems very remote and discomfort very present, and I can't believe we shall ever get beyond this.

'It is muddy here; all mud and flat dull fields, and when it rains, as it did last week, the wet comes through the roof, and we are uncomfortable and cross. It is an odd life. I don't know what to talk about; the Colonel is a regular, and so is one Lieutenant; all the other officers are either recruits like me or Territorial Reserve. They seem keen about everything, and the battalion in particular, and they are most of them pleasant fellows enough, but they make one feel a fool, and I don't like the way they talk; their values are so odd.

'Guy is enjoying himself on Salisbury Plain. I haven't heard from George lately.'

I could picture Hugo better after reading it. He was still alone, detached, half way between my attitude and Guy's. I felt sorry for him in his wet tent, inspecting tooth-brushes.

IX

Mrs. Sebright knitted a great deal. She belonged to a 'Work Centre'; ladies who met together three afternoons a week, and made shirts and bandages and socks.

She was patriotic, and talked about 'our brave boys,' and said that the British Army had never been beaten, and that the British Navy was something that the world had never seen before. She said, and seemed to believe, that English people were quite different from the people of other nations; much braver, and more high minded, less likely to do anything wrong or make mistakes.

I was puzzled by this attitude at first. I thought she was trying to encourage herself by saying these things; but I found she really did think they were true, and soon I got quite accustomed to hear them said by other people, all round, every day. I thought that there were good and bad people in our Army, and in other Armies; brave soldiers and cowardly ones; I did not find it a help to me at all to say more than that.

'If we were all good, and the Germans all bad, the War would matter less,' I said, one day, but Mrs. Sebright thought it unpatriotic to say anything like that.

'When our own boys are fighting in the trenches,' she said. 'You surprise me, Helen.'

Maud was much worse. She was not content with praising our own Army and Navy, she kept on abusing the others. She came to stay with us in the Christmas holidays, and told a great many stories of German atrocities. In every case she would begin:

'I know for a fact,' or, 'I have it on excellent authority'; but when I asked her how she knew, or on whose authority, she would get angry and did not explain.

She would say that the Germans must be taught a lesson. . . .

No civilized nation had ever behaved as they did . . . They were 'unique in history.'

'This policy of frightfulness is unparalleled,' she said, 'absolutely unparalleled. They have forfeited their right to existence as an independent nation.'

She had dismissed the German teacher in her school, and two little German girls were excluded also. 'Feeling runs too high,' she said. 'I could not, in the circumstances, countenance their remaining. I hope that German will be a dead language before long.'

X

Autumn passed into winter. The fall of Antwerp; escape

of the *Goeben* and *Breslau*; Declaration of War with Turkey; the bombardment of Scarborough and West Hartlepool these were landmarks in the sea of events.

People had begun to accept the War as a natural state, to cease expecting a sudden dramatic finish.

Mollie finished her three months' training, and was drafted to a War Hospital in Wales. She came to see me before she went. She was serious and intent.

'I wish I could do more,' she said. 'I hate to be safe, when the others are in danger, don't you feel that, Helen? I do hope they will send me to the front.'

I said:

'You are doing much more than I am. You are in it, not outside, like me.'

Mollie said:

'Yes. I am sorry for you, Helen. It must be terrible for you to be outside, and not able to help. Of course you can't,' she added quickly, 'your work is just as important really, more perhaps,' and she smiled her delightful smile that was like George's.

'I feel,' she went on earnestly, 'that I can never do enough, if I worked myself to the bone, when I think what the men out there are going through already; what is waiting for George, and Guy, and Hugo, when they go out. It seems horrible to me to sit safe at home when they go, just nursing in a hospital.'

I said:

'It will be pretty ghastly in a hospital if the War goes on,' and I was surprised at myself; I had not thought consciously about the wounded men before.

Mollie shuddered.

'I know,' she said. 'I have seen some of it already. There were some my first month—blinded—it seemed so soon.'

And I thought:

'Could Hugo be blinded?'

I was glad to have seen Mollie. She brought the War home to me more clearly than anything else had done. She understood what it meant, how dreadful it was, and yet she was sane. I wondered if I could help in a Hospital too; but I was nursing Eleanor still, and very much tied.

I went for a time with Mrs. Sebright and sewed shirts; then I did bandages myself, at home, instead.

In January, Guy crossed to France; George Addington sailed for Gallipoli in April; Hugo's battalion went out as a reinforcement in the second battle of Ypres.

I did not see any of them before they went.

XI

That Easter we went away for a week. Walter was so tired, I was anxious about him. He had extra work at the University, for several of the lecturers had gone to the War, the young unmarried ones, and he was working at his book on inscriptions as well, in the evenings chiefly. He would go straight upstairs to the study after dinner and work till late.

'I may not have time to finish it,' was all he said when I urged him not to. 'I must work while I can.'

We went up to the Wall. The weather was bad, and Walter could not leave the War behind him; he seemed obsessed by it; he could talk of nothing else all the time.

I tried to cheer him up, to tease him a little, and make fun and play as we used to at first; he had liked me to before, but he did not care for it now. He smiled rather absently, and turned back to his book; when he spoke it was only of the advance in Gallipoli.

I felt that it was my fault that I could not cheer him up. I could not feel gay myself; I could not make spontaneous fun, and so it was no good, and I worried about my baby, left for the first time. I kept imagining disasters that were not probable at all. One night I woke up in a fright, and thought that the nurse might have left the tap of the gas fire half on, and the gas be escaping; and another time, I thought that a cat might have jumped into the cot, and the nurse not noticed it. I was jumpy and nervy, I knew it, and so no use to Walter. I thought about Hugo and Guy in France, and George in Gallipoli; and that made it worse.

We sat one day on the hill-side beyond the Wall, where we had often sat before, and looked out to the North. We could see the place when we had walked together, that first day when we had met at the camp and I had gone down with Walter, into the barbarians' country. It seemed a long time ago. I remembered how exciting it had been, and how I had felt that I had begun to know Walter, and understand him. I knew him much better now, but did I understand him? I slipped my hand through his arm and laid my cheek against his.

'Dear,' I said, 'what has happened to us both? Why are we so dull and sad?'

Walter looked round at me slowly.

'We are tired, I think,' he said. 'That is all and we can't rest; nobody can rest just now.'

I stroked his hand, I remember; I felt very sorry for Walter; I felt that, perhaps, I had not thought of him enough, in thinking of Eleanor so much. He looked so tired and unhappy now.

'It would be easier for you if you could fight,' I said.

He flushed and looked away.

'I know,' he said shortly, 'it would, but I can't.'

I was astonished at the sharpness of his tone.

I said:

'Of course not, Walter, nobody thought of it.'

He said:

'I have.'

And I felt a cold shiver run through me. I had not thought of it, and yet, somewhere at the back of my mind, this terror had been there. I held my breath and waited. I could hear the sheep cropping the rough grass a hundred yards away.

Then I said:

'Yes? Do you really want to go?'

And Walter nodded his head.

'I would give anything to go,' he said intensely. 'When Harland was coming home last week a girl gave him a white feather.'

I tried to laugh:

'But that is absurd,' I said. 'Surely he didn't mind?'

'He did mind,' said Walter.

He kept his eyes to the ground; he was tearing up the grass into little tufts and throwing it away.

'I don't suppose I should be any use even if I wasn't

married,' he said. 'I don't suppose they would pass me at the Medical Board, but I hate to stay behind! It makes me ashamed of myself, and I am not used to feeling ashamed.'

I tried to think clearly and dispassionately, but I couldn't. My impulse was to plead with him, to implore him not to leave me, not to go to the War, but I checked it. I felt that he would go, that it was inevitable, that I had known all the time that he would, and that I could do nothing.

'You know,' I said, 'it seems to me almost braver not to go; just to go on doing dull essential work, that somebody must do. All the sentiment and enthusiasm goes to soldiers, but "they also serve". . .?' I felt sobs in my throat. I stopped short.

Walter said:

'Yes, I know that too; I know I ought to stay; that my duty is with you, and my mother; I am not free to choose, but even my students are going, and those friends of yours have gone.'

I said:

'That was different; they were not married,' and then I thought of Cousin Delia, and Mollie.

'Dear, I won't keep you if you want to go,' I said, and I suddenly cried.

He put his arms round me and kissed me, again and again.

'I know you wouldn't, my darling,' he said, 'but I can't go.'

And I felt him nearer and more precious than before, and I thought he felt me so.

'My poor, poor dear,' he said, 'if only the War would end soon.'

And I said:

'It must end soon. I am sure it will.'

XII

Walter said we must cut down expenses, and put all possible money into War Loan. It was the least we could do, he said. So Eleanor's nurse was dismissed. I would look after

Eleanor myself; I was glad to do something definite, and enjoyed looking after my baby for a time.

It was a wet summer; from all sides came complaints of the floods; crops ruined, cattle drowned, people suffering already from the strain and anxiety of war longed in vain for sunshine and kindly weather.

'It is the guns,' they said, 'the big guns cause the rain.'

Rachel was coming now. I tried to look forward to her as I had to Eleanor, but I could not. I thought again and again:

'How shall I manage two children, who am so pressed with one?'

Eleanor would wake up early in the morning; she would talk and jump and keep us both awake, and she was getting very heavy to push in her perambulator. By the end of the day I was very tired. When she was in bed I could not think or read; I would drop down on the sofa and wait for Walter to come home.

I thought:

'It cannot go on much longer now; it is bound to end very soon.'

XIII

In October Walter volunteered under the Derby scheme. He told me before he went out that he should not be taken.

'I know they will not pass me,' he said. 'I know I am a crock'; but his voice was excited, and his eyes very bright. I knew that he hoped, in spite of what he said, that he might be taken.

All that afternoon while he was out at the Recruiting Office I sat indoors with Eleanor and tried to sew. It was a wet afternoon, and I could not face the heavy perambulator walk, pushing up hill to the Heath through the mud and rain.

I sat in the nursery with her, and she played on the floor. She had a cart on wheels that she pushed up and down, the wheels squeaked; I remembered that I had meant to oil them, but the oilcan was downstairs in the kitchen. I was too tired to go down and fetch it, and come back up all the stairs.

Eleanor made a great deal of noise; she upset chairs, and

banged on the floor with bricks; she unwound reels of cotton, with which I was trying to sew; then she upset a bowl of flowers, and I had to go down to the bathroom and fetch a towel; and she screamed and screamed, though I had not scolded her at all. Her shrill, piping little voice pierced through my head like needles. I felt that I must scream or hit her, if she would not be quiet.

Then I thought:

'How horrible that I should feel like this about my baby! I should not have believed, a year ago, that I could feel like this.'

At six o'clock, Walter came in.

I stood up and waited. I heard the front door slam, and then I heard him moving about in the hall. He opened the drawing-room door and looked in, and then I heard him coming up the stairs.

He opened the nursery door and stood still in the door way; and I stood still too, and looked at him.

There was an odd confused expression on his face that I could not make out. I did not know if he was glad or sorry; relieved or disappointed. He came in and threw a bunch of papers on the table in front of me.

'C3!' he said, with a laugh. 'We need not have bothered!' and it seemed to me as though my heart had stopped beating, and now suddenly it began with a rush.

And I said:

'Oh, Walter, are you sorry?'

He sat down in the chair beside him, and faced me across the table.

He said:

'Sorry? I don't know; nobody likes to be C3, I suppose. Thank you for nothing—that is about all——'

I said:

'I can't be sorry. I can only be glad,' and I put out both my hands to him, across the table.

'It isn't your fault,' I said, 'you have done your best. I think I may be glad.'

His eyes were fixed on the table, and he did not answer me; then he pulled his hands away, and buried his face.

'I am not sorry either,' he said huskily, 'that is what is so awful. I thought I wanted to go. I thought I wanted to prove, to myself and every one else, that I could fight, and be a fine fellow. I made myself believe it, but it wasn't true. I know now that I was afraid all the time!'

I went round beside him and kneeled on the floor and I leaned my cheek against his arm. I felt as though he were a child, as though he were much younger than me, and weaker, as I used sometimes to feel with Hugo, when we were children.

I said:

'Dearest, does that matter? Isn't every one afraid? It is the people who are afraid and go, that are the bravest; and you tried to go.'

He said:

'Yes; but I haven't gone. I don't suppose now that I shall.'

Eleanor pushed herself against his knees.

She called:

'Dadda, Dadda,' and beat him with her brick.

At last he noticed her and picked her up on to his knee.

'Well, Baby,' he said, 'are you glad that Dadda is not going to the War?'

'Dadda dee-ar,' Eleanor repeated; she laughed and grabbed at his glasses.

Walter put her down again and she began to scream.

Walter put his hands to his head and stood up.

'Do make her be quiet, Helen,' he said. 'I can't stand the noise.'

I tried to quiet Eleanor, but she went on crying. Walter made for the door, distractedly, and went out.

When at last I had pacified Eleanor, I sat down again in my chair and tried to think; but I could not. It seemed to me then, that I was too tired even to realize my own relief. I felt numb and stupid.

Then Eleanor stumbled over a footstool, and fell, and again she began to scream. I looked at the clock on the chimney-piece; it was bedtime, past bedtime. I picked Eleanor up, but she was angry; she kicked me, and went quite stiff. I struggled with her and carried her off to bed.

XIV

Walter got work at the Admiralty. He deciphered telegrams. He went there immediately after breakfast, and did not come home till eight or half-past eight. He made a point of arriving sooner than the other people in his room, and of leaving after they did. He was paid much less than his University salary, and that he would not take.

His College offered to pay him some proportion of his salary while he was at Government work, but he refused it.

'It is the least I can do,' he said. 'Other men have to leave their work, whatever it is, and lose everything. We must manage to live more cheaply.'

We decided to do without the gardener who came one day a week; I said that I would keep the garden tidy.

Walter said he would dig on Sundays.

XV

Just after Christmas Guy was wounded, and came home for six weeks. He was shot in the shoulder; it was not dangerous. He was sent to a hospital at Southampton. Cousin John applied for leave to have him at Yearsly, a private hospital now, but that was against the regulations.

Cousin Delia went down to Southampton and stayed in an hotel. I went down to see him one day, before he went back.

He was sitting with Cousin Delia, and his arm was in a sling. They were in a little room with a balcony looking out on to the sea. Guy was laughing when I came in I saw his face sideways against the light, and I thought:

'How dear he is, and how just the same as before.' I don't know why exactly, but I had been afraid of his seeming different.

We had tea together, Cousin Delia and Guy and I, and we were very happy. The War seemed a long way off; we did not talk about it. Guy had another month ahead of him before he need go back. He went to Yearsly at the end of his leave; he had a fortnight there, but I did not see him again that time.

XVI

Maud was running a Canteen at the Station at Lessingham.

Troop trains came through there every day, and very often at night. She took the night shifts as a rule, and did her school work by day. That was like Walter.

'One likes to do one's bit, you know,' she said.

She talked a great deal about the 'Tommies.' What fine fellows they were; what splendid single-hearted fellows. It was true no doubt, and any way, even if they were not, it was a good thing to give them cakes and hot coffee; they were unfortunate enough, poor things, and I admired Maud for her work for them, and yet somehow, when she praised them, I wanted to run them down. I felt so sure that she did not understand in the least what they were like; difficult, intricate creatures, part noble, part ignoble, just as we all are; some brave, some cowardly, some understanding what they were doing, others not understanding at all; and Maud lumped them all together as 'fine fellows,' just because they were English soldiers, and we were at War; and I knew she would have called them that, whatever they were like.

Miss Mix used to visit the wounded soldiers in the London Hospital; she read to them, and wrote letters for them, and she took blinded soldiers out for walks. Good old Miss Mix; she too thought them all splendid, but it was quite different with her.

She said to me one day:

'They have all done what I could not do. They have been through things I know I could not stand; and it is partly for my sake, for lots of old women like me, who seem not much use in the world, that they have done it; and it makes me very grateful to them, that is all I know.'

I went with Miss Mix several times, and wrote letters and read to them too, but I could not leave Eleanor much, now I had no nurse. Louise took her out for me then, but after Christmas Louise left us, and went into a Munition factory, and for several weeks I could get no one in her place. When I got another maid, she was very incompetent, and Sarah, the cook, did not like her at all. They quarrelled, and complained about each other a great deal; and then Sarah gave notice. She too went to work at Munitions; it was natural, I suppose, for they earned much higher wages. Mrs. Simms, the charwoman, cooked for us for a time, and at last I got a cook who was very old and deaf, and could not cook very much; but I was glad to get her, and she stayed for some time.

There was no time to do anything else while this was going on. I did part of the housework even then, for the old cook couldn't, and the young maid was very slow. I did it badly, and it took me, too, a long time. I hated the housework; I hated the brooms and dusters; dreamed about them at night; and about the kitchen sink, where I had helped to wash up, while we had no cook. The brooms were kept in the bathroom, for we had no other place to keep them. There were pegs for them there to hang on, and a shelf I for polishes and dusters. I began to hate the bathroom too. It was a squalid bathroom, with a painted bath, that was painted green, and was chipped.

We had meant to put in a new bath, later on; but now of course we could not. The green bath worried me, and the paint wearing off; it seemed to get worse week by week, and the wall where the brushes hung was dirty.

Walter worked always in the evenings now. It was the only time he got for working at his book.

'If I leave that altogether,' he said, 'I can't live. It is the only thing that takes me away from the War.'

While he worked in his study, I sat downstairs and sewed. There was always mending to be done, and I mended. I did not mend well either; it seemed to me, at this time, that I could do nothing well.

And then, at the end of March, George Addington was killed.

XVII

I heard the news from Mollie, in a letter. The letter came

at midday, by an unusual post, and I thought:

'A letter from Mollie. How nice to hear from her!'

And I took it upstairs with me to read. Eleanor was asleep in her pram.

I sat down on my bed, and opened the letter. I thought of Mollie and how much I should like to see her.

'George was killed on Wednesday,' she wrote. 'Shot through the head, leading an attack. He was killed instantaneously, and probably did not know that he was hit. I have had a telegram, that is all, from the War Office. It will be a long time before I can hear any more; three weeks at least, the letters take from there.

'I can't believe he is dead. It seems so strange, that one knew nothing about it on Wednesday, that one had no dream, no premonition nor anything. Oh, Helen, I wrote to him yesterday, and he was dead already——I should be glad, I know, that he was killed at once. It would be worse, much worse, if he were wounded and missing, as it might well have been; I keep telling myself that. I have written to Hugo at Ypres, to tell him of it. He will be badly cut up, I am afraid. He loved George very dearly; but he is bound to know soon; and to Guy too. I wish for Hugo's sake, they were together.'

I sat a long time with the letter in my hand. I had not expected this, I had not somehow envisaged it at all. It seemed to me impossible, and not to be borne.

'George dead! George killed!' I repeated the words over and over to myself, and they had no meaning; and then I thought:

'I shall never see George any more; never as long as I live; no one will see him any more.'

And then I thought:

'I was unkind to George.'

I thought of George as I had last seen him, on the doorstep at Campden Hill Square. How he had come out with us, to say good-bye, and how he had smiled, that wide delightful smile, and yet he had looked sad; and how I had wondered what was the matter, and whether he had known the War would come.

And then I had not written to him when he joined the Army. I had written to Hugo, and to Guy, but not to him. I had meant to, of course. I had kept on meaning to, and putting it off, and then it had been too late.

I had written since, of course; I had written twice, and sent him a parcel of food; but that was not enough in a year and a half, I had meant to write oftener; he had said he enjoyed getting letters; I had meant to write regularly, but I was always bad at writing letters, and little things had got in the way.

Eleanor was asleep in the garden in her perambulator. I left her and went out; up the road, towards the Heath.

The road seemed full of soldiers, blue wounded soldiers. All roads were full of them at this time and when I came nearer I saw that they were blind. I dreaded the blinded soldiers; I hated to see them, for I had an idea, somehow, I don't know why, that Hugo might be blinded. I passed the blinded soldiers, and got beyond them to the Heath. The trees were coming out; light green buds on the branches; and there were crocuses in the grass.

The sun came down through the branches, and shone on the crocuses. It was a fine day, and warm for March. I sat on a seat, and thought about George, and I thought:

'It is all very well for the flowers, and for the buds on the trees; they come again after the winter; they are born again. There will be other boys growing up, and other men, but never George again. If the world goes on for millions of years, there will never be anyone who is what he was.'

And a sense of wild anger and indignation possessed me. I felt:

'This is wrong and wicked and a horrible mistake, this War that has killed George. What is it worth? What is it for? What can it ever achieve that will make up for him?'

And I felt:

'It must be stopped. I have been asleep and woken up. I can't let this War go on that has killed George.'

'George killed! George *dead*!' I repeated the words again. I felt as though the world had begun to reel, as though the foundations of my life had begun to crumble.

'What next?

Guy too and Hugo . . . .' The encroaching reality of the War struck through my last defences. I felt that I understood what it was, for the first time.

A clock in a church struck one, and I went home again. Eleanor would be waking up; she would be crying for me. I must hurry; I would be late, and all the way home I was thinking:

'What can I do? I must do something to stop this War.'

Eleanor was awake and screaming. I went to her and got her up from her perambulator, and washed her, and gave her her dinner; and after dinner, I dressed her to go out, and put her back in the perambulator, and pushed her out on to the Heath. I had no time to think any more, for she kept talking to me in her insistent baby way, that in my heart I loved, but to-day, I wanted to be quiet. I wanted to get away somewhere and think. I felt excited, elated, somehow, as though I had discovered a truth of immense importance; something that was the key to all our trouble.

'The War must be stopped. We must stop it now.'

The words kept repeating themselves through my head all the afternoon, and I felt that in a moment, if only I could get away by myself and be quiet, I should know how this could be done.

When Eleanor was in bed I could be quiet, and think about it. It would not be long now till she was in bed.

And then when I got her into bed, Walter came home.

He was unusually early, more than an hour before his time. He had such a headache, he said, he could not work any longer, and so he had come home. I was up in our bedroom when he came in, tucking Eleanor up. I sang to her always when she was in bed. She did not understand very much what I sang, so I sang all sorts of songs, and to-night I was singing the Agnus Dei that Guy and Cousin Delia used to sing. It seemed to fit in with what I felt to-night; the sins of the world; our sins; and the hope that help was at hand.

Walter came in heavily, and sat down on the bed.

'Daddy came,' said Eleanor, and popped up her head.

I looked round at Walter, surprised to see him there so soon. And then he told me about his headache. I could not take in what he said; it seemed unimportant and trivial; little things about some one a long way off.

I said:

'George is killed,' and stood looking at him, across Eleanor's little cot.

He drew in his breath sharply, and put his hands up to his head. That was a gesture of his, familiar to me now.

I gave him Mollie's letter, and he read it in silence.

'For you'—he said at last, 'and for me——'

And he dropped his hands limply on his knee.

I was astonished at the expression of acute personal sorrow on his face; he had not seemed to care much for George when he was alive. I went across to him, and sat beside him on the bed. I stroked his shoulder, I know, and tried to console him. I don't know what I said. It happened like this so often now; these fits of despondency, almost of remorse, and my attempts to encourage him. It had become in a sense automatic. It seemed to me, at times, that I had no more to give; that I was drawing water from a well that was dry; but to-night it was different; I felt somehow beyond all that. I did not speak to him of my conviction, of what I felt myself about George, and George's death. It was no use speaking to Walter of things like that, I knew.

We went to bed early on account of Walter's headache. I, too, was glad to go.

'Now I can be quiet and think,' I said to myself.

And I lay awake a long time after Walter was asleep and looked up into the darkness.

And I thought:

'What is it I must do? What is it I am just going to understand?'

It was very quiet in our road. There was no sound of traffic; only a dog in a garden not far off barked for a little while, and a cat called somewhere from a roof. A taxi hooted turning a corner at the end of the road, then it changed gear for going up the hill; there was a grating, grinding noise as it changed gear, and then that passed out of hearing. Some one walked past on the pavement, a man it seemed to be, walking very fast. Then again there were cats, and again a taxi horn, and after that for a long time, it was quite quiet.

And as I lay still and listened to the noises in the night, all my excitement seemed to ebb away, and I understood that I had discovered nothing, and that there was nothing I could do.

I could not stop the War, and nobody could. We were caught in it all of us, all nations, all people in the nations; it would go on, and more and more people would be killed; hundreds and thousands of people would be killed every day, and I could do nothing at all, and I understood too that George was dead, and that I had loved him dearly, and that he who was so full of promise, such a fine, splendid nature, would do nothing with his life; he was just at the beginning, and there would be no more.

XVIII

The next day, Walter had influenza. He was in bed for a week, and after that the cook got it, and then the housemaid. They were a long time getting better.

News came of a Republic in Ireland; fighting in the Dublin streets, repression, retaliation; then the fall of Kut. Then the Conscription Bill was passed.

In June, Claude Pincent was killed in Mesopotamia. A week after he was killed, they gave him a V.C. We had not seen him for a long time; people said that he had taken to drink or drugs or something, but I don't suppose it was true.

Then Anthony Cowper was killed. He was a dear, merry fellow and enjoyed his life.

'Guy will miss him very much,' I thought.

Freddy Furze came home on leave in July. We saw him several times. I felt since George's death, the precariousness of life and was grateful for people still alive.

In August, Rachel was born. I had hoped again for a son, but I minded less this time; perhaps because I had expected less, and had felt less about it altogether. I had been afraid that the baby must be affected by the War, and by my own state of mind all through the winter, but she was a fine child, even larger and stronger than the first.

Mrs. Sebright came to stay and look after Eleanor while I was in bed. She was very competent and managed Eleanor very well. She looked after the house too, and ordered the meals, and I had nothing to do; and I thought:

'If only I could lie here for ever, and never get up and never have to go out into the world again.'

I did not want to read or even talk very much, only lie still and do nothing; and sometimes for nothing at all, I would lie and cry.

And then Hugo came home on leave, and I did not see him.

I did not know he was coming, and he came to see me.

I was resting in the afternoon. They had drawn the curtains and put me to sleep, but I was not asleep. I heard the front door bell, and heard the door open, but I did not know it was Hugo, and they sent him away.

They did not know him, of course, they did not know who he was; and they told him I was resting and could not be disturbed; it was too soon too to see visitors, the nurse said, he must come again in a few days.

And Hugo went away.

'Tell her that I came,' he said. 'Give her my love.'

He did not come again in a few days, for he was down at Yearsly all that week and half the next, and then he was sent for to go back to France; his leave was cut short by four days, and he could not come again.

XIX

I must have been in a foolish state those first weeks after Rachel was born. I don't believe I was ill really, but I felt very ill; and things worried me that should not have worried me at all.

I got bothered again about the bathroom; about the paint coming off the bath, and the wall that was dirty where the cedar mop hung up. I kept thinking about that bathroom over and over again; I could not get away from it. I thought how nice it would be to have another bathroom; all white tiles with nickel taps and glass shelves, like bathrooms I had seen in shops. I had never lived with a bathroom like that, for at Yearsly the bath was a big old-fashioned one in a wooden casing, and at Campden Hill Square it was the same. I don't know why this got into my head, or why it stayed there, but it became an obsession. I kept planning how it would be, and where the glass shelf would be, and how many white tiles would be needed, though I knew, of course, that it could not be done; even if we had the money to spend, our bathroom was not big enough to be like the one I planned; but it kept me from thinking of the War, and about Hugo, and Guy, and George; it kept me also from thinking about getting up again with two babies to look after instead of one, and Mrs. Sebright gone away.

Walter found me crying one day when he came in to see me, and he asked me what was the matter, and I said that I did not like the bathroom, and the paint peeling off the bottom of the bath. That sounded so silly, that it made me cry more.

'And the wall is all grey behind the mop,' I said.

Walter put his hand to his head in his tired, bewildered way.

'But, Helen dear,' he said, 'you can't be crying about *that*?'

And I nodded my head.

'I do so want a bathroom, all white, with tiles and glass shelves and shining taps,' I said.

'But, Helen, you know we can't afford that sort of thing,' he said, 'even if it were reasonable to do it. Tiles are very expensive.'

I said:

'I know; I know they are expensive; I know I shall never have a bathroom like that; that is why I am crying.'

Walter was trying to be kind.

'You know, Helen,' he said, 'I sometimes think you don't quite understand; quite apart from the question of whether we could afford it, do you think it would be right to spend a lot of money on white tiles and shelves when the War is going on? Do you quite realize what the War means? Hundreds and thousands of people being killed every day and maimed and blinded.'

I put out my hand to stop him:

'No, no,' I said, and my voice sounded unnatural and shaky and I could not control it. 'I know all that; I know it would be wrong. Please don't let us talk about it any more.'

Walter looked hurt and puzzled with me, and I could not

explain.

That night I could not go to sleep for a long time, and when I did, I dreamt of Hugo being blinded.

Mrs. Sebright was very kind to me. She seemed to like me much better when I was ill and silly; some people are like that; they do like anyone better who is ill; and the Doctor was kind, the Doctor Chilcote whom I had had before. She said I must go away for change when I got up, and I said I couldn't, I could not leave Walter and the house, I said; but she arranged it all.

I was to go with the children to Cousin Delia, to Yearsly, where I had not been for over a year; and Mrs. Sebright would stay with Walter, and the nurse would go with me for a week.

I was glad to have it arranged; I tried to look forward to it, but it did not seem real to me somehow; and when the nurse went away after that first week?

What would I do then, I wondered.

XX

Yearsly was now a hospital. Less serious cases were sent on from the big General Hospital, or convalescents. The garden was full of bright blue suits, as the streets in London had been. There were ten wounded soldiers there at this time. One of the Lacey girls was there with Cousin Delia to nurse them. How she made room for us I do not know, but there was room, and I had my own bedroom, and my old bed that I had had always when I was a girl.

It was quiet at Yearsly, and the War seemed further off; even the soldiers did not bring it close, for they were getting better, and they were happy to be there.

It was like a dream somehow being there with the babies and the soldiers; the same and yet not the same; and the men were gone away from the garden and the farm.

I went down to the village with Cousin Delia, and saw the same people that I used to know, but they too were different. Old Joseph's son had been killed, and John Elliot from the farm was missing, and all the young men were away.

It seemed more changed in a way at Yearsly than in

London, or I realized the changes more distinctly.

The horses were gone too, commandeered by the Government, except Guy's hunter, which he had got with him; and the flower garden was partly growing vegetables and partly run to grass, for old Joseph was alone now, with no young man to help him.

The roses were still the same, and the High Wood, and Cousin Delia was the same herself, as always.

It was like stopping still awhile to be with her. I did not think ahead; I tried not to think of going home.

Cousin Delia kept the nurse for a fortnight longer. She said I was not fit to look after the children myself.

I thought:

'It is wrong; I ought to do it'; but I blessed her for the decision and was glad.

She spoke to me of Hugo's visit. 'You must see him on his next leave,' she said.

She said he was well, but unhappy, how could one expect otherwise. She spoke of George too, and Mollie.

She said:

'I wish I could have seen Mollie, but she cannot get away from her hospital. She is going to Salonika soon, that is better for her I think.'

XXI

When the time came for me to go home, I found it very hard.

I thought:

'Supposing I were a soldier going back to the War.'

And I felt ashamed, but I did not dread it less. Cousin Delia too did not want to let me go. She said that I ought to have more help at home, a better maid, who would help me with the children; I said I would try to get one.

I dismissed the little girl I had, and got a good maid, who took the children out in the afternoons for me. It was much better while she stayed, and she stayed for about a year. Then the Air Raids began, and made her nervous, and then she went away.

Walter had been for his ten days' holiday while I was at Yearsly. He went to the Roman Wall again, and walked about it by himself. He came back refreshed, and more cheerful for a time.

The battle of the Somme was in progress at this time. Guy got a D.S.O., and Freddy Furze was killed.

In September, two Zeppelins were brought down on the East Coast.

Prices were rising fast; food, and clothes, and wages. Coal was expensive too; it became more and more difficult to manage with the money we had. I tried to manage; I kept accounts of all I spent; I tried having herrings for lunch, and tea instead of coffee for breakfast I tried jam instead of butter; but it seemed to make no difference.

I had no new clothes this autumn, and Walter had none. He didn't mind about it, but I did. I darned and mended, and it took me a long time; but Eleanor needed new clothes, and I had no time to make them when the mending was all done; it never was done.

I had to help Ada with the housework, as she helped me with the children. I was tired all the time, and that upset Rachel. I had not milk enough, and she began to flag. She slept badly at night, waking and screaming at four, at three, at two o'clock. Then I weaned her, and the interminable business of prepared foods began. It seemed to me that I spent hours in the day measuring and mixing milk, and cream, and water. No food suited Rachel. She lost weight, she was cross, she was sick. I grew anxious about her, and then frightened. I began to think she would die.

At last the food was right, and she recovered; but she was always a more restless child than Eleanor had been. She would not lie still in her cot when she was awake, but cried to be picked up.

Since the gardener left off coming, the garden had got untidy. I tried to cope with it, but there was so little time. The grass grew long and ragged, and we had no mowing machine. Walter said we could not buy one, till after the War.

I tried to cut the lawn with shears, but it was not a success. They would not cut it properly, and the stooping made my back ache. It ached very often now, and my feet ached and my head.

I thought:

'It can't go on much longer. It must end soon now.'

XXII

In December, our balance at the Bank was overdrawn.

Walter came in with his face all white and tense. He threw the pass-book on the table in front of me.

'There,' he said. 'Overdrawn at last. I have been expecting this.'

I felt as though he had hit me, his voice was hostile; he looked as though he hated me.

I said:

'Walter, I am sorry; I have done my best.'

'I can't understand it. Other women manage, why can't you? Other women on smaller incomes than ours; my mother did.'

I said:

'I know they do.'

He said:

'I must earn more, I suppose. I must do examining or something of that sort in the evenings; I must give up my book—that was the last thing that kept me alive!'

I said:

'Don't do that, Walter. I will try again; perhaps we could manage better without a cook.'

He said:

'You couldn't cook; you can't manage as it is; and your grandmother keeps telling me you are overworked.'

I did not know that Grandmother had said so. I did not know that she had noticed it at all.

I said:

'I could learn to cook. I would rather do that than housework.'

He said:

'Don't talk nonsense!'

He clasped his head in his hands, and leaned across the table.

'It has never happened before,' he said, 'to be overdrawn. It is a disgrace.'

I said:

Cousin John was overdrawn quite often; I don't think it mattered much.'

He said:

'Damn your Cousin John! *They* have capital behind them. We have not.'

I said:

'I have a little, Walter; couldn't we use that?'

He said:

'I won't use your capital, and I won't be helped by your relations. Do you know,' he asked suddenly, 'your grandmother offered to pay for a nurse for the children?'

I said:

'I did not know.'

'Yes,' he said very bitterly. 'She did, and I refused. I told her that you could manage without, as my mother had managed. I think I was rude to her. She was displeased with me.'

I wondered vaguely when all this had happened.

I thought:

'How dear of Grandmother.'

We had stopped having lunch with her on Sundays. I had not seen her often since Rachel was born.

He got up again, abruptly, and left the room. I stayed alone and cried, and wished that I were dead.

Afterwards Walter was sorry.

He said he was sorry; he said he hardly knew what he had said.

He said:

'I had such a headache, and the pass-book was the last straw. I was awfully upset. I was a beast.'

'Dear, dear Helen,' he said suddenly, 'you must forgive me. You don't know what you are to me.'

I said, of course, that it did not matter. I said again that I was sorry; but I felt him still unkind.

I thought:

'He does not love me for what I am. He wants me different all the time. What I have and could give him is of no use to him.'

That winter wore through somehow, as the last had done, and on January 31st came the announcement of 'Unrestricted Submarine Warfare.'

Walter looked grim.

He said:

'We shall begin to feel it in earnest now.'

Prices were rising still, but gradually. There was no visible difference after this for some time.

Then the Russian Revolution came. That made me think of Sophia Lane Watson. I wondered where she was. I remembered her old enthusiasm for Russian Revolutionists. Would she be pleased at this, I wondered?

And then America came into the War.

XXIII

In June Guy came home on leave. He was at Yearsly first, and then three days in London. He stayed with Grandmother in Campden Hill Square. I went to see him there and he came up to me. He wanted to dance, he said, it was so good to be at home. 'Let us be jolly,' he said, 'I have only two days more.'

So I went with him to a club, somewhere near Bond Street it was. We had dinner first in Soho, and then we went and danced. I had no dancing clothes now, except very old ones, but Guy did not mind.

'That is the dress you used to wear,' he said, and he was pleased.

It was like being born again to dance with Guy. The years between, and the War, seemed to fall away; it was as though all that had happened was wiped away, and we were back again in 1912 before the War, before even I was married.

We danced till two o'clock; then Guy saw me home. We would do it again the next night, we said.

Walter was in the study working, when I got home.

He said:

'You are very late, you will be tired to-morrow.'

I said:

'I think that I shall not be tired any more. I have come alive again.'

And I laughed, and kissed him.

Rachel woke up at half-past five, but I did not mind.

I thought:

'We shall dance again to-night.'

And we did. We went to the same restaurant, and the same club, and we danced till nearly three.

'This has been good,' Guy said. 'Thank you, Helen.'

And I said:

'Thank you, Guy.'

He went back the next day, at a quarter to twelve. Mollie was in Salonika now; he had not seen her; I was sorry about that.

Cousin John and Cousin Delia came up to see him off. I saw them at the station. Then I went back to Walter, and the house, and the children, but for a long time it was better after that.

I wished that Walter could dance; he had promised me once that he would learn.

I asked him now; it was foolish of me.

He said:

'I have no time to dance, and I don't want to. I don't understand, Helen, how you can bear to dance at a time like this.'

I said:

'If Guy can bear to——'

He said:

'Oh, Guy!' and stopped short.

'I think it is abominable,' he said.

Afterwards he was sorry. Walter was always sorry afterwards, when he had been cross, but I could not forget the things he said. He broke his glasses soon after this, the rimless ones that he had bought to please me. He would not buy any more. He went back to the old spectacles with the black steel frames. I could not bear him in those spectacles.

XXIV

The children had whooping cough that summer. When it was better we went to the seaside. We took lodgings on the Norfolk coast; it was cheap to go there because of the War; people were afraid of the German Navy, and bombardments from the sea, and Zeppelins.

There was no bombardment, nothing while we were there, but it was very dreary. There were soldiers there as everywhere, and barbed wire along the cliffs. It was cold too and rainy.

Walter came down for a fortnight. The children still coughed a great deal, they coughed especially at night. Maud came for a bit too, and helped me with the children.

I thought:

'That is kind of Maud—I have been horrid about Maud'—but even so, I was glad when she went away.

I was glad to leave that place. London was much better than that. We came home in September.

I went to see Grandmother at Campden Hill Square. She was away and there was a new maid who did not know me.

Mrs. Woodruffe was in the country, she said. She was expected back next month.

I knew she had been at Yearsly. I had hoped that she was back. The maid did not offer me tea, and I did not ask her for it. I felt disappointed to an absurd degree. I walked across Campden Hill to Kensington Church, and thought of my wedding there four years before. I took a bus from there down to Chelsea and walked past Mollie's flat. The blinds were down and there were no flowers in the window-boxes. That was natural, of course, with Mollie far away. I turned back again towards the bridge. I went into the little tea shop where we used to have meals very often. Here too the waitress was new, everything was changed; different and strange. It seemed as though I had been away for years and years.

And then as I sat and waited for some tea, I caught sight of my own face in a looking-glass that was hanging on the wall; and I realized suddenly with a shock that my own face was changed. I looked so shabby, so provincial, somehow, and dull. I had not realized before that I looked like that now. I had hardly thought of my own appearance for so long.

I stared at myself in that looking-glass, and felt ready to cry.

How was it that I had not seen myself like this before?

I looked at myself every morning, of course, when I did my hair, but I had not really looked for months, even when I dressed to go out with Guy. Was I getting old? I was nearly thirty now, was that really old?

I had seen myself so often in the same looking-glass before, an oval looking-glass it was, in a dark lacquered frame. I had sat so often at this same table with Mollie, and George, and Guy, and Hugo. Would they all be changed when I saw them again? If I did see any of them—George I would never see.

I tried to remember his face as he had last sat there, in that little restaurant, at that same table; but I could not remember any particular time as the last.

He at least had not faded nor tarnished:

'They carry back bright to the coiner the mintage of man,
The Lads who will die in their glory and never be old.'

I repeated the lines to myself, and they made me happy, with their familiar beauty. I remembered the first time that I had read them, lying on the sofa in the drawing-room, at Campden Hill Square. A big, deep sofa with a green Morris chintz.

I had had a bad cold; it was winter and the fire was burning in the grate. I had watched the light flickering on the ceiling as I lay on my back, and repeated the lines with wonder and delight to myself. All this came back to me.

I had thought them so true, so full of meaning; and how little I had really understood.

Now I was oppressed and overpowered by the dread of old age, of deterioration, and change, and loss. It was gone already, the wonder of youth, and light, and life; it was slipping through my fingers before I had had time to realize and enjoy it. This was not life, this daily drudgery, this struggle to keep going, to get through, to exist. I was marking time, we were all marking time, waiting and waiting for the strain to relax, for the War to end; and meantime our youth was going.

Before in the old days we had been waiting, too, but that had been different. We had been waiting then for something to begin, to happen, this was waiting for something to end, to stop happening.

The waitress brought my tea. The toast was spread with a very rank margarine. The cake tasted of cocoa butter, and I remembered what delicious bread and butter they used to give us here.

I sat still for a long time after my tea, looking out at the familiar view; the trees, the wide road, and the river. Then I paid my bill and walked up the street to my bus.

XXV

A few days after this the Air Raids began.

We had heard, of course, that they would come. There had been the Zeppelin raids; people had talked of bombardment from the air; of London being destroyed; of German plans for more and larger aeroplanes than anyone had seen; but it had not seemed very real. And now, when the first raid came, I did not realize what it was.

I was undressing in my bedroom; it was about half-past ten, and I heard the warning whistles. Then came the shouts through a megaphone, 'Take cover; take cover,' a rhythmical, rather melancholy shout, like a sort of refrain. I stood still with my hairbrush in my hand; I remember that I was brushing my hair. The gas was turned low for fear of waking the baby, Rachel was the baby, in her cot at the end of the room; and it flickered a little in the draught from the open window, though the blinds were tightly drawn. I was thinking, I don't know why, of a summer holiday when I was a child, with Guy and Hugo, at Yearsly. I was thinking of the high trees, and the swishing sound of the branches against the house; and I remembered how at first, when I was very little, I had been almost frightened of that sound, and afterwards I had got to love it.

It was a quiet place, unshaken, unshakeable, so it seemed to me; even being a hospital had not changed it really.

And Cousin Delia too, she was always the same. I thought of her calm face with the mass of grey hair swept upwards from the forehead, and those great grey eyes of hers, that were like Guy's, but quieter. I could picture her face older, sadder, with more shadowed eyes, but I could not picture it harassed or worried or upset, nor marked with the fear or strain of the War.

And a great longing for Cousin Delia came over me, a longing for the quiet security of Yearsly, for the old high trees and the swishing branches, the sun-dried brick of the walled garden, the pear trees outspread against the wall, and the jasmine gate, and the droning of the bees. Inside that garden it was always sheltered and warm, outside the wind rocked through the beech trees, the clouds trailed rolling shadows across the wide green lawns, the high grass swayed and bent, like waves at sea, but the peace and quiet remained unbroken.

I thought of Guy and Hugo as boys, as they had been in those early summers when first I was there, boys in the branches of the beech trees in the High Wood, calling to each other among the calling of the rooks; and regret came over me, poignant, impersonal regret, at the inevitable pathos of existence; the relentlessness of time, and change, and the haunting dearness of the past.

I thought:

'It will never be so again. Never in millions of years.'

I heard the shrill prolonged whistling in the street, and the hurrying rush of feet, the sing-song, almost musical cadence of the 'Take cover,' as it drew nearer and louder, and then passed further on and away down another street, but I did not give my mind to it; it did not recall my thoughts; and then the guns began; first one, then another, then a third, at intervals of a few minutes first, then closer together, then in bursts. One big anti-Aircraft Station was close behind us on Parliament Hill. The report of its gun boomed out, with an almost deafening roar; the windows rattled and the doors shook.

And then I realized that an Air Raid had begun, and I felt excited, and wondered if I should be afraid.

I crossed to the window and looked out. It was a brilliant moonlight night, searchlights still swung across the sky, crossing, intersecting, passing each other, but the moonlight dimmed their brightness, and I thought:

'How beautiful it is.'

I looked up in the sky for Zeppelins or aeroplanes, but I could see nothing; only the tiny fleecy clouds, high up, incredibly high up, luminous and unearthly in the moonlight.

The street outside was empty, but further down in the bigger thoroughfares I could still hear the whistles and the warning cries and the shuffle of feet.

I felt my heart beating, but I was not afraid. I wondered:

'What next? What will happen now?'

Then there was a stir inside the house; feet on the stairs, the opening and shutting of doors.

Walter came in from the study. I had forgotten Walter; and Maud came downstairs from her bedroom; I had forgotten that Maud was staying with us just then.

They pulled me back from the window.

Maud said:

'Quick, we must get the children downstairs.'

She went to the cot and picked Rachel up.

She said:

'Ada has taken Eleanor down already.'

Walter said:

'That's right, Maud: that's right. Hurry up, Helen, why are you waiting?'

He took me by the shoulder and pushed me in front of him across the room, turning out the gas as he passed, and I went where he pushed me. I felt quite passive, and as though I were a long way off, and looking on We sat downstairs in the dining-room; the servants were there already with Eleanor. She was pink with sleep and rather puzzled. They had wrapped her up in a rug, and she sat on Walter's knee. I took Rachel on mine; she was still fast asleep.

We could hear the shrapnel like hailstones on the roof, and in the street, and the long wail of the shells, and then between, came the sound of engines, a droning sinister sound.

And I thought:

'A bomb might fall and kill us any moment; it might fall now, while I think.'

But it had no meaning for me at all, and I thought:

'How funny we look sitting here in our dressing-gowns.'

For only Walter was still dressed, and I thought how funny the old cook looked with her hair down her back, and I thought Maud looked much nicer than she did in her ordinary clothes.

Maud was trying to talk to the maids, to distract their attention from the noise, and I noticed the tremor in her voice.

And I thought:

'How funny that is; Maud is quite frightened.'

Now came a dropping of bombs, louder, more reverberating explosions, one after another. I counted seven in quick succession, then there was a lull. Again we could hear the whizzing of the engines, louder and louder, and then less loud, and again the barrage and the wailing of the shells and again the pattering like hailstones in the street.

Ada and the cook shuddered and shut their eyes.

Eleanor asked:

'Why is there such a noise?'

Maud said:

'Gun practice, my dear child. They are practising with guns.'

And she seemed satisfied, she was still half asleep.

And I thought:

'Those bombs have fallen somewhere; they have fallen on something; people must have been killed.'

But it did not mean much to me even so.

Maud said violently:

'And they call this War. I don't.'

I said:

'But what else is it?'

Maud said:

'Murder. Massacre.'

And the cook and Ada nodded their heads.

The funny old cook with her grey plait of hair sat up very straight in her chair.

She said:

'I could find it in my heart to be a second Charlotte Corday.'

I was surprised at her, and I could not remember what Charlotte Corday had done.

She shook her fist and said:

'That Emperor William.'

And I thought again:

'How funny it all is.'

And then I thought:

'It is wrong to think it funny.'

And we sat there till the firing died away.

There was silence for a while and then 'All Clear' sirens were sounded.

Maud drew a deep breath and stood up.

Walter passed his hands across his forehead.

He said:

'At last. Now we can go to bed.'

And I thought:

'It is over now. That was an air raid.'

And then I thought:

'George is dead; and Guy and Hugo are out there, where it goes on all the time.'

And I shivered and felt cold.

Walter said:

'I wonder how Mother stood it.'

And Maud said:

'She ought not to be alone.'

XXVI

The next night there was another raid, and every night that week. Walter was all on edge.

The children became fretful with their nights disturbed. I thought it would be better to stay in our beds, quietly, as though nothing was happening, but Walter said that was silly.

He said we must take the reasonable precautions. So we sat downstairs, night after night, Walter and I, and the servants, with the children half asleep.

Maud had gone to Mrs. Sebright, and taken her down to the school. 'People should leave London, who could,' she said, 'it was foolish to stay behind.'

And then the raids stopped for a bit, and the nights were quiet, and we slept again and were glad.

Afterwards, when they came, we stayed in bed.

Food was now difficult to get. There were voluntary rations. I spent hours every week weighing and measuring them out. People who kept to the rations put cards up in their windows. We kept to the rations, but we did not put up a card. The taste of beans and lentils became sickening to us all.

Ada gave notice, on account of the air raids, and it was a long time before I got another maid.

The long months of the winter passed on slowly, harder and more difficult than the last. No sugar, no fat, no fuel, and the weary hours of waiting in a queue for the horrid food we got.

I got to loathe the shops where I had to market; the butcher's shop in the High Street, where I waited every Tuesday and Saturday, the grocer's where I waited hours, to be told in the end that the margarine had given out, that there were no beans, that tea had risen again in price; I had to take the children very often, and Rachel was heavy now to hold. I watched the other women in the queue, working women mostly, more tired and draggled than me, with children more fretful than mine, and wondered at their patience; and sometimes I wondered if they really minded it all as much as I did.

It was so cold that Winter. I had never known such cold; perhaps it was the lack of fats that made one cold, Maud said so anyway; and there was so little coal. We shut the drawing-room up, and the study too, and lived in the dining-room downstairs. There we could have a fire; and Walter at his office was warm; but I was always cold; and I thought of Guy and Hugo in the trenches; Hugo had always felt the cold so much, and then I thought:

'George will not feel cold any more, at all.'

Walter and I saw each other very little. He worked almost always in the evenings after dinner; examination papers now, to make more money, not his proto-Hittite Script; and on Saturdays and Sundays as a rule. He was not happy, I knew; how could he be? but we were like people in a fog; we could not see light, nor each other, we could only struggle for breath, to keep alive; and again we said:

'It cannot last much longer. It is bound to end very soon.'

My grandmother was still at Yearsly. Cousin Delia had kept her there.

XXVII

In February, Hugo came home on leave, and I saw him. He wrote to me that time and said he was coming. He would be in London for a few days first, and then at Yearsly.

His letter came at breakfast time amid the clatter of plates and feeding the children. I opened it, and could think of nothing else.

Three days later, Hugo himself came. I was coming back from my afternoon walk with the children, pushing the heavy perambulator up the hill, thinking, wondering if he would come to-day. Suddenly I saw him at the end of the road, coming to meet me; a long way off still, but unmistakably Hugo.

I had not seen him in khaki before, and the silhouette was strange, and although I had expected it, it was a shock; but I knew his walk, and I knew the poise of his head. I stopped the perambulator and stood still.

My heart leaped up and throbbed. I had a wild impulse to turn round and run away. I had been counting the hours until this moment, but now that it had come, I was afraid. I dreaded this meeting with Hugo in a way that surprised myself. I felt it to be charged with emotion, painful, stirring emotion, as of all the past revoked; of lost youth, and lost joy, and that terrifying sense of regret for the passage of time and of life. As I hesitated, he saw me. He took off his cap and waved it and I had no choice, I waved back and went on to meet him.

We seemed a long time reaching each other. Then we shook hands, and stood still. I looked into Hugo's face, and he looked into mine; it seemed at first, as though we had nothing to say.

Hugo's face frightened me; he was smiling now, the faint half hesitating smile I knew so well, but there was something new in the very smile, in his mouth, above all in his eyes, a desperate, haunted expression, that I had not seen before.

I said:

'I am glad to see you, Hugo, it is good of you to come up here.'

He said:

'Why, of course I came.'

He turned to the children, and looked at them with an amused, half puzzled expression, and then back to me.

'I can't get used to the idea of you with children, you know,' he said; and then he added abruptly: 'they are neither of them like you.'

I said:

'No; they are like Walter's family, both of them.'

I had not admitted this before, to anyone, nor yet that I minded about it, but I did.

'I wish I had a child,' said Hugo suddenly, staring away across the street. 'A son—you must have a son, Helen.'

And he turned back to me.

I said:

'Yes, I hope I shall, next time.'

We walked on slowly, towards the house. The children were unusually quiet, staring with round eyes at Hugo.

We talked of Guy; Hugo had seen him at Amiens, and of Mollie, still nursing in Salonika. We did not talk of George. Then we reached the door of the garden and went in.

I pushed the door open and we went inside. The garden with its uncut grass looked sordid and forlorn. I was sorry Hugo should come to it like that.

I opened the door of the house with my latchkey, and lifted the children out. Eleanor ran tumbling up the steps and across the hall, Rachel I had to carry. I set her on a chair in the hall and came back for the perambulator.

Hugo helped me to lift it up the steps, and past the umbrella stand.

He hung up his hat and coat, and shut the door. I watched him as though it was a dream. It seemed so strange to see him there. I took him downstairs to the dining-room where tea was being laid.

'We have shut the drawing-room up,' I said, 'because of the coal,' and I wished I need not have him in that room where the ugly sideboard was. It looked so dull that room, and so crowded up now we used it altogether, and I wanted to have Hugo in a beautiful room.

I left him there while I went upstairs with the children. Their undressing and preparing for tea seemed to take longer than usual that day.

When I came downstairs, Mrs. Sebright was there. I had quite forgotten that she was coming to tea.

Mrs. Sebright asked Hugo about his journey, about the length of his leave, about his billets in France. Hugo answered her questions quietly, smiling very faintly his hesitating smile. Mrs. Sebright talked about submarine warfare; she asked him if he knew what the latest inventions for catching submarines were; Hugo did not know.

Mrs. Sebright seemed to find no difficulty in talking to Hugo. She asked him things that I could not have asked.

I could not talk to him at all while she was there. I sat and watched him while he talked to her. I felt the precious moments slipping away, precious, irrevocable moments, and wondered what it was that had happened to him.

'Is it just the War?' I wondered. 'Is that what it is?'

I felt a passionate longing to talk to him of the War, of my soul and his, to help him and be helped.

Tea was over, and cleared away. We drew our chairs up to the fire. Nobody spoke much. Eleanor and Rachel played with wooden bricks on the floor behind us. Hugo helped them to build a little while, then he stood up to go. I went with him up the stairs into the hall.

I said:

'Hugo, I must see you again.'

He stood looking up at me from the lower step.

'Yes,' he said. 'When? Let us go and see some pictures.'

I said:

'Yes; to-morrow, after lunch I will come.'

'I will meet you at the station; at Charing Cross, at the Tube.'

I said:

'I will be there at half-past two.'

'Right. Good-bye till then.'

'Good-bye.'

I stood, and looked after him; his figure was lost quickly

in the shadow of the darkened street.

And I thought:

'He has come and is gone; but I shall see him again.'

I thought:

'To-morrow; at half-past two.'

Then I thought:

'Hugo.'

I asked Mrs. Sebright if she would look after the children for me the next afternoon. She had done so sometimes before, when there was no maid I could trust, and she said she would.

'I want to see Hugo again, down in London,' I said. 'He will only be here for two days, just now.'

'Poor young man,' Mrs. Sebright said, 'he looks very ill. Has he had shell shock, do you think, at any time?'

I said I didn't think so, but I felt a rush of gratitude to Mrs. Sebright for her kindly tone. I bent down suddenly and kissed her, and she looked surprised.

'Poor boys,' she said, 'poor boys, I pity them indeed.'

And it struck me as very strange that she should class Hugo in any group—as one among others like him—he who to me had always seemed unique; so wholly different from all other people.

XXVIII

Hugo was waiting for me on the platform. We made our way through the hurrying crowds of people, and out of the station, hardly speaking a word.

It was a grey day, a heavy overcast sky threatened rain. We crossed Trafalgar Square, to the Admiralty Arch; then we went through it, and turned to the left, across the open space of the Horse Guards Parade. We walked along where the water used to be, by the War Trades Intelligence Department, those strange piles of Government buildings that usurped the bright coolness of the water. In one small remaining corner the pelicans still lived, crowding with ruffled feathers on their little clumps of rock.

We walked along to the end, to Buckingham Palace, then we turned back, to the right, along the Mall.

I felt a new excitement and delight at Hugo's presence; at being with him again after so many years, and so many changes. The sympathy and understanding that had been so much a part of our relation before seemed there as strong as ever, now we were together again. We spoke very little; there seemed no need for speech. From time to time we looked at each other and, as our eyes met, a sense of assurance and security seemed to pass from one to the other.

It seemed to me as we walked as though we two were alone in a world of desolation and ruin. I felt my thoughts and my emotions of the last three years rising up, formulating themselves, seeking expression. I was possessed by a sense of experience, of our separate experiences, to be shared now, to be unified, and made whole.

We crossed Piccadilly and turned into Bond Street.

Hugo had chosen an exhibition of Raemakers' cartoons as the pictures we were to see. We took our tickets at the door, gave up our umbrellas, and were inside.

We walked round the two small rooms for a long time. Hugo looked at the pictures, dumbly, intensely, and I watched Hugo.

We stopped before a picture of a wood in autumn; the leaves falling from the trees, and a dead soldier, a German, lying on the ground.

'When the leaves fall, you shall have peace.'

The words from a speech of the Kaiser's were below it. I felt a cold grip at my heart, at my throat, and the picture swam before me . . .

'When the leaves fall, you shall have peace.' The words echoed through my brain, emptily, metallically. I saw the dead soldier, huddled, hunched up in the wet ditch, and the leaves falling over him, and I felt suddenly that I must cry out, scream, that it was more than could be borne.

I turned to Hugo: his eyes were fixed on the picture, and again I saw that haunted, terrified expression that had struck me when I saw him first, but it was more now. I felt suddenly, that my own emotion was somehow a reflection of his emotion, that my own despair was an echo of his despair.

'You shall have peace . . . You shall have peace . . .'

I felt at that moment that I was seeing with his eyes and

feeling with his mind. I was fascinated, horrified, paralysed; then I broke the spell:

'No, Hugo,' I said, and my voice sounded rough and unnatural to myself, 'come away, come away quickly!'

I seized hold of his arm and pulled him after me, through the swinging glass doors, and down the steps.

Outside, the rain had begun to fall, a thin, drizzling rain . . . we paused here and drew breath: I felt as though I had woken up from a very ghastly dream.

I laughed, nervously, I knew, and shivered——

I said:

'Those are terrible pictures—they make one remember and think——'

Hugo stared at me, with sombre, unseeing eyes.

'Yes, they make one think,' he repeated.

We walked out into the street; I kept my hand on his arm: I felt dizzy, and still frightened at my own thoughts and feelings, and almost frightened of him.

As we turned into Piccadilly the rain came on more heavily, beating and pattering against our faces; we remembered suddenly that we had left our umbrellas in the gallery; we turned and hurried back again.

When we came out for the second time, we were calmer, and more established.

We turned into the nearest tea shop, Stewart's, at the corner of Bond Street, and went upstairs. There was an empty table by the window; we went to it and sat down.

Hugo leaned his chin on his hands, and looked across at me.

He said:

'That is a wicked picture, Helen,——do you know what it is to want peace?'

I said:

'I think I begin to know.'

'I won't give up,' he went on, as though he were talking to himself, 'I won't; I am not going to be killed; I am going right through to the end. Nothing can be worse now.'

He buried his face, and shivered.

I asked:

'Do you want very much to be killed?'

And he bent his head.

'I am frightened sometimes,' he said, 'I think I am going mad in the night; even here; I see things, and hear them, over and over again; I am afraid of doing it on purpose; of letting it happen. . . . George would never have got like this. . . .'

'No, George was different. I think, perhaps, it was easier for him.'

'Yes, George was braver than me, and now, you see, he has finished. He has not got to go on afterwards as I must. I must go on, partly because of George, and can you think what it will be like, Helen, afterwards, when we are sane again, and realize what we have been doing?'

I said:

'I can't think about afterwards at all, Hugo. I can't look ahead at all beyond next week.'

We were silent then, looking out of the window at the rain in the street. It pattered on the tops of omnibuses, on umbrellas, on mackintoshes, on the grey paving stones. The humming noise of the traffic rose up to us, muffled, through the double glass, and all those people, and the hurry, and the busyness, seemed very far away.

The waitress came to take our order; we asked for tea, and turned back to the window.

I said:

'Yes; we must go on; it is all we can do now; just wait and hold out . . . on and on and on. . . .'

And he repeated:

'Yes; that is all; somebody must go on; that is the only way to look at it, I think.'

I said:

'Oh, Hugo, is it possible that all this is only three years?'

Hugo looked up with his hesitating smile.

'Three years has not much meaning now,' he said, 'has it? We didn't know anything then; we hadn't begun. We don't know much now; afterwards, if we can go through with it till the end, we may know something, perhaps.'

He added abruptly:

'I am sorry for you, Helen.'

'And I, for you,' I said.

'It is the same for us both, in a way; for everybody, I

suppose.'

'No, not quite everybody, I think; but for you and me. I am glad we have met again, Hugo, so glad.'

He put out his hand across the table and took mine.

'I wondered if you would come to-day,' he said.

The waitress had brought our tea and put it down, but we had not noticed her.

There was to us both, I think, great consolation in this clasping of hands: strength and companionship in a world of destruction.

After tea we went out in the rain, and walked in the Green Park.

We walked up and down, backwards and forwards, talking a little, not very much, of casual, trivial things; comforted and upheld by each other's nearness.

At last we went back to the station, and Hugo saw me into the train.

I said:

'Let me know when you come back,'

He said:

'I shall come back in ten days.'

'In ten days?'

'Yes, in ten days.'

XXIX

The next days passed, unreal and dreamlike to me. I was happy, elated, filled with a renewal of youth. Hugo was there, Hugo was alive, I had found him anew after this long time, and I would see him again in a few days.

It seemed to me during those ten days that everything was easier and pleasanter than before. Nothing worried or irritated me; I lived in a world of my own.

Even Walter noticed a change. Something had come back, I think, that he had missed.

He said to me, one day:

'You are happier than you were, Helen . . . .'

And I was pleased and laughed.

'Yes, Walter,' I said, 'I am so happy at seeing Hugo

again.'

Walter looked at me queerly, and sighed.

'You ought to see more of your friends,' he said, 'I know that. It is natural you should miss them.'

I stroked his cheek.

'I shall see them again, after the war,' I said. 'We shall all meet together then, except George . . .'

'Poor George,' said Walter, and he sighed again.

At last the day came, and a note from Hugo, at Yearsly. He would be in London that morning, by twelve o'clock; crossing that night to France.

I took the next train. I left the children in the care of Mrs. Simms.

Hugo was there to meet me; he had come straight from Waterloo. We lunched together, and then we walked in the Park.

This day it was fine. A clear, cold winter's day, with tiny transparent clouds, high up in a pale sky. We walked quickly, rejoicing in the cold air and the warmth of walking.

Then we went to the National Gallery. Most of the pictures were hidden away in bomb-proof cellars; that was a disappointment; but we were happy to-day.

We went to tea with Grandmother, at Campden Hill Square; we enjoyed the familiarity of the room, of the atmosphere, and the china, and the cat.

The hours passed; how we did not know. It was evening already, and we stood on the steps of the 'Coliseum,' going in to the Russian Ballet. It was the Scarlatti Ballet, 'The Good Humoured Ladies,' that we saw. The music and the dancing excited us; it was perfect. All was perfect, on this most wonderful of days.

We left the lighted theatre, and went out . . . out into the dark night and the shaded streets.

We made our way across Trafalgar Square, bare and empty in the shadow, through the Admiralty Arch again, and across the Green Park.

Hugo's train was to leave at midnight.

We were silent in the darkness of the trees. The bitterness of ending was over our joy now.

We walked close together, bumping against each other as

we walked. Hugo took my hand and held it, and we walked like children, holding hands. We passed out of the Park, and down the road, into the hurry and rush of Victoria Street, past the Underground Station, and under the vaulted roof of Victoria Station.

Smoke from the waiting trains swirled in white eddies under the shadowy roof. Whistles sounded: calling voices and heavy footsteps: the churning noise of engines, getting up steam, and the clanging of luggage barrows on the platforms.

There were soldiers everywhere; waiting groups, sitting and lounging about, loaded with their service kit; bags, rifles and helmets slung about them in a shapeless mass; tired, anxious faces, and joking voices; one was telling a story to a listening group; it seemed to be a funny story, for bursts of laughter interrupted him.

Hugo inquired about his train. No one seemed to know. We wandered from one official to another; there was no train to leave at midnight, they said.

At last some one came who knew about it; the leave train was postponed till the morning, at 7 a.m.

I felt an immense, disproportionate relief; I glanced at Hugo; he was looking at me with his whimsical, questioning expression.

'Seven hours more,' he said.

'Seven hours,' I repeated.

What should we do for seven hours?

'I told them not to expect me back till they saw me,' I said. 'I must wait and see you off.'

'Helen? I should like it.'

'Will you, Helen?'

We turned back to the Hotel, where Hugo had a room reserved till the next day. I would stay there too. He engaged another room.

We walked up the stairs like people in a dream. The stuffy hotel smell, the thick, shabby carpet, the dull glare of the electric light, stamped themselves on my mind, but dazedly, as fantastic, unreal things.

In the long, deserted passage we stood still. Rows of shut doors stretched on either side of us. Boots stood outside some of them, military boots, and empty water cans. One bulb of electric light shone at the further end.

We read the numbers on the doors. 247 was my room. We reached the door, and then stood still again. It seemed a waste of precious time to sleep, but we were very tired, suddenly, unbearably tired.

'Good night, Helen.'

'Good night.'

We paused, and waited again.

Dumbly, instinctively, I raised my arms to Hugo's neck. He grasped me, and we kissed. It flashed through my mind, as something very strange, that we had not kissed each other since that time we did not kiss on the evening of Guy's birthday, beside the Jasmine Gate. We had before that always, without thinking about it.

'My dear, dear Helen . . .' Hugo murmured; and I said nothing at all. My hands clasped each other, hard, behind his neck; I felt just then that I could never let him go . . . and then it seemed suddenly that something snapped . . .

'Good night, Hugo,' I said, and my arms dropped to my sides.

'My dear, good night.'

I waited a moment longer with my hand on the handle of the door; it seemed to us both, I think, that there was something more we must say; but we could not; no words came.

I opened my bedroom door, and pulled it to behind me. I dropped into a chair by the window, and sat there, quite still, for a time. Then I roused myself, took off my hat and shoes, and lay down on the bed.

I lay still and listened to the stir of the traffic outside. The rumble of trains, the perpetual hoots of taxi cabs turning round the corner, in and out of the station. From the open window, came the acrid smell of train smoke, drifting in with the night fog. I felt cold, and shivered; then I got up and threw my coat over the quilt of the bed.

It seemed to me that I must have lain awake all night, but at last I fell asleep.

A maid woke me at a quarter to six, with a can of hot water. I woke with a start of terror, and plunged myself awake properly in the hot water.

A few minutes later I met Hugo in the 'Breakfast Room' of the hotel. There were other people there; about a dozen other officers, two or three women with them. We smiled faintly at each other, and sat down. Outside it was still dark, and an early morning fog obscured what lights there were. We drank hot coffee and ate fried bacon, and then again we went into the station.

The train was there this time. Hugo found a place and put his luggage in. Then we walked up and down on the platform till it was time to start. The morning was raw and chilly. The cold fog got into our throats and eyes. It seemed to enclose us in a deadened solitude; to shut out the world beyond; to muffle even the footsteps of the other waiting people.

'It must not be so long till you come again, Hugo.'

And he looked at me with his odd little questioning smile.

'Remember,' I said suddenly, 'you are going through with it. We have got to go through to the end.'

'Yes,' he replied quietly, 'we have got to go on. I will, and you will too,' and he turned abruptly to me.

I bent my head.

'Yes, I will too, of course.'

'Guy will be having leave soon,' said Hugo.

'Yes, and Mollie is coming home this summer.'

'It would be good if we could all be here together.'

'After the war, anyhow.'

'Yes . . . after the war. . . .'

The train was going to start. The guard waved to all the waiting passengers to get in. Hugo jumped in quickly. He leaned out of the window and took both my hands.

'Good-bye, Helen.'

'Good-bye, Hugo . . . till next time. . . .'

The train jerked and puffed. A porter hurried along, slamming the doors. Hugo drew back his head, the train jerked again, and moved slowly forward.

I stood where I was, looking after the train. Hugo did not look out of it again, and I did not wave my hand.

I watched it drawing past me; carriage after carriage reaching the bend of the line where a station lamp threw a glittering light upon the windows; then out into the fog and darkness; and the smoke drifted back, chilly, mockingly, along the empty lines.

There were other women on the platform, walking back towards the barrier now, and I walked with them, dazed, hardly sensible, not knowing where I went.

And I never saw Hugo again.

XXX

In March, peace between Germany and Bolshevik Russia was signed at Brest Litovsk.

Maud said the Russians were traitors. She said she would be ashamed to be a Russian.

I thought:

'Some Russians will live, now, who would have died . . . that is some good in a world gone wrong. . . .'

But then the great offensive began in France. The tension and anxiety grew acuter, day by day. More news of the German advance, more Americans arriving in France, and we wondered which would come the fastest. Even in the streets, when one went out, one could feel the general anxiety, and see it in the people's faces as they passed.

In April, came the famous Army Order of Lord Haig, when he said:

'Our back is to the wall.'

Walter came in with the *Sunday Evening Telegram*, and threw it on the table, and a sense of dread and insecurity came with him into the room.

He said:

'This is the end of everything!'

And I thought of Guy and Hugo, out there in France, with the Germans pressing them back, step by step. There seemed so many Germans, and so few with them.

I said:

'There is still a chance.'

And Walter answered wearily:

'I suppose there is!'

So the spring wore on. Every week I wrote to Hugo, and

every week he wrote to me, and from those letters I drew strength and courage and happiness.

Walter said that he could not understand it; now, when the news was at its worst, I seemed so cheerful and serene, he said. I could only smile and admit that it was true.

It seemed to me that I was bound by my compact with Hugo. I had pledged myself to carry on with my job; I would make a success of my marriage with Walter, for Hugo's sake, and the determination to do so gave a new purpose to life.

I did not look far ahead, I did not make plans for the future, the present was enough in itself, with Hugo's letters as points of light to look for, and mine to him, as the expression of a week's fighting.

I could give much more to Walter now, and I gave it, and I felt him turn more and more to me for strength.

When I was in bed at night, I could see Hugo so clearly sometimes, that I could hardly believe it was not true. It was as if the war was between us, noise and confusion, and horror . . . and I could get through that, and somewhere behind it, I found Hugo . . . and there were shell holes, and barbed wire, and all that sort of thing about, but it didn't matter . . . Hugo was there, and it was all happy, and wonderful, and I knew that he was alive.

My son was born on the 15th of July, the same day that the German advance was held. In the strange serenity and confidence of these last months, I had felt sure that it would be a son this time. He was called John, after Walter's father, but I counted it partly for Cousin John as well.

It seemed to me that this son was a symbol of victory . . . not of Foch over Ludendorf, nor the Entente over Germany; these things were again remote to me, and unreal, but of peace over war, strength over weakness, light over darkness. I was filled with a sense of fulfilment and triumph, and of peace.

I thought:

'This is what they mean by the "Peace of God."' And I wrote all I felt to Hugo, and I told him about my son.

XXXI

In August, Guy was wounded and sent home. He was badly wounded this time. Cousin Delia wrote to me; he was sent to a hospital for officers in Park Lane. Cousin Delia came up to be near him; she stayed with Grandmother, in Campden Hill Square.

They would not let me see Guy at first; they said he was too ill. I saw Cousin Delia, and I saw in her face that she did not think he would live.

I said:

'Is Guy any better?'

She said:

'Not yet; he may get better.'

Guy did get better, very slowly indeed. He would live, they said, he would walk again, but he would be lame always. I could not imagine Guy lame, walking about with a stick.

Cousin Delia said only:

'I am so glad that he will live.'

There was, it seemed, something unconquerable in Guy.

I saw him in September. He looked ill, and almost old. Guy on his back, not moving, seemed all wrong; and his hair was turning grey.

He smiled at me.

He began, at once, to joke.

It was bad luck, he said, to be laid out like this, just at the very end.

'I might have been in at the death,' he said, 'when I had kept going so long! Hugo has beaten me, good old Hugo!'

I talked about Hugo, and the letters I had had from him lately, and of the war ending, and how every one was saying that it must end very soon.

Then Diana came in. She was a V.A.D. Her eyes danced and sparkled under her white coif; she was so tall and strong and full of life, and she moved as though all movement were delight. She came to bring Guy tea, in a feeding cup, on a tray.

Guy introduced her to me, and she smiled at me, and at him. She put her arm under his head to raise him up; she gave him his tea to drink like a little child. She arranged his pillows deftly, with her strong white hands, and I watched Guy's eyes as they followed her about the room, and I thought:

'Guy is going to marry that girl . . .'

And I thought of Mollie, at Salonika, with George dead. And I thought:

'What chance has Mollie, against that joy and youth?'

And I thought:

'Guy has forgotten Mollie . . .'

And I thought, as I watched her walk:

'I know what she feels like. . . . I felt like that, once. . . . I can remember it. . . .'

And then I thought:

'That is why Walter wanted me . . . do they always want that in us?'

And then I thought:

'Guy is like Walter, now, in that way, and he wants her . . .'

Guy smiled at her as one might at a loved child.

'You see,' he said to me, 'I have good care; I ought to get well very soon, oughtn't I?'

She said:

'You are getting well; we are very pleased with you!'

He said:

'She loves the war; she thinks it is a splendid war, don't you, Dinah?'

And she laughed, and her eyes danced.

'Oh, top hole,' she said, 'simply topping!'

Guy said:

'That is so refreshing. "*A quelqu'un le malheur est bon!*"'

And I thought:

'She is not horrid; she doesn't understand.'

I thought:

'She is very lovely, and very young.'

She said:

'There's a dance to-night, at Bengy's . . . you know . . . jazz of course . . . simply divine! simply divine! Old 31 is coming . . . his leg's nearly all right. . . . It's rotten,' she said, 'that you can't come!'

And Guy said:

'Awfully rotten!'

I thought:

'How can she talk like that to Guy? Doesn't she know that he will not dance any more?'

It was time for me to go, and Diana came with me to the top of the stairs.

'Awfully good of you to come,' she said, 'he wanted to see you. . . . Come again when you can; he gets awfully blue, you know, at times. . . I buck him up a bit, chaff him, you know, and that sort of thing, but it's jolly rotten really . . . bucked him up no end seeing you. . . .'

She was kind to me, she meant to be kind. She was explaining Guy to me; he was hers now, but she would not shut us out.

I wondered if she was kind to Cousin Delia too, and what Cousin Delia thought of her.

About a fortnight later they were engaged. Her name was Diana Sotheby; her father was the captain of a battleship; she was very 'well connected,' people told us, and twenty years old.

Cousin Delia said:

'She is lovely, and I think she is fond of Guy. They will be married when Guy is better; when he is out of hospital.'

She wrote to Mollie in Salonika, and so did I. I don't know at all if Guy wrote too.

Cousin Delia went back to Yearsly, and still the war went on.

We invited Diana to tea. Walter did not like her.

'A dreadful young woman,' he said, 'I don't know what Guy is about!'

I said:

'You see, she is not lame, at all, in any way.'

Walter said:

'Don't be silly, Helen! There are plenty of young women who are not lame. I suppose Guy thinks her pretty.'

I said:

'She is pretty.'

XXXII

News of the war kept coming; better and better news. The Germans were falling back now, all along the line. The German Front was breaking, the Allied troops were pressing forward everywhere. Bulgaria made peace, then Austria. President Wilson and the German Government were exchanging notes on peace.

'It will end now very soon . . . any week . . . any day. . . Germany is beaten. . . . The war is won now. . .' people said.

And then, on October 11th, Hugo was 'wounded and missing.'

I read his name in the Casualty List, in the morning, at breakfast:

'Hugo John Laurier, Second Rifle Brigade.'

Wounded and missing . . . wounded and missing . . . wounded and missing . . .

I thought:

'It is not true . . . it is quite impossible . . .'

I thought:

'It is quite certain that there must be a mistake . . .'

I thought:

'. . . But the war is over now . . . so nearly over . . . that could not happen now . . .'

I stared at the words till my eyes ached. They seemed to grow larger and darker than the other words on the page.

I had not expected it.

Walter said:

'Is there any news?'

And I said:

'Yes . . . there is something . . . about the Americans . . . they have been fighting somewhere, I think.'

Walter said:

'That is not important, what about the German retreat??'

I turned over the pages of the newspaper, and began to read aloud. My voice sounded to myself very odd, and remote, and unnatural, but Walter did not notice it.

I read that the German Front was breaking, that Allied

troops were pressing forward at all points. I could not tell if the words I read made sense, but he seemed satisfied.

I could not tell him about Hugo. He did not care for Hugo enough.

After breakfast, I bathed the baby, and took the little girls for their walk. The morning passed so uneventfully, in so ordinary a way, that I thought again:

'That could not have been true!'

When they were in bed for their midday rest I took the paper up again and looked, and it was there:

'Hugo John Laurier, Second Rifle Brigade . . .'

And I turned all cold . . . cold like a stone . . . and I thought:

'I must see Guy . . . I must see Guy at once . . .'

I could not go out yet, not till the afternoon; then I went upstairs and put on my hat and coat; then I went out and along to the tube station, and got into the tube. I changed at Leicester Square, and got into another tube, and that went very fast, and I got to Dover Street. Then I got out and walked into Park Lane, and along Park Lane to the hospital where Guy was. It was not the time for visitors, not for another hour, the nurse told me so at the door, but I said it was important, I said it was bad news. She looked at me hard, oddly I thought too, and then she told me to wait. She went away and came back, and then she told me to go upstairs. I knew my way to Guy well enough by this time, and I walked up the stairs, wondering what to do.

Diana met me at the top of the stairs. She smiled her flashing smile.

'Hulloa,' she said, 'what a funny time to come!'

I said:

'Has Guy seen the paper yet, this morning's paper I mean?'

And she said:

'I don't know; I don't think he has yet to-day.'

I said:

'His brother is missing . . . it is in the paper to-day. . .'

She said:

'I say! . . . how rotten! . . . how absolutely rotten!'

The smile died from her face.

'Poor old chap,' she said, 'he'll be awfully cut up! He thought no end of his brother . . . must have been jolly decent,' she said, and then: 'I suppose you knew him too?'

I said:

'Yes, I did know him.'

She said:

'Was he like Guy?'

I said:

'No, different from Guy.'

And then I sat down on the stairs . . . and the whole place seemed to swim . . . the stairs and the banisters . . . and the doors of the rooms in the passage . . . bright mahogany doors with panels that shone like glass . . . and she said:

'I say, what's up? I say, you do look rotten!'

And she stared at me, perplexed.

Then she said:

'I'll get you some tea . . . that'll buck you up no end!'

She said:

'Come on to my room, I've got a decent chair.'

I said:

'I'd rather stay here, thank you. I'm going away in a minute.'

She said:

'Aren't you going to see Guy?'

I said:

'You had better tell him. I don't think I can.'

I said:

'His mother will be coming. She is sure to come and see Guy.'

Diana gave a whistle.

'Lord! There will be an upset! . . . Our wedding'll be put off . . . if Guy's brother's killed . . . sure to be, don't you think?'

I said good-bye to Diana.

She gave me a cup of tea.

I thought:

'I must go to Yearsly, to Cousin Delia now. . . .'

I got into a bus in Piccadilly, and off it at Waterloo. I walked up the long sloping entrance, under the bridge.

The station was very big and full of people. The wide

arch of the roof seemed bigger than usual, higher, and further off. It seemed very full of smoke and noise.

I went to the booking-office where we always went for our tickets, but it was shut.

I thought:

'There is no train . . . I cannot go to Yearsly . . .'

I came out again from the booking-office, to the open space of the station.

There were lights in the station, and people shouting; a porter was shouting at me; then he knocked me with a barrow, and hurt my knee.

I thought:

'It is no use going . . . why should I go to her? She has Cousin John . . . and the people . . . and the garden . . . and the trees . . . everything there will be sorry . . . everything there loved Hugo . . . what use could I be to her . . . or she to me?'

I thought:

'It is beyond that . . . beyond being good at all. . . .'

And I turned and went out of the station, and down the long sloping road, and under the bridge again. And there was the noise of the traffic, of trams, and buses, and cars, and people thick all round me, and shops, and the smell of fish . . . and there was mud in the street, and the pavement too was muddy. . . . The shops gleamed darkly through the chinks of the shutters, and the people jostled and bustled round me, about the shops.

I thought:

'I must get away . . . I cannot bear these people . . .'

It was beginning to rain now. I turned down a side street, away from the crowd and the noise. The rain beat against my face, cold, steady October rain. I thought of the open country, in France, as I had seen it in pictures. Shell holes half full of water, distorted piles of wire, stunted remnants of trees . . . and the cold rain beating down. . . .

I walked on, faster and faster; I was almost running now. I knocked into some one . . . a policeman . . . I begged his pardon and hurried on. I felt that I must get away, by myself, alone, and the longing for this, superseded everything else. But there was nowhere to go . . . only houses, and streets, and people . . . and at home, there was no room where I could be alone.

I began to be out of breath. I stood still. My skirt was all wet now, it clung about my knees. I leaned with my hand against a lamp post. There was a seat beside it, and I sat down. I bent down in the shadow, and covered my eyes; and still I could not think. The rain beat down on the nape of my neck. It trickled down my back under the collar of my coat . . . and then, I was calling Hugo. . . . I called to him through the rain and the darkness, across the expanse of sea and land. . . . I stretched out my hands to him, and called again, and I felt that he must hear me, if he was anywhere. Was he somewhere lying alone, deserted, and wounded? I pressed my hands against my eyes, trying to see in the dark, to force myself to see, to hear his voice, answering me through the emptiness of the night. But I saw and heard nothing. Only whirligigs of light, as my fingers pressed against my eyeballs, and the splashing sound of rain on the pavement and in the puddles, and it was very cold.

I got up again from the seat, and turned to go home. I had come much farther than I knew, and it took a long time to find the way.

When I got home, Walter opened the door. There was light behind him in the hall, and I saw him black against the light.

He said:

'Where in the world have you been? I waited an hour for dinner!'

The rain dripped off from my clothes, in a pool, on the step where I stood. I saw it dark, like a blot, growing bigger, in the light from the door.

I said:

'Hugo is missing. You didn't know, I think.'

Walter stood very still; then he pulled me into the hall.

'When did you hear?' he asked. 'How do you know?'

I said:

'This morning, at breakfast. It was in *The Times*, you know.'

He said:

'You never told me! Why didn't you tell me then?'

I said:

'I couldn't tell you. It was too bad for that.'

We stood and looked at each other.

I thought:

'He doesn't care . . .'

He put out his hands towards me and drew me close to him.

'My poor dear Helen,' he said. 'Oh, my poor dear!'

XXXIII

The next day, came a letter from Cousin Delia, a short, quiet note, that was like her.

'You will have seen yesterday that Hugo is missing. We have no further news of him,' she wrote. 'His father has been to the War Office, but they can tell him nothing more. Hugo was missing on the ninth after the taking of Cambrai. They could not collect all the wounded on that day, and when they did so, he was not among them. There was very heavy shelling on both days, and it is probable that he was killed. I am making inquiries at the hospitals for men of his battalion who were in that fighting, and I will let you know if I have any news.'

I read and reread her letter, and I wondered, as I had often wondered, at the calm of Cousin Delia, and I thought that she would die if she lost Hugo. Quietly, calmly, as she had lived, she would die.

And I thought all day of Yearsly, of the old brick walls, and the apple blossom, and Guy and Hugo, calling from the trees; and I thought of Cousin Delia in the garden as she had been when we were little, with her long yellow gloves, and her shady garden hat.

And I thought:

'That is all over. The world has gone on since then.'

And my own grief became part of the world's grief, and my own loss, part of the world's loss.

And then, when Sunday came, I wrote to Hugo. I had written to him every Sunday since February, when he came home.

'Hugo, my darling . . . they say that you are dead . . . killed . . . blown to pieces . . . not there anywhere any more. . . . I can't believe it, for the world is going on . . . it looks just the same now, as it always did . . . and I can't believe in a world without you in it . . . anywhere at all, for I think, Hugo, that you were the world to me. . .

'They said: "When the leaves fall, you shall have peace." Do you remember that? . . . they are falling now. . . .I can see them . . . from the poplar tree at the gate, yellow, dirty leaves that fall in the street . . . but you said that it must not be like that . . . we came away from that picture. . . . Have you got peace Hugo, now? . . . silence and peace, after tremendous noise? . . . I try to think of it like that, but it is difficult. . . . I can only think that you are gone away . . . out of everything . . . that I shall never see you again . . . and then it seems as though some one was laughing at me . . . .some horrible devil, and it can't be true. . . .'

I addressed the letter and posted it. I don't know where it went, or what happened to it.

Two days later, a letter came from Hugo. I saw it on the hall floor, where it had fallen through the letter-box.

And I thought:

'He has answered me. He is not dead at all!'

I broke the envelope open, and I tried to read it, and I could not read it at first . . . the letters swam together, it seemed all blurred and indistinct, and I had to stand still and wait. And then, I tried again, and I read the date: October 8th, 1918. October 8th. That was more than a week ago. That was before he was killed. . . .

I looked at the address, and it told me nothing; illusive, non-committal as the addresses always were, but the writing was Hugo's:

'Helen dear,' it ran, 'I must write to you to-night, for I think we shall be busy to-morrow. Here it is quiet for the moment, and I have had a happy day. I saw cows and an old woman in a village . . . a piece of a village still . . . and I saw an old orchard that had been destroyed last year . . . and the stumps of the trees had flowered, the broken stumps of the trees . . . they had apples growing on them, round red apples, and there was grass over the stones already, and moss. I was glad to see it. And there were dahlias flowering at one end of the orchard, where there had been a garden, and there was a little tree, the sprout of a tree, where a clump of trees must have been. It was a birch, very tiny, by the edge of a pond, and its leaves were falling, tiny, golden leaves, and floating on the water.

'There was a robin and a mouse, a wild mouse. It has made me very happy. It was like Faith and Hope and Charity . . . do you know what I mean? I wish I could see you to-night, Helen . . . but I believe I shall soon. Somehow, I don't mind the thought of to-morrow as much as I generally do. It is nearly the end now.

'The mouse was sitting up, looking at me in the shadow of the birch tree, and then it scuttled away under the leaves. Do you remember the mouse at Yearsly, in the Frog Pond? on the stones? It made me think of that. And now, good-night, my dear. . . .'

And that was all.

I thought:

'Hugo was happy.'

It seemed to me at the moment, that what happened afterwards, could hardly count, and I felt his letter, after all, an answer to mine.

October wore to a close. The certainty of peace grew clearer day by day, but no news came of Hugo. No news ever came.

Cousin Delia came to see me once, and I saw Guy. He spoke of Hugo a little but not much; Diana was there.

He was to leave the hospital soon, in two or three weeks, they said. He was to go to Yearsly. They would be married later, after the New Year.

XXXIV

And then, on Armistice Day, something seemed to snap inside my head. I was out with the children at eleven o'clock, when the guns were fired and the bells began to ring. And it was then, at that moment, that it snapped, and it seemed as though I was mad for a time, and I did not understand what I was doing.

I thought:

'It is too late . . . it is a month too late! . . . I do not want it now. . . .'

I thought:

'If Hugo is killed, why should not all be killed? . . . it is silly to stop the fighting now . . .'

I took the children home and put them to rest. Then I took John, who was tiny, with me, and went out into the street. I walked to the Tube station, and got into a train. I got out at Charing Cross and walked across St. James's Park, towards Victoria. It seemed to me that the world had gone mad. People were shouting, and yelling, and waving their hats; the bells were ringing still, there was a hubbub of noise; lorries crowded with munition workers whirled past me, one after the other, with shouting and singing and the raucous whirr of rattles. The king had been addressing the crowd at Buckingham Palace, and I found myself caught in the rush of people coming away. Taxi-cabs dashed past me, crammed to overflowing; officers hung out of the windows or sprawled across the roofs, blowing whistles and cheering. The crowd seethed and pressed along Victoria Street; people on the tops of omnibuses stood up and waved their arms.

And I thought:

'Why do they do it? What do they understand?'

I thought:

'They did not mind the war . . . they could have stopped it, these hundreds and hundreds of people, waving their arms. . . .'

I thought:

'They did not mind it or they would not shout like this . . . they would make war again, these people that shout. . . .'

And I felt that I could not bear it, that I must get away.

I wondered why I had come, and where I was going. I did not know. I had no plan. I think I had come to Victoria because of Hugo, because I last saw him there. But now, I did not go into the station. I turned aside, and went along outside it, by the high, blind wall in Buckingham Palace Road, and then I turned over a bridge, the railway bridge that is there. I walked on and on, and I got away from the crowd, but the noise was everywhere.

John seemed very heavy, much heavier than I had thought. He began to cry and I rocked him, and still we went on through the grey, drizzling streets. We came to the Embankment, not far from Chelsea Bridge, and there was a seat. I sat down on the seat. I fed John there, and rocked him to sleep. I felt suddenly, now, quite weak and exhausted, as though I could not go on, and it seemed to me that I understood now, for the first time, that Hugo was dead.

I do not know how long I sat there. I know I was very cold, and so was John. He woke, and cried again, and I walked on. I came to Albert Bridge, and passed it, towards the chimneys. When I reached Mollie's flat, I looked up, and the windows were open. I was not surprised at all.

I went up the stairs, with John, and knocked on Mollie's door, and the knocking sounded loud, in a pause of the noise outside.

Mollie opened the door.

She cried out, as though she were startled, and stood back.

I walked past her into the room, and dropped down on the sofa. It was a low sofa, and I felt as though I were falling a long way, down and down and down.

Mollie was kneeling on the floor beside me. She took John from me, and laid him on a cushion. She made up the fire and put the kettle on to boil. Then she rubbed my hands, and asked me questions, in her low, quiet voice, that I had not heard for so long. And I lay back and watched her, as she moved about the room, and I felt in a strange dream, as though the past had come back.

I said:

'Hugo is dead.'

She said:

'I know. I heard from his mother.' Her clear eyes darkened: 'And you?'

I said:

'Oh, that is all . . .'

Mollie was looking at me, and I looked at the fire.

'I see,' she said at last. 'Poor Helen!'

I said:

'Yes, that is all . . . I can't bear it any longer. . . .'

Mollie asked:

'Did you know you would find me here?'

I said:

'No. How should I know? I just came away.'

Outside, along the Embankment, the shouting lorries passed, and the crowds, and the rattles, and the noise rose and fell, in irregular, intermittent waves. Bursts of singing floated in at the window, drunken, vulgar singing, of loud voices, cat calls, and shrill, unnatural laughter.

And I shivered, and buried my face, and Mollie comforted me.

She gave me tea to drink, and I felt better, and I realized then, for the first time, that it was strange to find her here.

I said:

'So you are back!'

She said:

'I came yesterday.'

And then I looked at Mollie, and I saw that she too was unhappy, and then I thought of George, and I put out my hand to her:

'Mollie,' I said, 'George too. . . . I had not forgotten George . . .'

She said:

'You should not forget him. He cared for you most of all.'

I said:

'He never told me . . .'

She said:

'What was the use?'

I said:

'Guy is going to be married. You know that too, I expect??'

Mollie bent her head.

'Yes, I know that too,' she said.

I said:

'Mollie, how can you bear it? What have you left at all?'

Mollie looked away. She was kneeling still on the floor, and the firelight danced on her cheek, turned so, away from me, and up the lines of her hair. And I saw that she too looked older, and I saw grey streaks in her hair; and I thought of Guy and Diana, and I felt that I hated Guy.

She said:

'I don't know yet. I shall find something soon. Life will go on again. I know in my mind that it must.'

She said:

'Is Guy very happy? What is Diana like?'

I said:

'She is very young, lovely, and hard as steel.'

She said:

'We can't choose for Guy. Perhaps that is right for him.'

I said:

'It is not right! I think Guy's soul has died!'

Mollie smiled at me:

'You are not changed so much, really,' she said, and touched my hand. And then John stirred and cried, and I picked him up again, and laid my cheek against his, and I felt that I had John, and that he was life for me.

Mollie said:

'You are lucky, Helen, to have that baby!'

I said:

'Yes, and I have two others . . . but they are not like this.'

And then I talked to Mollie, about everything that had happened; about Walter, and Maud, and his mother, and how I was beaten by it all, and how little use I had been.

And then about Hugo's coming, and all that we did together.

I said:

'We saw pictures, and heard music, and then we walked about and talked. We went to the station, and there was no train, but there was one in the morning, and I saw him off in a fog . . . it was all foggy' . . . and I seemed to see it again, as I talked about it, the station filled with smoke, and the lights, and the thin, sharp fog . . . and Hugo's train going out, away, round the bend of the line . . .

And she said:

'Is that all, Helen?'

I said:

'What more could there be? Only everything was

different for me after he came and went. You see, we had made a promise, both to go on to the end. It seemed to me, at first, that he had broken his promise; but he hadn't really, of course; I see that clearly now. It was the end for him, for the war was really ended; but I must go on longer. . . . We had to do different things. . . .'

She said:

'Is that Hugo's baby?'

And I said:

'How I wish it were! But not all my wishing can make it . . . and he had no child of his own!'

She said:

'Forgive me, Helen!'

I said:

'It's no case of forgiving. These things don't happen really . . . not with people like us.'

'No, not with you and Hugo. . . . I should have known,' she said.

We sat and talked together till very late that night. The lamps were lit outside, those cheerless, darkened lamps, and the noise in the streets went on.

We bathed John by the fire, in George's big blue basin and we put him to sleep on the sofa, and then we made our supper.

And Mollie talked of Salonika and what she had done there, and we talked of little things, little everyday things, and I stayed there that night, and in the morning, it was better.

The next day I went home. I told Walter where I had been. I told him that I got caught in the crowd, and that Mollie had come back, and he did not ask me questions.

I wondered sometimes, with Walter, how much he understood.

And that was the first day after the Armistice. The beginning of the time that has been, since the War.

Part Four

They came and went and are not,
And come no more anew,
And all the years and seasons
That ever can ensue
Must now be worse and few.

I

THE days that followed were confused and anxious, as the days before had been. There was no sudden change in life because the war had stopped. The change from war to peace was as hard to believe as the change from peace to war had been, and less complete.

Christmas came, and we had a Christmas tree. We had crackers and cakes, and we danced round it in a ring.

'It is the first peace Christmas,' we said. 'It ought to be gay.' And I think the children enjoyed it, though Eleanor did not care much for things that were not useful.

Early in the New Year we had influenza again; everybody had influenza about then. Eleanor and Rachel had it first, then Walter and the maids, and last of all, John. He was the most ill, and I thought he would die; but in the end he got better, and our life went on as before.

Guy was married in February. He was married at Portsmouth where Diana's father was stationed; in a red-brick church on a hill. I went to the wedding, but Walter did not go.

Before that there was a party at Yearsly, to welcome Diana. It was not a real party, because of Hugo; a dinner to the tenants, but no dancing in the hall as there would have been. There were presents for Guy and Diana; a silver tray, and a tea-pot; and they all came to see Diana.

She stood with Guy in the hall; he could stand with crutches now, and they all came and shook hands with them. Old Joseph came, and Mathew, both their sons had been killed, and the Elliots from the farm, whose son was missing, like Hugo. The young men were not back, those who were still alive, and the girls were mostly away, in factories and shops, but all the old people came, and I thought how old they looked.

I thought they liked Diana, and for the same reason that Guy did. She stood very straight and tall, in a white, shimmering dress. She wore a string of pearls that Cousin John had given her; she had chosen that as a present.

'I adore pearls!' she said.

Cousin Delia too had given her a necklace of old paste, little old pieces of paste set into flowers; it had belonged to Mary Geraldine, and Cousin Delia used to wear it, now she gave it to Diana, and she did not care for it.

She called me into her room—that was the evening before. . . .

'Oh, my dear!' she said, 'just look what she has given me! It's quite too marvellous, and awfully quaint, of course, but I simply couldn't wear it, could I? Will the old duck mind, do you think, if I don't? I wouldn't hurt her for worlds!'

She clasped it round her neck, and made a face in the glass.

'I should look too awfully odd, shouldn't I, now, like that? Belonged to some old grandmother, she says. . . . I'm no good at the antique stunt!' She flashed round at me, with her laughing, dancing eyes. 'Not my line, you know, is it? Don't you agree?'

And I didn't know what to say, for what she said was true; it didn't look right on her; it made her look loud and crude; she made it look weak and poor. But I loved that necklace so, on Cousin Delia. She had worn it when we were children, and Hugo had loved it too.

I said:

'I can't judge. We knew that necklace too well. . . .'

And she put out her tongue at me, and laughed again.

'You are a priceless crowd!' she said. 'You live in a world of your own, all long ago, and out of date, and things as they used to be! . . . Guy'd be the same, if I'd let him, but I won't, I warn you, so there! . . . I suppose I must wear this to-morrow, and I shall look a fright!'

But she did not wear the old necklace. She wore the new big pearls, and she did look very lovely, and Guy was proud of her.

I asked what she thought of Yearsly, for I could not make out what she thought.

She said:

'Oh, simply topping, but it does give one the hump!'

I said:

'I think of it as such a happy place.'

She said:

'Do you? What a scream! I feel like being in church. Perhaps though, you like being in church, and feeling very good?'

I said I didn't think so.

She said:

'It's so subdued, it makes me want to shout . . . and that die-away sort of music that Guy and his mother do . . . oh I know it's very classy . . . but it doesn't appeal to me, too much like church, again . . . Guy's got a decent voice too, he sings a lot with me, jolly different songs,' and she smiled mischievously, his mother wouldn't like them!

'Of course, the garden's jolly, but the house is awfully dark. I'd cut down half the trees . . . they give me the creeps at night, all swishing on the windows . . . and I'd put on new paint, and lots of jolly curtains instead of those faded things that look as though they'd fall to pieces. I like stripes,' she said, 'I'd have a red carpet, or perhaps black, if the walls and curtains were bright. . . . I love doing up rooms! I've done them all at home; the "mater" doesn't mind.'

And then she laughed again.

'I love to shock you,' she said. 'You look as though I'd burnt a bible! Ta-ta!'

And she ran away.

Guy said:

'Isn't Dinah lovely? I love to see her run!'

He came up just then, limping, on his crutches.

We turned along the terrace, and walked on, slowly.

'You know, Helen,' he said, 'I can't think what she sees in me . . . I must seem such a dull old buffer to her . . . especially now. I wish you could see her dance! You know, Helen,' he said again, 'she reminds me sometimes of you, when you used to dance . . . and I can't dance with her!'

I thought:

'What can I say?'

I was very sorry for Guy.

I said:

'She is very good tempered, and she even laughs at herself. . . .'

Guy said:

'You don't much like her, and I don't think Mother does, but you will when you know her better, I feel quite sure of that.'

I said:

'Yes, I am sure we shall; she takes a little knowing.'

I said:

'I expect she is shy.'

But I did not think she was shy.

Mollie was at the wedding, and Ralph Freeman and I, and some cousins of Cousin Delia's, and Grandmother, of course, and that was all on our side. The rest were Dinah's people. She told us to call her Dinah; she said that every one did.

II

That Summer, Walter was appointed to a Readership at Oxford. It was a better post than the one he had before, at Grey College, and he was glad to get it.

He said:

'I shall have time at last to write my book.'

And so we left our house in Hampstead, and I was glad to leave it. It looked shabbier and more forlorn when we left it, than when we came. For a time, when we lived there first, it had been better; when the garden was in order, and the bulbs came up in the Spring; but the grass was all ragged again now, and I had planted no bulbs that Autumn. The paint we had put on, inside the house, was chipped and scratched already. Outside, it had never been done as we had meant to do it, and the extra wear and dirt of six years was over everything. The bath was more worn than ever, for we had not had it re-enamelled, and the greasy patch on the wall, behind the cedar mop, was bigger and darker.

I was glad to go, and I did not mind much where we went. There were schools for the children in Oxford, and Walter longed to be there.

He said:

'It is the only place where people think.'

I did not find that at all, but I suppose that they thought about different things.

We went down to Oxford and looked at houses. We did not enjoy looking at them as we had the first time. We stayed at the hotel, where Mollie and I had stayed with Cousin Delia for our Commemoration dance. It seemed quite different now, and all the town seemed different from what it used to seem when Guy and Hugo were at college and we used to come and see them. We looked at a great many houses and at last we took this one, where we live now. It is strange to me to realize that we have lived here, already, almost twice as long as we lived at Hampstead; so much was happening then and so little now; one year is like another now, only the children grow bigger, and we grow older, and I suppose it will go on, just like this, until we die.

We moved to Oxford in November, just a year after the Armistice. We moved our furniture and our pictures and our books, and put them into new places in the new house. I put the alabaster bowl on the new chimney-piece, and the candlesticks that George and Mollie had given me. They looked all wrong in this room with the ornate chimney-piece and the coloured panes in the window.

And I thought:

'What does it matter? What does anything matter now?'

Cousin Delia sent me Hugo's statue of the Delphic charioteer, and I put it in the corner, on a shelf all to itself just as Hugo used to have it in his room at Clifford's Inn; our room was not like his even when that was there, but I liked to have it there.

People came to call on me, a great many people. They meant to be kind to me, I knew that. They wanted me to join all sorts of societies and to do all sorts of things. They asked me if I was musical; if I took an interest in politics, or infant welfare. And it seemed to me, when they asked me that I was not interested in anything at all.

They thought so too, I think.

Walter was vexed with me. He said that I ought to make friends with some of the ladies that came to see me; he said they would think me stuck up, that I gave myself airs. I didn't understand how they could think that. I don't now. Walter said that I would find that I had lots of things in common with some of them, if only I would try, and I expect that is quite true, but somehow I couldn't do it, I couldn't make the effort. I felt then, and I still do, as though there were no room for new people in my life any more. I should never care for new friends as I did for the old ones. When one has had the best of all, second best seems not worth having.

Mollie came to see us. She helped me with the house; we arranged the books together, and the pictures, and all the little things. She stayed a little longer, and I thought:

'There is still Mollie . . . if she can go on, I can.'

But she could not stay long. She was going to work again at her Biological institute, and she had to go back. She said she would come again, she said she would often come, and she does come, and stay with us quite often. Even Walter is glad when she comes; he says it is her intellectual interests that have kept her so sweet and serene; he calls it so intelligent. I should not put it in that way, I think it is something much deeper and more fundamental in Mollie, than her interest in biology, that makes her what she is; but it does not matter much what we call it, we mean, really, the same thing. And often when she is not there, when I am discouraged and downhearted, and wonder if it is worth while going on, I think of Mollie, as I do of Cousin Delia, and I am ashamed of my own poorness of spirit, and I think again, how wonderful they are.

III

Just before Christmas time, my Grandmother fell ill. She had grown very old and frail in the last years. The war had worn her out.

I went to her at Campden Hill Square. It was like long ago, before I married Walter; I had not been to stay there, for more than a night, since then.

Grandmother said that she was glad to have me there.

'It is like old times,' she said.

They said she would not get better; they said that she was too old. She might last a few weeks, not more, the doctor said.

And so I stayed with her, and she talked a great deal to me, mostly about my father when he was a little boy, and all that had happened then, nearly sixty years before, and when she was first married, and about my grandfather, when he was young.

And I thought:

'Time does not matter. There is no time for her.'

And I thought:

'It will be like that for me too, before long.'

Two days before she died, I was sitting in her room, her sitting-room upstairs, where she always used to sit, and she was by the fire, in her own big armchair, for she would not stay in bed, and she began to talk of much more recent things, of the War, and of Hugo, and then of Walter and me.

'Dear child,' she said, 'I am glad that you married him. . . . I have wondered, but I am glad. He will always be the same . . . you know the worst of him, and it is not a bad worst.'

I don't know what I said. I was on the floor beside her, and she stroked my head as she talked.

'You know,' she said, 'poor Hugo . . . that never would have done. I was very much afraid, at one time, that you would marry him. Poor, dear Hugo . . . he would not have been a good husband . . . it is better as it is. . . .'

And I felt that I could not bear it . . . I felt I must tell her everything, that it was all a mistake . . . that everything was wrong. . . . I looked into the fire, and the words rose up to my lips, and I nearly told her then, but I am glad that I did not.

I thought:

'Why should I say it? She is so very old, she is going to die . . . she need never know at all. If souls should be immortal, she will know about it then . . . but I don't believe they are. I think that she will end . . . I think Hugo has ended.'

And so I smiled at her.

And she said:

'You are happy? I think that you are happy, my dear?'

And I said:

'Yes, Grandmother, I am quite happy, now.'

She said:

'There are ups and downs. . . . There are always ups and downs . . . one must take the bad with the good. It will all be better now that the War is over.'

And then she said:

'Poor Delia! I am truly sorry for her. She idolized her Hugo . . . she never saw his faults . . . and now, I don't believe that she cares much for Guy's wife.'

I said:

'She never says so. I am sure she tries to like her.'

Grandmother looked up sharply; she smiled, more as she used to smile:

She said:

'I have seen her, you know. She would not be easy to like! But there it is, my dear, . . . you must take the bad with the good! . . . Guy is alive and married . . . that is much better than being dead.'

And then she talked again about my father when he was little.

And I thought:

'How odd it is, that she did not care for Hugo.'

I thought:

'You can never tell why people like each other.'

Two days later, she died. She was buried at Yearsly. The house in Campden Hill Square was sold, and some of her things were sold. I had not room for much. Cousin Delia had some, and she helped me with it all. And that was a chapter closed.

Cousin Delia did not die. She did not seem very different

from what she had always been, and she often talked of Hugo as though he were still alive.

IV

Guy's first baby was born that Spring. It was a girl, and it was called Delia. Guy and Diana lived in London now. Guy had gone into business; Diana said he must make money, and there was no money in the Bar, at least, not for years and years. She said that she knew very well what it was like to be poor; she said that her 'Pater' was poor, 'poor as a barn-door rat, and that's no fun, you bet!'

So Guy gave up the Bar; he said that he did not mind about it, and he went into business. I don't know what he did in his business, but it seemed that he made more money in that way, though Diana said that it was still not enough.

And then, Cousin John died too. He was hardly ill at all, only a few days.

I thought:

'Every one is dying. Who will be left alive? Young people died in the War, and old people now it is over.'

And there was another funeral in the little Yearsly church, and a tablet for Cousin John, on the wall, near the tablet for Hugo.

Now Guy and Diana were to move to Yearsly. Cousin Delia would not stay there, though Guy had asked her to.

She said:

'It would not do, it would not do for Diana.'

And so she packed her things, and I went and stayed with her, and helped her pack. I took John with me; he was three years old then, and he played in the fields at Yearsly, as Hugo used to play. We went through all the things, Cousin Delia and I. We sorted out the cupboards, and the drawers, and the boxes of letters. It had all to be left in order for Diana to take it over.

'I hope she will care for the place,' Cousin Delia said. 'I hope she will get to love it, in time, as I have loved it.'

We were both thinking of Hugo, and how she had not known him, and how to us he was there in every place and thing.

I was with her there, for a week. It was in October, and the trees in the High Wood were red and bright, like flames. I have never seen the trees so bright as they were then.

I went and walked in the wood, the last day I was there. I went and sat down on the leaves, beside the Happy Tree. The tree trunks stood out clear in the spaces of the wood, grey and distinct against the flaming leaves, and the sun was shining down through the brilliant leaves and underfoot as well, the ground was red, and shining, and I felt, suddenly, that beauty was still alive. It was like a flare of trumpets or a shout of triumph.

And I thought:

'Is this "A lightening before death"?'

And I thought:

'Death does not matter—death and life are one!'

And I thought:

'This is truth, this glory of flaming trees!'

And I felt a burst of joy.

I felt:

'This still goes on.'

I felt:

'What do I matter, or all that matters to me?'

And I felt that it was for Hugo, this chorus of his trees.

I felt:

'This is his wood. The trees are singing for him.'

And I felt:

'I have understood . . . I have understood at last!'

And I went down from the wood, after a long time. And I met Cousin Delia coming out of the walled garden. Her arms were full of flowers, dahlias, and chrysanthemums. Smoke was rising up, very blue, from behind the garden wall, and she looked happy too.

I went up to her and said:

'I was in the wood. The trees were like trumpets blowing. . . "And he went over, and the trumpets sounded for him, on the other side." . . . It was like that to-day!'

And she said:

'I know. I was in the wood, this morning.'

And I went indoors with her, and we put the flowers in

water. And the next day, I went back to Oxford, with John.

Cousin Delia went away to a little house, near Bath. Nunky went with her, and Mrs. Jeyes, the cook. She took the deerhounds with her, and she made a garden. I go to see her sometimes, and sometimes I take John.

V

I have been back twice to Yearsly since Cousin Delia left.

Guy has asked me to go oftener, and Diana is kind and friendly, but I do not think she would like it if I were to go there often. That is quite natural; I should not fit in with her friends.

But, she says:

'Come when you like . . . just send a P.C. and turn up!'

And I say:

'Thank you, Dinah, that's awfully good of you!'

But I know she wouldn't like it if I did, and I think she knows that I know, and anyhow, apart from that, I should not want to go often.

It is all so different now, and I loved it as it was. I suppose it is growing old that makes one dislike changes. Diana has changed a great many things, just as she said she would.

The house looks smarter now; there is new paint and new wall-paper. It is not exactly ugly, for Diana has a taste of her own, and I think she has taken trouble to make it just as she likes. The old brocade has gone, but the curtains are not striped; they are of a brilliant cretonne, with very big, pink flowers, and the paint inside, is yellow, bright yellow like mustard. Diana says it is the latest thing, pink-curtains and yellow paint; she says that every one is having that now.

She has put chairs in the hall, big leather chairs and tables; she calls it a lounge hall, and they sit in there a great deal, and smoke. Diana is always smoking, and all her friends smoke too. They sit on the little tables, as a rule, instead of the chairs. And there is a very big gramophone; I think it is the biggest gramophone I have seen. Diana's friends are all very well dressed, and most of them paint their faces; Diana does not paint; her own colour is too lovely to need it; I think she grows more lovely every time I see her.

She has five children now; three girls and two boys. She is nicest with her children; she romps with them like a big tiger with cubs.

The eldest boy is called Hugo. He is not at all like our Hugo. Diana thinks he is, but she never saw him. She says that the people round all say that he is; they would say that, of course, because he has the same name. He has dark eyes, that is true, but not the least like Hugo's. He is just like Diana, and his eyes are like her eyes. He is a splendid child, big and strong and merry. He laughs and fights his brother and sisters, and he is always running. He breaks things and does not mind, he hurts people and isn't sorry. It sounds strange to me to hear them call him Hugo.

They are all fine children, all strong and well and cheerful. The house is full of noise, laughing and screaming and scuffling. I am glad there are children at Yearsly. There are five of them, and there were only three of us. I am glad they are there and yet it is almost more different than if they were not. They live so differently from the way we used to live, and they never play in the wood at all. But I think sometimes, that they are better fitted for life than we were. I think they are tougher than we were, and less illusioned.

One of the children, the second girl, is unlike the others; she is only five now, hardly more than a baby, but she is much gentler than the rest and more devoted to Guy. I think that she will be a help to Guy some day, and he, perhaps, to her, when she grows up, and I sometimes wish that I could see more of that little girl.

They have put in central heating, and electric light. It is more like an hotel now, and less like a loved house, but it is very comfortable, and there are two new bathrooms, white-tiled, like the bathroom I used to want.

Old Joseph is still there, I think Guy has insisted on keeping him, but Mathew is pensioned off, for there are no more horses now. There are two motor-cars, one big, and one smaller, and a very smart chauffeur, called Septimus Ward. Jayne, the butler, died soon after Cousin John, and there is a smart new butler, quite different from Jayne.

There are lots of little dogs, Pekingese, with bows, but

no big dogs. Diana plays games a good deal, but she never goes for walks. She has her own car, the smaller of the two. It is a 'Sports model Lancia,' painted red, like a pillar-box, and she does speed tests, and hill trials, in a fur cap with long ear-pieces. She has a red leather coat, with fur up round her throat, and very big fur gauntlets, right up to her elbows. She always goes about in her car, even into the village. There is only room for two, and she sometimes takes one of the children. She has a very loud horn, and she blows it a great deal.

I think she enjoys her life; she is often laughing. When she is annoyed, she is cross and sulks, like a child. She makes scenes with Guy, in public, and doesn't mind who hears. At first, I minded that very much, I was so sorry for Guy, but it doesn't seem to matter, it is just like a child in a temper; she forgets all she has said, and every one has to forget, and they do, apparently, and it all goes on as before.

They have made a racquets court out of part of the old stable. Diana plays racquets well, and Guy can still play a bit.

Guy is still in business. He goes up to the city every morning, and comes back in the evening. I think he must be quite rich; they seem rich, when one is there.

I think Guy is happy; it is very hard to know. He walks about with a stick, and his hair is quite grey; he looks older than he is, and he is now forty-four. I wonder very often what he thinks about it all; but of course he does not tell me, and of course I do not ask.

The trees have been thinned out, and many have been cut down. There are none close up to the wall of the house now, as there used to be, and the branches would not tap now on the window-pane of my window if I slept in my old room; but Diana's maid sleeps there now, and I dare say she likes it better without the trees.

The first time I went back, they had not touched the wood, but the last time that I went, the Happy Tree had gone. I went up in the wood as soon as I got there, and looked for the Happy Tree, and I could not believe it had gone. It gave me an odd feeling, as though I must be asleep, and I walked all about, to try and find where it was, and there was the place where it used to be, and just a big stump was there.

And I found Guy walking about, with his stick, in front of the house.

And I said:

'Oh Guy . . . the tree . . . you know, the Happy Tree. . . .'

And Guy looked at me so queerly, for a moment, with his face screwed up, and I was not sure at first, if he was angry. . . .

And then he said:

'Yes. It was cut down while I was away, last autumn. Dinah had it done. She did not know, of course, that it was a special tree.'

And I said:

'No, of course not . . . she could not have known.'

And I thought:

'He had not told her that!'

We did not talk about it. We just walked up and down, and Guy talked about his children, and I talked about mine.

The seats in front of the house were all painted bright green. They were painted every year, and the paths were always raked.

It is right to rake gravel paths, and to keep the edges trimmed. It ought to look much nicer, but I don't think it does, somehow.

VI

And now it is ten years since the war ended; ten years all but a few weeks. These years have gone much more quickly than the years before them did. People always tell one that, that the years go faster and faster, as one grows older. Nothing happens now, and so much was happening before.

The children are growing up; even John is ten. He goes to school here; there is a good school, but I suppose he will have to go away when he is a little older. I don't know what I shall do when John goes away. But I suppose when the time comes it will be like everything else. One thinks:

'I cannot bear it, if that happens!'

And then it does happen, and one does bear it, and everything goes on, just the same as before.

I don't know how I should have lived all these years without John. He is often very naughty, much naughtier than Eleanor or Rachel have ever been. I am not clever with my children as Cousin Delia was with hers. I often wish that he could have the childhood that I had, at Yearsly, with her, he would understand that, he understands a great many things. I read stories to John that Cousin Delia used to read to me, and poetry sometimes too. I think he will like poetry; not as Hugo did, not so much nor so young, but he sees the point of it even now as Eleanor and Rachel never did, and of all that kind of thing. It is a pleasure to me to read to John, and I think sometimes, of all the books we will read together when he is older, books that I read with Hugo in the hay, at Yearsly, in the long summers, and then sometimes I am afraid that I am building too much on his being what I want him to be, and that he will not be like that at all when he is older . . . but I shall always love John, whatever he grows into. . . . Mollie said that I should be thankful for John, and I am, I have been always.

Eleanor likes books that give her information. She likes facts and statistics, and she does very well at school, much better than John or Rachel. They say she is very clever, that she will get a scholarship. That will please Walter. He is proud of Eleanor, but I think he loves Rachel best. She is more alive; she is not so good as Eleanor, nor so naughty as John, not so fair as Eleanor, nor so dark as John. She does her lessons well, but she likes to play at games. I don't think life will be hard for Rachel.

I think Walter is happy. His book came out last year. It was published by the University Press, and that was just as he wanted. Not many people bought it, but he said that did not matter, he had not expected that; it was praised in learned journals, very highly praised. Several German professors wrote to Walter about it. Two came to see him, with special dispensations from the Home Office, because they were Enemy Aliens still. They were very polite to Walter, and complimented me on my 'so distinguished man'; they said he was 'world-famous' for his proto-Hittite script.

I am glad Walter is happy, or at least, happy for him. . . . I don't think he could be happy, as Hugo or I would be. He is less cross now, and kinder. He likes his work in college, and he has time for work of his own as well. He has started another book that will last about ten years, and he goes for walks with his friends: those two friends of his both came back; one of them teaches Ancient History, and the other Philosophy, but it doesn't make much difference; they like to talk to Walter, and he likes to talk to them.

Walter is not different, really from what he was when we were married; he is less fierce, perhaps, because he is more assured; he knows more where he is, and other people know. But he is not really different, though he said that he would change, and I said people didn't, and yet I have myself . . . I have changed much more . . . that is funny, I think, how little people know.

Last Spring, when the blossom was out, I went down to New College, and looked at the cherry tree that we used to see from Hugo's window. I suppose it is just the same now, as it always was, but I do not feel the same about it now. There are other young men in Hugo's college rooms, three generations of young men have been in those rooms since we came here, and others, of course, before that. It is twenty years now since Hugo was there.

And now it is my birthday, and I am forty; and Hugo, if he were alive, would be forty-two and a half. That seems impossible; I cannot think of Hugo as not young.

And there are the leaves coming down. There are always leaves and trees . . . and always coming down . . . naturally . . . every year . . . why do I notice that?

And this is all that has happened. It does not seem very much. It does not seem worth writing about. I was happy when I was a child, and I married the wrong person, and some one I loved dearly was killed in the war . . . that is all. And all those things must be true of thousands of people.

THE END

www.ingramcontent.com/pod-product-compliance
Lightning Source LLC
Chambersburg PA
CBHW051319130726
47987CB00004B/1870